NETHERWORLD
FAE

BRIDE
OF
DEATH

USA TODAY BESTSELLING AUTHOR
LEXI C. FOSS

Bride of Death

Editing by: Outthink Editing, LLC

Proofreading by: Katie Schmahl & Jean Bachen

Cover Design: Cover by Sanja Balan of Sanja's Covers

Title Page, Background Art & Chapter Headers by: Anna Spries

Illustrated Map by: Ricky Gunawan

Published by: Ninja Newt Publishing, LLC

Digital Edition

ISBN: 978-1-68530-349-5

Print Edition

ISBN: 978-1-68530-407-2

AI Disclaimer: This book does not contain any elements of AI content. All art was designed by real artists, and all of the words were written by the author.

To Poseidon, for always being my favorite. Don't tell Hades.

BRIDE
DE*of*ATH

A Netherworld Fae Novel

BRIDE
— of —
DEATH

A Persephone & Hades Retelling with a Faelicious Twist...
One where Hades has to learn how to share with his favorite Enforcer and the God of Dreams.

The God of Death says I'm his long-lost bride.
His soulmate.
A Goddess who betrayed him two thousand years ago.

He believes my memories are the key to our survival.
Only, they're memories I no longer possess. Because I'm not who he thinks I am.

I'm Serapina, not Persephone.
A human, not a Goddess.
And that knot he keeps talking about? Yeah, that's not coming *anywhere* near me.

Except Hades isn't the only one threatening to claim me with his knot. Morpheus, the God of Dreams, says I belong to him, too.

And don't even get me started on Maliki, the sexy fae assassin in charge of my captivity. That deadly fae has a body crafted in sin and a smirk that makes me question my sanity.

All three men want access to my nest. To my heart. To my mind.

It's that last part that scares me most. Because if I truly am the one who betrayed my own kind, then I'm not worthy of being a Goddess. Let alone *their* Goddess. And what happens then?

Author's Note: *Bride of Death* is book one of the Netherworld Fae trilogy and ends on a cliffhanger.

WELCOME TO THE NETHERWORLD KINGDOM

Persephone is mine. Don't let my cousin tell you any different. He seems to think he has some sort of claim on my mate, but he's wrong.

She's been mine for thousands of years.

She's my soulmate.

My flower. My Omega. *Mine*.

Only, once upon a time, she tricked me. Deceived all of Mythos Fae kind. Hid the Omegas from their Alphas. *Destroyed* the world we once called home.

I may never forgive her.

But I love her.

It's my weakness. My curse. My *blessing*.

Ah, Persephone, darling. You may be locked away in a human shell, but I will set you free. Even if it means I have to break you first.

As you may have guessed, this story is complex. Dark and twisted. Layered with myths and lies.

I wasn't always God of the Netherworld Fae. But I'm not here to provide a history lesson, just a glimpse of what to expect.

Because you're in my universe now, loves.

And all you need to know is that my Persephone has finally come back to me. Perhaps unwittingly, but she's here. If there's one thing I know, it's that fate always wins in the end.

Welcome to the Netherworld, my darling soulmate.

It's filled with death. Darkness. Gloom. All the things that make you suffer.

I will be your source of light. Your savior. Your home.

Together, we'll undo the sins of your past.

Together, we will suffer.

Together, we will thrive.

And in the end, you'll remember what it's like... to be mine.

Below are some themes you may find in the Netherworld Fae trilogy. Please note that this list applies to the **trilogy**, so some of these themes will not appear in *Bride of Death*. However, I wanted to share what you can expect from this three-book series.

Themes include:

✔ Slow-Burn Romance (This one might surprise some of you; it surprised me, too.)

✔ This is a Hades and Persephone retelling with a "why choose" twist (much to Hades's chagrin)

✔ No MM, but there are group scenes (Some of these scenes may have slight MM play for the benefit of the heroine.)

✔ Consent between the heroine and her mates

✔ Psychotic Hero (Maliki)

✔ Celibate Hero (Hades) — But he likes to watch...

✔ Hero who loves CNC and sleep play (Morpheus)

✔ No Other Woman or Other Man Drama (No Cheating)

✔ Possessive Over The Top Alpha Males

✔ Touch Her and Die Vibes
✔ Alpha/Omega Dynamics
✔ Knotting, Nesting, Purring & Growling (because yes, please…)
Enjoy! <3

PROLOGUE

"WHAT GAME ARE YOU PLAYING NOW?" MY COUSIN ASKS AS he collapses onto my favorite couch.

"Why are you here?" I counter, my gaze narrowing at his sudden and very unwelcome appearance in my personal quarters.

This has become a regular occurrence over the last few months.

And I am not pleased.

"You know why I'm here," he drawls, kicking up his expensive shoes to rest on my table.

A table made of ancient lava rock.

A table that is not made for shoes.

A table that's meant to be looked at, not touched.

My jaw ticks. "Stop worrying about things that aren't yours to worry about, Morpheus," I tell my cousin. "And kindly fuck off."

He snorts. "Are we truly going to have this conversation again?"

"You're the one who insists on popping in uninvited every few days to discuss my mate," I reply as I pour myself a shot of Hellfire.

I don't offer Morpheus one.

Because he won't be staying long.

"Go back to your dream world, Cousin," I murmur. "That's the only place you'll ever be safely allowed to indulge in your fantastical ideas."

"Mmm, dreams. An interesting conversation, that." He cocks his head to the side, causing his long silver hair to cascade down over one shoulder. "Our mate still thinks you're a figment of her imagination. Why?"

I still, the Hellfire grazing my lips as I pause mid-drink. "How do you know this?" I ask as I slowly set my drink down on the en-suite bar and give my cousin every ounce of my attention.

Morpheus merely grins. "How do you think?"

I take a step forward. "Stay out of her fucking head." The words are uttered clearly. Slowly. *Precisely*. "She is not yours."

"She's not yours either," he tells me, suddenly very serious. *Too* serious. "She doesn't even know you exist. Not really. You let her think that first night here was a dream, and you've spent the last thirteen fucking months brooding over what to do with your precious little flower."

My gaze narrows even more, a warning lingering on my tongue.

But my cousin isn't done.

"I used to find it amusing." He drops his fancy shoes to the ground and leans forward, his forearms on his knees. "I'm no longer amused, Hades."

I stare down at him, evaluating. Because that's a threat

underlining those words. A threat I'm not sure I like. "What are you saying, Cousin?"

He gives me a look and stands. "Family terms won't save you today, *Cousin.*"

"Save me from what exactly?" I press.

His blue-green eyes swirl with an emotion, one I identify far too closely with. *Possession.*

Serapina is my Persephone. My long-lost mate. Her soul knows mine, even if the human shell she currently wears feigns confusion. Our kind is destined—an Alpha with his Omega.

The problem is that my cousin seems to think she's his Omega, too.

"Alphas form circles for a reason," he tells me as he steps around the table and into my personal space. "I suggest you remember that."

I arch a brow. "Are you threatening me?"

"Not yet," he replies, a lethal note underlining his tone. "But I will if you let this progress." A book appears in his palm, one I recognize as the Netherworld Fae Registry. He slams it against my chest. "Page four thousand and seven. Read it."

My eyebrows come down. "Why?"

His vibrant gaze captures and holds mine. "Because if you don't fix it, I will." He takes a step back. "You have forty-five days, Hades." He vanishes before I can reply, his essence leaving a permanent aroma in my space, like he's marked my fucking office.

That is a threat. Just as much as his words. *Forty-five days.*

"To do what?" I ask the space he just occupied.

Part of me wants to magic the book back to where it belongs in the heart of the Netherworld Village. However, my interest is piqued.

"Fucking Morpheus," I ground out as I walk over to my desk to set the book down.

I return to the bar to grab my drink, fully aware that I'm going to need it, and take it over to my chair. It faces a slate of mahogany stone, the texture similar to wood yet hard as rock. A unique craftsmanship, one I brought with me from my home realm.

Settling, I stare at the ominous text. The pages are encased in a silky, leatherlike black fabric—*netherite*. It's a quality binding, one I'm very familiar with, as I created it.

Smoothing my hand over the skull etched into the front, I find the book's hard edge and carefully flip it open to reveal the fiery scrawls littering the magically enhanced pages.

Numbers appear at the bottom, shifting before my eyes without actually turning the papers. The book knows what I want—page four thousand seven.

My cousin's desire becomes clear as the script appears, the red letters revealing a name we both know very well.

Serapina Everheart.

"Lie," I mutter. But my eyes linger on her false name for only a second before scanning the details scrawling across the page. She's listed her next of kin as *Alina Everheart*, which is also false. They're not related by blood. However, I skip over it and home in on the next line.

A line that has my heart stopping in my chest.

And my blood running cold.

Mate Status: Single.

A growl vibrates my chest and echoes out into my office.

"Single?" I repeat aloud, my voice deep and guttural and *furious*. "You are *not* fucking single."

I suddenly understand my cousin's threat. He's giving me forty-five days to *fix this*.

"*Fuck.*"

I've given Persephone time to grow into her accommodations and allow her soul a chance to come out to play. She's an Omega and I'm her Alpha. It's only a matter of time before she goes into heat and calls for me.

However, it's been over a year since she arrived in my domain, and nothing has happened.

Nothing except *this*.

An entry into the Netherworld Fae Registry.

One whereby she's marked herself as *single*.

Because she wants to join the Netherworld Kingdom ranks.

My jaw clenches. "And do what, my darling soulmate?" I wonder out loud, my gaze scanning the page once more. "Live in the Netherworld Village?" I huff a humorless laugh. "You have to be joking, love." That's no place for a Goddess—*my* Goddess.

No, this waiting period has lasted long enough. It's time to act. And I know exactly what move to make.

"By the time I'm through, your mate status will be known by everyone in all the realms," I promise my soulmate. "Because I'm going to mark you as my fucking bride."

Several Weeks Later

MY FIST CLENCHES AT MY SIDE, MY DESIRE TO HIT THE dead guy in front of me igniting my nerve endings.

I'm not a particularly violent person. Actually, I've been called meek more than once in my life. Quiet. *Shy*, even.

But this guy is asking for an introduction to the new me.

Sera, as I've introduced myself to everyone here.

The old me, *Serapina*, died in the Monsters Night universe.

"Look, all I'm sayin' is, you could use a mate like me," Dead Guy drawls, his glass of ink sloshing dangerously close to the rim as he moves his hand in a dramatic gesture toward himself. "I'd be very good to you, little human."

There's that term again. *Little human*. He keeps tossing it around like it's some sort of endearment.

But being the sole mortal in Death's Den isn't an endearing trait. It's basically akin to wearing a shirt that says "Weakling" across the chest.

I'm not, of course. Wearing that shirt, I mean.

I'm wearing a tank top.

And jeans.

I shudder. Whoever invented this fabric deserves a date with the Blood River.

I never thought I would miss my clothes from back home—or anything, for that matter—yet here I am, yearning for my long skirts and laced-up tops.

Regency fashion, as my sister's mates call it. That's what Alina and I grew up wearing. But since relocating to the Netherworld Kingdom, she's been slowly inflicting this world's attire upon me.

Including the infamous skinny jeans hugging my legs now.

Ugh.

"I can save you from the games," Dead Guy goes on. "'Cause ya know they're gonna draft y'all, right? Serve you right up on a platter for us to pick from."

I stare at him. "What games?" I ask, finally responding to his babbling nonsense.

"The mating games," he tells me, his white eyebrows waggling over his reddish-brown gaze. "Ya haven't heard about King Onyx's plans for all the unmated brides?"

Unmated brides.

I'm not sure if he's talking about women left over from the canceled Hell Fae Bride Trials or the innocents that were kidnapped during Monsters Night last year.

A lot of the patrons in Death's Den assume that's where I came from—the Monsters Night event.

Since they're partially right, I don't correct them. They

don't need to know that I'm a charity case brought here by my sister and her overly generous mates.

Nor do they need to know that I'll be exempt from whatever "event" King Onyx might be planning. Alina's men would never allow me to play. Stars, they barely let me move into my own place last month. I can't even imagine what they would say if I told them I wanted to participate in *mating games*.

Though, it shouldn't be up to them what I do or don't do.

But that's a consideration for later.

"They're not games," a deep voice interjects from down the bar. I squint at the newcomer, hardly able to discern his masculine form in the shadows. But he's there, his golden eyes seeming to flicker like the flames dancing throughout the room.

Death's Den certainly maintains its reputation and ambience with its crypt-like decor.

Obsidian stones laden with bones decorate the bar counter. Solid black slabs of marble rest over ivory-colored poles—which may also be bones—for the tables. And black wood frames the booths as well as the bar stools and high-top chairs.

The walls also resemble a cave. The light is predominantly provided by candlelit chandeliers. And the floors are stark gray slate.

When I first entered this place a few weeks ago, I shivered.

But I needed the job behind the counter.

The manager of Death's Den—a Corpse Fae named Gnarls with pretty green eyes and bright red hair—took one look at me and hired me on the spot.

I thought I got lucky.

That illusion disappeared on my first night after dozens

of male fae showed up to enjoy the new "eye candy" at the bar.

Turns out I was hired for having boobs.

Yay me.

"Not really, anyway," the voice continues, his sensual baritone easily carrying to my ears. "They're more like trials to see if any of the women who have settled here are ideal mates. There's a difference."

I frown at the shadowy figure. "And these *trials* are mandatory?" Because this is the first I'm hearing about *trials* or *mating games*. And I've worked this bar every night for nearly a month now.

"That's the rumor," Dead Guy murmurs. "Heard it m'self earlier today."

Myself, I think, longing to correct this fae's grammar. I think he's a Corpse Fae, hence my nickname for him. But the squid shot he requested earlier seems to be a favorite of the Death Fae patrons. So maybe he's a mix.

"King Onyx told Lars, who told Munch, who told me that we've got ourselves a fun little time comin' up," Dead Guy drones on. "But as I said, I can save ya from all the trouble, if you're lookin' for a good mate."

The shadow at the bar grunts. "This courtship is almost too romantic for my ears." He leans forward, his gold eyes catching and holding mine as a candle illuminates the sharp lines of his jaw. "Would you mind pouring me a spider ale, sweet mystery? I'm going to need one to make it through this awful proposal."

Sweet mystery.

As far as nicknames go, I'm... I'm okay with that one. It's a lot better than *sugar tits*, *babe*, and *little human*. All of which I've been called tonight.

"Oh, feck you, Ghost," Dead Guy mutters. "No one asked you."

"And thank the fae for that," the shadowy one drawls, leaning back into the darkness. It seems to wrap around him like a blanket, hiding him once more from view.

But I won't be forgetting that handsome jawline of his anytime soon.

All the males around here are gorgeous, even the dead guy seated at my bar. I'm pretty sure it's a requirement, honestly. However, *Ghost* certainly possesses some of the sharpest features I've ever seen.

Outside of my dreams, anyway, I think.

With a mental shake, I clear my head—because no, I will *not* be thinking about *that* right now, thank you very much—and focus on pouring Ghost a spider ale, just like he requested.

The smoky liquid flows from a tap and somehow pools inside the glass I'm holding. I'm not quite sure how it works. Though, I've long stopped questioning the magic in this realm.

It's vastly different from that of the world I'm from but not necessarily alarming. I grew up knowing supernaturals and monsters existed. I just never expected to live freely among them.

I have my sister and her mates to thank for that.

Unless I'm drafted for this mating game…

Frowning, I walk over to set the spider ale in front of the one called *Ghost*. "What have you heard about this rumor?" I ask him directly. "Will all the women be forced to participate?"

"Not all of them," he murmurs, accepting the drink from me.

"Only unmated ones," Dead Guy inserts from down the bar.

But I'm not focused on him. I'm staring into a pair of glittering gold irises instead. "Only unmated ones?" I repeat the words as a question, curious to hear his take since he seems to know something about these supposed *mating games.*

"All unclaimed females will be considered eligible," he tells me. "Assuming King Onyx and King Skull can agree to terms before the nuptials take place."

I stare at him. "Nuptials?"

"Indeed," he murmurs.

"Our lord's wedding," Dead Guy helpfully explains. "Apparently, he's found a bride. Have I mentioned that I'm invited to the main event?" When I finally look at him, his eyebrows waggle again. "I can bring you as my plus-one, if ya like."

Ghost snorts before taking a long swig of the venomous drink I poured for him.

Gnarls warned me when I started not to imbibe anything at the bar. "All of it will kill you," he told me with a grimace. "So just be careful, yeah?"

That was the extent of his managerial training.

Everything else I learned from Claws—a Death Fae who very much lives up to his name.

"Don't think she's available, Jacky boy," Ghost drawls, his golden eyes still on me. "And definitely not interested."

I frown at him. I mean, he's not wrong. But I can voice my own opinions, thank you very much. And I'm about to tell him that when Dead Guy growls. "Why don't you mind your own business, *dog*?"

Ghost slowly sets his glass down and turns within the shadows, his vibrant eyes suddenly on Dead Guy. "Are we going to have a problem, Jack?"

My brow furrows. *Jacky boy.* I didn't think much of the nickname before, but now that he's called him *Jack*, I'm realizing that's Dead Guy's name. *Seriously? Jack?*

"There wasn't a problem until you showed up," *Jack*—

I'm never getting over that name—mutters. "I was having a nice conversation with the little human until you arrived."

And my hand is now a fist again.

"She was about to accept me proposal, too," he goes on, causing one of my eyebrows to lift upward. Not only does he not seem to understand the proper use of pronouns, but he's also implying that I'm actually interested in him.

Which I'm not.

At all.

I don't want a mate. I just desire freedom. Independence. Some time *alone*.

Because my entire life has been dictated by someone else's actions. From the moment I was born in Nightingale Village to the fated Monsters Night to being rescued and brought here, I've never been given a choice.

And now this asshole wants to steal my voice from me, too.

"No," I say, interrupting whatever nonsense he was just spouting at Ghost. "I'm not interested in your proposal. I'm not interested in mating games. And while we're on the topic of things I'm not interested in, I do not enjoy being called *little human*."

He blinks his long, dark lashes at me. "If the mating games move forward, you won't have a choice as an unclaimed female."

"Who says she's unclaimed?" Ghost asks conversationally, his drink now near his mouth. Or I assume it is, anyway. He's almost entirely covered in shadows again, but the glint of the glass winks at me from where I imagine his lips should be.

Full lips, I think, recalling his features from a few moments ago. *Set in a too-handsome face.*

Just like all the fae here.

No one ages beyond their thirties, at least as far as appearances go. And everyone is attractive. At least on the outside.

But I learned long ago that looks can be deceiving.

In a universe full of supernatural beings, nothing is ever what it seems.

"The Netherworld Fae Registry," Jack says, his comment sending a tremor down my spine.

It's… it's an irrational reaction. I already went through the process of providing my information and classifications to the Netherworld Fae Registry last month; it was a requirement for me to seek housing in the Netherworld Village.

But it's impossible not to compare the list to the one I grew up fearing—the list of eligible candidates for the Day of the Choosing.

And that dreaded Chalice…

I wince with the thought, my mind conjuring up an all-too-familiar stage. The Viscount. My name being chosen for Monsters Night.

The confusion that followed…

"Says she's not got no attachments," Jack goes on, yanking me back to the present with his gibberish-like statement. "Which means she's unclaimed."

"Perhaps the one who has a claim on her hasn't made that declaration clear," Ghost murmurs, leaning forward and leaving the shadows behind. "Maybe she has no memory of him—or is it them?—at all."

I frown, his words feeling a little too intentional. A little too *personal*. Like he knows something about me. *Something about my past…*

"Or it's entirely possible that all of this is a game," he goes on with a shrug. "Regardless, the Netherworld Fae

Registry isn't all-knowing. And more importantly, Jack, I don't think she's interested in what you're offering. So it's time for you to move on and fuck off."

Jack bristles at the bar. "This has nothing to do with you, Ghost."

"Unfortunately, that's not entirely true," he drawls, a flash of metal appearing in his hand as he twirls a blade. "Don't make me ask again, Jack. I may enjoy the experience, but you certainly won't."

Dead Guy visibly pales, which is a feat considering his too-white complexion.

I swallow and take a step back. There's something very deadly pouring off of Ghost. It's not tangible. Not even an aura. It's just… *him*. He exudes violence. And there's a hint of madness in his gaze, one I didn't notice before but clearly see now.

Or maybe it's not madness so much as malice. Danger. *An eagerness to kill.*

Those golden orbs swing my way, his lips curling into a soft grin that belies the cruelty radiating from his eyes. "Don't worry, little mystery. Jack was just leaving."

"You're an asshole, Ghost."

"I am," he concedes. "But in this case, I'm trying to save your life."

"By threatening it?" Jack scoffs as he slides off his stool. "If ya wanted the female, ya could have just said so. No need for all the theatrics."

Ghost finishes his drink and slowly turns toward Jack. "I adore violence, Jack, but not even I would be suicidal enough to flirt with the Bride of Death."

SERA

I BLINK.

Bride of Death.

"What?" I blurt out as Jack takes a shaky step backward.

"She's… she's…" His pupils blow wide, turning his eyes black. "I didn't know, Maliki. I swear on the crypts, I had no idea."

"As I said, I'm just trying to save your life," Ghost drawls. He cants his head. "You can go now, Jack."

"Thank you." Jack bows and vanishes, leaving me bewildered in his wake.

My bewilderment grows as I realize everyone is staring at me with obvious curiosity.

"You really shouldn't flirt with your bar patrons, little mystery," Ghost tells me as he sets his empty glass on the counter. "Unless, of course, you want to watch your fiancé kill them all on your wedding day."

I gape at him. "What?" It's the same word I already

uttered, but I... I don't even know where else to start. "Fiancé?" That word seems appropriate. As does the title he mentioned. "Bride of Death?" I shake my head. "I think you've confused me with someone else."

That's the only explanation.

Yet everyone is watching me now because of Ghost's commentary.

Thorns, I think with a mental sigh. *This is the last thing I need right now.*

I told Alina I would be fine on my own, that I could survive here without her supervision. If word of any of this gets back to her, she'll send her mates to the village to retrieve me. And won't that be fun?

I nearly growl at the prospect.

Or maybe the sound released from my chest.

Because Ghost arches a brow like he heard it. "I know exactly who you are, Persephone," he says, his blade disappearing as he leans forward and folds his arms along the counter. "Though, I hear you prefer to go by Sera now?"

He phrases it as a question, like he's trying to have a polite conversation with me.

The brutality he exuded seconds ago is entirely gone now. Instead, he appears harmless again. Normal. Studying me with those alluring irises. Smiling.

But he just called me *Persephone*, a name I hear every night in my dreams.

With him, I think, shivering.

My fated dreams with the mysterious Godlike Alpha started after a woman who claimed to be my mother saved me from Monsters Night.

Or did she kidnap me? I wonder, not for the first time.

My memories of everything that happened are murky at best. I vividly remember the Day of the Choosing and the Nightingale Village Viscount calling my name. The next clear memory is of Alina waking me up in the palace.

I recall bits and pieces between the two events as well, like Alina finding me in the garden, and my dreams of *him*.

Persephone, he calls me, his cultured tone a caress that makes me tremble even now as I think about his deep voice in my head.

"How do you know that name?" I ask Ghost in a whisper, wondering where he's heard it.

"I've heard you refer to yourself as *Sera* to countless fae in this bar," he replies with a shrug. "Usually after they call you some sort of pet name like *little human*." He waggles his brows. "Not very true, is it?"

I swallow. "That's not the name I meant." I'm still whispering, my voice barely carrying to my own ears.

He smiles. "I know." He picks up his empty glass and studies it. "Your fiancé has tasked me with escorting you to your new accommodations. Shall we go now?"

"I…" I frown, his words slowly registering through the fog of my mind. "No. I'm not going anywhere with you."

Not after seeing that lethal side of him peek out and terrify Jack.

Not after he called me Persephone *like the man in my dreams…*

I shake my head and take a step back.

I should call… The thought trails off in my mind, my lips tightening. *No. I'm not calling Alina.*

I need to handle this on my own, not rely on my sister for help. This is *my* life, and I'm done living in my sister's shadow. I love her. I do. But I need to take care of myself.

And that starts with surviving in this kingdom full of deadly creatures.

Ghost lifts a shoulder in a shrug and settles back into

his chair. "All right, then," he says. "Can I have another spider ale, please?"

I stare at him. "I'm not going anywhere with you," I repeat.

"Yes, I heard you the first time." He gestures to his rounded ear. "Your decline is noted."

"And accepted?" I ask slowly when he doesn't elaborate.

His lips curl. "For tonight."

I narrow my gaze. "I'm not sure I like that response."

He shrugs again. "Not my problem, mystery." He leans forward once more. "Now, about that spider ale?"

"You want me to give you a drink after you threatened to drag me off to a fiancé I've never even met?" I grunt. "No, thanks."

I turn to go serve someone—*anyone*—else at the bar and run right into a hard chest.

Jumping backward, I gasp as I stare up into a pair of golden irises.

The same ones that were behind me a second ago.

"I didn't threaten you," Ghost says casually. "I *offered* to escort you to your new accommodations."

He takes a step forward, causing me to move backward another step.

However, he doesn't advance on me. He simply pivots to his left and grabs a glass instead.

"And you definitely know your betrothed," he adds as he toggles the spider ale to life. The smoky tendrils flow in ripples that build dangerously close to the rim. But he cuts off the essence just before it spills, then twirls the glass and vanishes.

I spin toward where he was sitting mere minutes ago to find him lounging in his seat once more.

"Cheers," he says, toasting me before taking a sip and

relaxing into his chair. "Thanks for giving me the night off, mystery. I needed a bloody break."

I… I don't know how to reply to that or to him. He's obviously insane. Psychotic, even. *And powerful*, I think, shivering at the residual touch left behind by his overwhelming aura. It's as though he's wrapped me in the shadows along with him, his essence bleeding into my exposed skin.

Only, a glance downward suggests it's all in my head.

He's playing with me.

Just like all fae do.

My jaw tightens.

This is ridiculous. I turn away from him again and resume my responsibilities behind the bar. That guy can go sit in a patch of thorns for all I care. I don't have a fiancé. I'm not interested in any mating games. And I'm definitely not going anywhere with *him*.

Ignoring Ghost, I go about fixing some refills for the regulars in Death's Den. But all they do is gape at me as I bring them their drinks. No flirtatious banter. No comments. Just wide eyes as they study me through a new lens.

I do my best to act normal and simply smile while distributing the glasses.

Then I return to clean up what I can behind the bar.

All while everyone watches, including the one who ruined my night.

It takes all my energy to pretend like everything is fine when all I want to do is scream. A few words from this stranger have derailed my status. *Bride of Death*. What does that even mean? Does he think I'm engaged to a Death Fae? There are thousands of them here. Tens of thousands, even. How would I even begin to figure out which one he's talking about?

Not that it matters.

Because I am *not* engaged.

I'm just not.

I don't want a mate. I never have. Which was why my heart plummeted when the Viscount called my name during that infamous Day of the Choosing.

Serapina Everheart.

My eyes threaten to close as I picture myself in that white dress, walking down the aisle to answer my fate. Over three years later, and it's a stark memory in my mind. One I'll never forget.

Especially what happened after I boarded that train.

What came next reminds me of a dream, though. The way I was whisked off into a garden and introduced to my mother. Or rather, my *creator*.

I… I still don't understand how any of it was real.

It felt like a single night of sleep that just wouldn't end. At least not until I opened my eyes and found Alina walking through the flowers. Then it was like I drifted off again, only to wake up in a palatial bed with views overlooking the Netherworld Kingdom.

Swallowing, I shake my head and return to my surroundings, only to realize that everyone has left except Ghost. He's still seated at the bar, though he appears to be sipping a brand-new drink.

Narrowing my gaze at him, I say, "You have to pay for those, you know."

"Do I?" he asks, one dark brow rising. "But I've been serving myself."

"That doesn't make the drinks free," I tell him.

He smiles. "What if I told you the owner said I could have these for free?"

"I'd call you a liar."

"Would you?" Amusement deepens his question.

"Then what are you, Persephone? A liar? An excellent actress?" He cants his head, causing his unruly hair to fall across his forehead. "Or are you simply a mystery to be solved?"

I hold his vibrant gaze. "How do you know that name?" This time I voice it as a demand, my tone infused with a confidence I don't feel. But irritation is a powerful motivator. And this guy has more than earned my annoyance.

He studies me for a long moment, some of his amusement seeming to disappear behind a wave of curiosity. "Your fiancé calls you Persephone."

A chill skitters down my spine. "And who is my supposed fiancé?" I ask, a little less confident now. Because only one man refers to me as *Persephone* and it's the sexy fae who haunts my dreams.

The one who once called himself *Hades.*

When I woke up the next morning, I realized that name was a result of my new surroundings. My sister had just rescued me from my prison garden and taken me to her mates' home realm—the Netherworld Kingdom.

And *Hades* is the God here, the one whom all the fae worship.

He also happens to be related to my sister's mate.

So it was no wonder I chose that name for my figment. Some inane part of me clearly wished I could be claimed in a way similar to how my sister was. To become a cherished Omega with a mate-circle.

A fantasy, one that will never come to fruition.

Because I'm not an Omega.

"Death," Ghost says, drawing me back to our conversation. "Clearly."

My brow furrows. "What?"

"Hmm, yes," he hums as he sets down his drink. "I

have heard of this ailment, but I've never witnessed it for myself before. Not until now." He gives me a sad look. "You humans really do struggle with your hearing, yeah?"

I stare at him for a beat, then narrow my eyes. "You're as bad as a thorn."

"A thorn?" he repeats, his eyebrows lifting.

"Yes. Irritating, sharp, and inconvenient." And a complete waste of my time. Glancing around, I make a decision. "Death's Den is closed. You should leave."

He follows my gaze, then lifts his arm, which I realize has been concealed by a cloak this whole time. But now I catch sight of tan skin decorated in smokelike ink as he makes a show of checking his wrist.

My heart skips a beat at the sight of those familiar tattoos. The writhing lines remind me of Reaper, my sister's Death Fae mate.

He's psychotic. Deadly. And utterly obsessed with Alina.

Good thing, too. Because if he weren't, he would be terrifying.

Which doesn't bode well for me now.

If Ghost is anything like Reaper, I'm in big trouble.

"I can smell your fear," Ghost murmurs, his golden irises flickering up at me. "I warned you not to flirt with your patrons, mystery. Do you enjoy blood?"

I stare at him. "Are you going to pay for those drinks?"

His brow furrows, his gaze dropping to the glass on the counter before slowly returning to me. "Maybe. Maybe not. I haven't decided yet."

"Then I don't know if you're a patron of the bar or not," I tell him. "So your warning is null and void." Not that I was flirting with him.

Fear him, however, yes, I do.

But I refuse to admit that aloud.

I moved away from my sister and her mates because I need to be able to survive here on my own.

And that includes handling fae like Ghost.

This is all just part of the territory of being a human in a supernatural kingdom.

I can do this.

I have to do this.

I will do this.

The mantra is one I've repeated several times over the last few weeks, and I do so again now as Ghost grins.

"I like you, Sera," he informs me as he slides off his stool. "It's a shame our next meeting won't be as enjoyable." He pulls out several obsidian coins and sets them on the counter.

They spin like all the money in this kingdom does and disappear into some sort of enchanted vault in the back.

I guess he's a customer now, I grouse to myself. *Not that it matters.*

"When you see me again, try to remember that you chose the hard way," he adds, his hands sliding into the pockets of his jeans as his cloak rustles around his broad shoulders. "I tried to be a gentleman, and you refused. What happens next isn't my fault, yeah?"

He doesn't give me a chance to reply. Just vanishes into a cloud of smoke—one that flows toward me and wraps around my throat like a noose. It tightens, only to dissipate into a light mist against my skin before disappearing into the air.

The scent of leather and fiery embers tickles my nose, and I kind of hate that I like the smell.

"Blasted fae," I mutter to myself. They're all so hypnotic and sensual and *playful.*

Yet something about this one was different. Most of the

males just ask me out on a date or broadcast their abilities to protect me in their kingdom.

Ghost did neither of those things.

Instead, he insinuated that I'm already claimed.

By Death.

Either Ghost has the wrong girl, or *Death* has severely underestimated me. Because I didn't survive my world's version of the monster mating games just to find myself in a forced arrangement with a fae.

Once upon a time, I yielded to a higher power.

I learned my lesson.

The next time someone tries to make me bow, *I'll fight.*

MALIKI

Serapina Everheart is trouble with a capital *T*.

Her golden blonde hair, pouty lips, and sparkling blue eyes craft the picture of corruptible innocence. Couple that with her perfect tits and heart-shaped ass, and she's like a damn beacon in this otherwise dark world.

A beacon that seems to call to every available male Corpse Fae and Death Fae throughout the Netherworld Kingdom.

Letting her work in Death's Den was a fucking mistake. Hell, letting her leave the palace was a damnable offense.

Thankfully, Hades has finally come to his senses. Because I am fucking tired of playing babysitter. Or maybe *stalker* is the right term.

I follow the alluring female everywhere. Knock out any fae who tries to touch her. Persuade would-be suitors to look the other way. And also ensure the trees in her favorite courtyard don't accidentally ensnare her.

Fae, she's too innocent to be here.

Too naïve. Too sweet. Too *human*.

Yet, supposedly, that's all a façade.

I've questioned that since Hades first told me not to fall for her little game. Because if she's playing at her innocence, she's doing one hell of a job.

Her expression tonight when I called her the Bride of Death suggested she had no idea what I was talking about.

But that's not my problem.

It's Hades's issue.

One I wish he would take on himself.

Alas, here I am, standing just outside his personal quarters, waiting for him to join me.

He knows I'm here. Not just because he's omniscient in general, but because Ossa growled a warning the moment I shadowed onto the dark cobblestone terrace. She's not my biggest fan. Given what she did to my favorite pair of shoes, I'm not all that fond of her either.

Howl and Mort are fine, though. Which is the only reason I crouch as the three-headed beast comes scrambling toward me.

Ossa releases a complaint via a low whine, while the other two yip in excitement. I can tell she's trying to gain hold of the legs, but her two brothers override her choice, causing the furry mass of black fur to tumble right into me.

I'm ready with my hands, scratching their abundance of ears and scruff, all while Ossa grumbles in annoyance.

"I'll never understand her disfavor toward you," Hades murmurs as he walks out through his flowing dark drapes. "Most females find you irresistible."

I snort, then go to pat Ossa on the head. "She's just jealous of Fleur."

Ossa snaps at my fingers, trying to take a bite out of me.

Which only has me chuckling in response when Mort and Howl snarl right back at her.

The three of them begin tussling amongst themselves, which creates a large spinning ball of fluff, one that whirls with violent energy across the stone ground.

Fire erupts in their wake, causing Hades to shake his head as he sends a blast of magic after them to minimize the fiery damage. "Useless," he mutters.

"You adopted them," I point out.

"I did," he sighs. "They're intimidating when they need to be."

"If you say so," I drawl, my focus shifting to the view. That's why I chose his terrace for our meeting instead of his office or his personal quarters.

I love it up here. It's quiet. The air is crisp. And the pale moons look close enough to touch, their dull yellow light casting an ominous glow over the valley below.

A valley that houses all of Corpse Fae and Death Fae kind.

This is one of the only places that ever gives me peace.

I admire the deep red falls in the distance, the thick substance roaring with powerful force from the top of the Netherworld Mountains and dropping into the Blood River below.

It's deadly. Unpredictable. And riddled with violent intentions.

Just like me.

"Where's my mate?" Hades asks.

"Safely tucked into her village bed," I reply without looking at him.

After Sera locked up Death's Den, I followed her back to the one-bedroom hut she calls home, just like I do every night. She never notices, something I can't really fault her for, as no one notices me in the shadows. That's where I lurk and kill. Hence my infamous nickname.

Fortunately for Sera, I have no desire to harm her. At least, not in the traditional sense.

Sexually is another matter entirely.

Alas, she's not mine to touch. A shame, truly, as I would very much enjoy making her scream.

"What part of *bring her to me* did you not understand?" Hades asks, a hint of irritation coloring his cultured tone.

"You told me to *escort* her to you," I remind him, my gaze still on the village below. From here, I can barely pinpoint Sera's location. It makes me uneasy, likely because I've been guarding her for nearly a year.

Ever since Hades helped free me from the Hell Fae King's interrogation room.

Turning, I finally look at Hades and arch a brow. "*Escort* implies consent. She didn't consent. Ergo, I followed her home and came back here to provide my report."

He stares down at me, clearly unamused. "And your report is centered around the semantics of specific words?"

I smile. "No. My report is, Serapina Everheart states she is uninterested in the upcoming mating games—not that she'll be eligible to participate—and she doesn't want an escort to her new accommodations. She also seems to be hard of hearing, as she favors the word *what*."

I pause, considering what else I need to tell him.

"Oh," I go on, "and you owe me fifty ink coins."

He simply holds my gaze, saying nothing.

I shrug. "She demanded I pay for my drinks even after I told her the owner says I can drink for free. Rather than argue, I left her a fifty. Hence…" I hold out my palm.

Hades remains silent, but I can see the storm brewing in his eyes.

He's pissed.

Good.

Hades knows better than to leave me up to my own devices for too long. And this babysitting assignment has far surpassed our usual arrangements.

Forcing me to watch his betrothed without being allowed to touch is a fresh form of torture. I meant what I told her about his possessive side—he'll kill anyone who even looks at her wrong. Including me.

Which makes the task of watching her very fucking difficult.

"You're going to make me retrieve her myself," Hades finally says.

"Am I?" I ask, feigning innocence. "I suppose it's that or you give me permission to use force—which will very likely require me to touch her."

His jaw clenches, understanding flickering in the dark depths of his intense eyes. "I see. That's why the semantics matter."

"Semantics always matter," I counter. "But in this case, yes. I'm not about to test the limits of our arrangement."

"I would never kill you, Maliki." Soft words. An ominous promise.

"There are fates worse than death, Hades." And I'm all too familiar with those fates. Many of those tortured destinies are ones I've crafted myself, and I have no wish to experience those outcomes from the opposite side.

He exhales slowly and finally releases me from the intensity of his gaze, his focus shifting to the Netherworld Kingdom below. "I need her in my palace."

"Then perhaps you shouldn't have let her leave in the first place." It's a chastisement, one that very few fae would ever dream of saying to a God like Hades. But I'm not most fae. And our arrangement is far from ordinary.

"I wanted to see what she would do," he murmurs.

"That's been your excuse for the last year," I point out.

"It's not an excuse. It's a reason." There's a subtle bite to his tone, one that tells me I'm treading on thin ice with my commentary.

But I don't fucking care.

This has gone on long enough.

"Have you considered that perhaps she's telling the truth?" I ask him. "That she doesn't remember anything at all?"

He doesn't answer me, though a flicker of black flames dances along his fingertips as he continues to study the world below.

"Do you find it troubling that she hasn't gone into heat yet?" I press.

He told me last year that a few weeks in his presence should trigger her Omega soul to take over, which would likely result in a long-overdue estrous cycle.

The only reason he informed me of this was because he needed someone he could trust to guard him while he took care of his mate.

However, that event has yet to happen.

And from what I've witnessed in Sera, it won't be anytime soon.

Her petite stature may physically mark her as an Omega, but she lacks the timidness and submissive tendencies that Hades once remarked on.

Well, the submissive part remains to be seen. I'm certain I could make her kneel under the right circumstances.

"I find a lot of things about this situation troubling," Hades tells me, his voice low, like he's afraid his words may carry, thus revealing his weakness. "I sense Persephone with every breath, yet I don't recognize her human shell. It's so fragile. *Too* fragile."

"You're worried she'll die and her soul will move on to another host," I translate.

"Among other things, yes. But sometimes the best way to light a fire is to ignite a spark." He looks at me again. "You spoke to her tonight?"

His question takes me aback just a bit, as it's not one I expected him to ask. "Yes."

"So you've officially met, then?" he presses.

"Officially? Not quite. But she knows me as Ghost."

He nods. "Good enough. Keep talking to her." He turns, dismissing me with that task.

"And say what?" I call after him.

He shrugs. "Up to you." He glances back at me over his broad shoulder. "But you have one week to convince her to marry me."

I huff a laugh. "So I've been upgraded from babysitter to seducer now?" I mean it as a joke.

However, he simply replies, "Yes," and begins walking again.

This time I shadow to cut him off at the doorway—an action that has Ossa growling at me from the terrace. I ignore the fiercely protective animal and focus on the beast of a God standing before me. "Give me parameters."

"No," he tells me. "No rules."

"Then I can touch her?" I voice it as a threat, knowing he'll react to it.

His jaw visibly tightens, just as I expected. "If that's what it takes, yes."

I startle at that reply and take a step backward. "*What?*" It doesn't escape my notice that I'm now using

Sera's favorite word from Death's Den, but it's an appropriate response. "Have you lost your mind?"

He arches a brow. "Are you saying you're not up to the task, Maliki?" He tilts his head, his expression evaluating. "Her pale skin will flush nicely beneath your touch, yes?"

I narrow my gaze. "You're fucking with me." Actually, no, he's *punishing* me. I danced around his terminology earlier, so now he's leaving me to define this game.

"No, I'm asking you to get closer to her," he corrects me.

"And that means I can fuck her?" I demand, trying to throw him off course and force him to set some sort of boundaries.

But the asshole simply shrugs. "Perhaps eventually."

Now I know he's lost the plot. "I had no idea you wanted cause to kill me, *my lord*." The title is one I know he hates. It's how all the fae in this kingdom refer to him. But I only do it when I'm trying to irritate him.

His lips curl. "Nice try, Mal." The nickname is one he rarely uses for me. "I may not wish to share her, but if it's the means to acquiring her acquiescence, so be it."

He tries to step around me.

I don't let him, instead meeting him move for move. "Then why not call Morpheus?" I ask, aware that my question is a low blow.

Some of Hades's nonchalance finally cracks. "Because Morpheus has no claim on what's mine."

"And I do?" I counter.

"You could," he tells me, again shocking the shadows out of me. "The notion of watching you touch her does not appall me the way it probably should."

I snort. "That's motivational."

"Would you like me to make it a request, Maliki? To ask you to fuck her for my pleasure?"

I finally step out of his way. "I'm not going to let you make a demonstration out of me at your wedding."

He runs his gaze over me. "If I were to do that, I promise we would both enjoy it."

"I crave the death of others, not my own," I tell him.

His lips curl at the sides. "I'm the God of Death, Maliki. If I kill you in ire, I'll just bring you back after I've calmed down." With that unhelpful commentary, he vanishes.

A note appears a second later, the lettering resembling Hades's familiar scrawl.

There are only two words on the white parchment, both penned in black blood.

One. Week.

"Fuck my life," I mutter. "And fuck you, Hades. *Fuck. You.*"

SERA

THE SCENT OF DEATH ON MY PILLOW STIRS ME FROM SLEEP.

It's a pungent stench, one that tells me what I'm going to see before I open my eyes—a dead fire lily.

The first time this happened—which was right after I moved in—I screamed.

The second time, I screamed again.

The third time, I stayed up all night waiting for the culprit to show himself... and shrieked when I found the source of my torment laying the wilting flower on my pillow.

However, now I simply sigh and open my eyes to lock gazes with the bright orbs glowing at me from beneath a royal blue hood.

It's a ghost.

A spirit.

A lost soul.

Er, I don't know exactly. But he has a skull face with an

upside-down heart hollowed out where his nose should be and blue flame-like eyes. He doesn't seem to have vocal cords, so he never speaks. But he does know how to write.

And he apparently thinks this hut belongs to him.

However, rather than trying to force me to leave, he keeps bringing me gifts like a cat in the night.

There's just one problem—all of his gifts are dead.

"Thank you, Pip," I say with a yawn before stretching in the tiny twin bed.

My ghost creature twirls in happiness, pleased that I've thanked him. Or maybe he's just happy that I'm talking to him. I'm not quite sure. He seems lonely. Which explains why he follows me around the second I come home and welcomes me every morning with his dead gifts.

Rolling off the stiff mattress, I'm careful not to bump Pip, and head toward the bathroom with the cloaked figure on my tail.

"We've talked about this," I tell him as he tries to come with me through the threshold. "I like privacy in this room. I'll see you again after my shower."

Pip—the name I gave him after learning he had no identity—pouts.

"Ten minutes," I promise him. Then I disappear to engage in my evening routine.

My hours in this kingdom are all out of sorts. There is no sun, only moons, and everything is cast in perpetual shades of night. It's a stark difference from my world of sunshine, vibrant flowers, and lush greens.

I've tried nurturing some of the trees in the courtyard outside my home, but the skeletal branches are nothing like the wooded ones from back home.

Sometimes I miss my old life.

It's asinine. I was basically residing in a dream for

several years, imprisoned by a Goddess who called me her daughter.

And that was after surviving the infamous Monsters Night protocols of my old village.

My jaw clenches. *This place might be littered with death, but at least I have choices here.*

Only, last night's antics at the bar replay through my head in the next moment, making me question that mantra.

Mating games.

Bride of Death.

New accommodations.

Though, Ghost didn't try to drag me anywhere last night, nor did he come for me while I slept. So maybe it was all some big joke? A weird Death Fae prank?

Is he even a Death Fae? I wonder.

Shaking off the question, I focus on my shower, the chilled water making my movements quick as my teeth chatter.

Apparently, all the water in the Netherworld Village is like this. It makes me miss the warmth from the palace.

But I can't go back there. I love Alina, and I'm happy for her and her mates. However, I need to find myself. To learn how to survive. *To figure out where I fit in…*

Some of the fae at the bar have talked about other kingdoms and realms. I usually pretend to ignore them while listening to every word, searching for hints of a place I might like to go.

So far, none of them have appealed to me, though. At least not based on their conversations.

However, I know where some of the portals are that take fae to alternate worlds. They're in the tunnel—the one that links the Netherworld Kingdom to the Morpheus Kingdom.

I've walked over there more than once, tempted to go inside and find the portals for myself.

But each time, I've been spooked by the eerie sensations surrounding the entrance. It's almost like the tunnel is a portal in itself.

Turning off the water, I wrap a towel around myself and step out of the small glass enclosure to stare into the circular mirror above my sink.

The bathroom is definitely a downgrade from the palatial one attached to my guest suite in the palace. However, I prefer this space to that one because this room is mine. As is the bed and the couch and my small kitchen.

Gnarls sends my paycheck to the village fund to help pay for my rent and utilities. I'm also given a stipend at the local Skull Mart for my groceries. Fortunately, they have an aisle dedicated to human food. Apparently, a lot of the fae like "other-world cuisine."

If only I recognized half the items in the aisle. I don't. But that's mostly related to my home world being different from the Human Realm here.

So complicated, I think, not for the first time. *Alternate dimensions. Fae. Monsters.*

I shake my head. "It's a wonder I'm still standing some days," I tell myself as I brush my hair and finish up in the bathroom.

Pip is pacing right outside the door, his white hands tucked behind his back as he floats back and forth. His big, hollowed-out eyes meet mine, the bright blue flames flickering to life in what almost looks like a smile as he perks up.

"It was only ten minutes," I tell him.

But he twirls again like he did after I thanked him for the dead flower, his cloak whispering across the floor.

I smile, amused by his excitement. It didn't take long for me to accept his presence here. He's just so endearing. And it's clear he doesn't mean me any harm. Instead, he seems to want to help me.

Which is probably why I smell burning in the kitchen.

"Oh, Pip," I groan. "Did you try making me breakfast again?" Because the last time he did that, the toast ended up black and the eggs rotted in the pan.

I don't quite understand his lethal touch, but it's clearly not meant for living things.

Hence the reason I try to step around him and not through him. I don't want to end up like the flowers or the food.

Pip dances again, swishing around and leading me to the kitchen. "I told you before that I appreciate the gesture, but I prefer to—"

My words end on a yelp as a flame bursts from the stovetop.

"*Stars!*" I scream as I dart toward the sink, only the fire shoots toward me in an irregular arc, forcing me to jump backward. My towel whispers around my legs, the cotton loosely tied against my chest. I grab the fabric, thinking about maybe using it to smother the flames, when a loud boom echoes from the front door.

I spin toward the sound, my attention torn between the growing heat and the pounding coming from outside. I'm about to ignore it when Pip zooms toward the door in a furious flurry. Or maybe he's panicking. I don't know. I also have no idea how to put out the fire.

"*Thorns,*" I hiss under my breath as I dart after him, my hand clutching my towel against my sternum.

When I throw open the door, I find Ghost standing just outside with his arm resting against the hinge and his head angled down. "Do you have any idea what time it is?" he mutters at me.

I blink. "What?"

He sighs. "I'm beginning to think that's your favorite word, mystery." Then he lifts his head to look over me at the chaos in my kitchen. His eyes narrow, his back straightening. "What in the Styx are you trying to cook?" he demands, his hands suddenly on my hips as he moves me out of his way and saunters into my house.

Pip has completely disappeared, leaving me alone with this lunatic fae who... who appears to be wielding a shadow...

I stare, my lips parting as smoke whirls all around Ghost, the source seeming to be coming from his arms. *His tattoos*, I think, suddenly realizing that he's shirtless and wearing only a pair of gray sweatpants. The ink along his arms and back shifts, leaving his tan skin behind.

Along with a lot of muscle.

Holy fae, this male really is stunning.

The perfect specimen of a man, really.

Not that I'm noticing. Or observing. Or ogling.

Nope.

No.

I'm just watching him put out the fire with his shadows. *How in the fae is that even possible?* I wonder, half convinced I'm dreaming now.

Because there's only one other male I've ever met who is this good-looking or this powerful, and he only exists in my head.

A head I now shake as I try to clear it and figure out what in the thorns is going on.

In a blink, my kitchen is fire-free and smoke-free, and all I can see is the expanse of Ghost's defined back as his tattoos writhe back into place. The swirls are mesmerizing, their pattern seeming to form skulls all over his skin.

"Wow," I breathe, hypnotized by the magic.

"Understatement," Ghost replies. "What the fuck were you trying to make? Charcoal pancakes?" He turns toward me, allowing me to admire another vast landscape of muscular lines.

So many abs.

So defined.

Yet oddly tattoo-free.

Hmm.

"Sera." My name from his mouth has my eyes slipping up to his lips, which are forming a thin line. "What the hell were you doing?"

My brow furrows. "Taking a shower." The words seem to leave my lips on autopilot. This guy's body has temporarily fried my brain.

"While your pancakes burned?" he asks, one of his eyebrows inching upward.

The condescending quality of his voice has me frowning.

Which slowly brings me out of my stupor.

"What are you doing here?" The question comes out slowly, my mind still surfacing to override my errant hormones.

Ghost looks like he just woke up, his thick, dark hair tumbling in messy waves across his forehead. He's barefoot. Shirtless—*obviously*. And… and in my home.

"Apparently, I'm saving you from burning down the entire fucking village," he tells me, his arms folding over his chest. "Who leaves pancakes unattended on a stove?"

"Why do you keep talking about pancakes?" I blurt out.

"Why?" Both of his eyebrows rise as he steps back to gesture at my black stove. "*That's* why."

"Oh." *Pip*. Right. I shake my head. "He was just trying to make me breakfast again." It comes out in a defensive mumble. Because Pip means well, but he just, um, he struggles.

Where is he? I wonder, looking around as Ghost repeats, "*He?*" There's a hint of incredulity to his tone. "*He* who?"

I meet his gaze again. "Not that it's any of your business, but Pip. And why are you here, again?" No, wait, I have a better query. "*How* are you here?"

The look Ghost gives me is filled with disbelief.

"I woke up to the stench of burning, then heard you scream like a fucking banshee. So I got out of bed to bang on your door with the goal of scaring off whoever or whatever made you shriek, as I prefer not to get violent this early in the evening. But then you opened the door and..." He once again gestures to my kitchen. "You're welcome, by the way."

I simply gape at him. "I didn't call for help."

He grunts and looks around. "Who is *he?*" he demands, ignoring my words.

Granted, I ignored him as well.

Which I continue to do now as I say, "I still don't get why you're here. How did you hear me?" Maybe that's a ridiculous question. He's a fae. They all have unique gifts.

"Because my bedroom is right through that wall," he says, pointing to the stove. "Not that it matters. Your scream definitely carries."

I narrow my gaze. "Your bedroom?" I repeat, my forehead crinkling. "That's impossible. Tank lives next door."

He releases another snort. "Tank hasn't been home for nearly a month." Those golden eyes of his capture and hold mine. "I sent him on an all-expenses-paid holiday right after you moved in, and he thanked me by letting me crash at his place."

My eyelashes flutter. "You…" I trail off, unsure of how to respond to that. "You're living next door." The words come out stilted. Hollow. Confused. "*Why?*"

"Because I'm your pet bodyguard, mystery." He leans his athletic hip against the counter and folds his arms again. "I'm also apparently your new recruiter, too."

"Recruiter?"

"That is indeed what I said," he tells me before sighing and tipping his head backward to stretch out his neck. "Can you please explain the burnt pancakes now, mystery?"

"I don't think I need to explain anything to you," I reply. "You're the one who informed me last night that I'm supposedly engaged. Now you say you've taken over my neighbor's home because you're my bodyguard-slash-recruiter. And you basically barged into my hut without an invitation."

He slowly straightens his head and neck, his intense gaze landing directly on me. "I didn't *barge* in, Sera. You opened the door, I saw the fire, and I walked in to put out the flames."

I stare at him again. He's not wrong, but he's not correct either. I didn't ask for his help. He just foisted it upon me.

Which I should probably be grateful for, as I had no idea how to put out that magical flame.

But I'm not about to tell him that. Not with everything else hanging between us.

"You're not supposedly engaged either," he adds. "There's nothing *supposed* about it. You're betrothed. And you've been betrothed for a very, very long time."

I huff a laugh. "Oh yeah? To Death, right?"

He doesn't share in my sarcastic amusement. Instead, he levels me with a serious look. "Yes. To the *God* of Death."

Everything inside me goes cold. "The God of Death?" I repeat in a barely audible whisper, certain—*hoping*—that I've heard him wrong.

"Yes," he confirms. "Hades."

MORPHEUS

SERAPINA'S SCREAM ECHOES THROUGH MY MIND, THE SOUND one that almost made me mist into her home moments ago.

But Maliki was faster.

He shadowed to her porch within a second of her shrieking and tried to beat her door down with his fist. In his sleepy state, he missed the source of her chaos—the little instigator now floating around in the Netherworld Courtyard.

The errant soul zipped right by Maliki, using the in-between to hide its presence as it escaped.

Either Maliki was too consumed by Serapina to notice the skittering creature, or he didn't see it. I suspect the latter.

But I saw the troublemaker.

And I want to know what it did to my intended.

45

Once I'm sure Serapina is safe, I trail after the lost spirit. The soul is still dressed in that strange blue cloak, its movements agitated as the sound of teeth chattering comes from beneath his hood. It's almost as though the essence is trying to speak.

Odd. I cock my head, intrigued as the hooded creature makes several animated motions with its arms before hanging its head in defeat. The air moves with an audible sigh, one that has me arching a brow.

"Souls don't typically breathe," I say as I materialize beside the spirit in the in-between. It's a chilling space I don't particularly care for, as it resides between life and death, but as a Mythos Fae, I'm allowed to linger.

At least for a bit.

Blue flame-like eyes flash up to mine from beneath the hood of the thick cloak, then the creature darts backward several paces. Or, well, *floats* backward. Its feet are not exactly touching the ground since the soul is part specter.

Although, its face certainly resembles solid bone.

Not abnormal. Many souls in this kingdom still have some of their corporeal features. However, this one appears to be more solid than most.

"Did you try to touch Serapina?" I ask it, my eyebrow arching. That wouldn't explain the burning scent I picked up on when Maliki stepped inside, but it would explain her scream.

The soul—who I swear looked intimidated a moment ago—vibrates and chatters white teeth at me while narrowing its eyes. Then the creature holds up a finger and waves it at me in a trademark sign of warning.

I stare at the little soul. "Are you trying to tell me to back off?"

The soul dips its head, nodding at me. Then points in the direction of Serapina's home.

"You want me to go back to her?" I guess.

Which is apparently the wrong translation because the little soul vibrates aggressively again and sprints to my opposite side to stand between me and where it pointed a second ago. Then the creature lifts its arms, causing the cloak to expand like a proper ghost.

But I don't think that's its intention.

Instead, it's acting like a guard dog—vibrant eyes turning into burning crescents, jaw visibly clenched.

"You're telling me to back off of Serapina?" I ask slowly.

The little soul relaxes a bit, then nods again.

I huff a laugh. "I see. Hades put you up to this."

The being visibly shrinks backward, the blue flames inside his hollowed eyes going wide as it starts searching the courtyard, like it expects the God of Death to appear in the flesh.

My brow furrows as the soul begins to shake. It casts a forlorn look back at the village—I assume at *Serapina*—then continues to scan the courtyard, clearly frightened.

"He scares you?"

The soul nods with a more frantic energy now.

"Because he forced you to watch Serapina?" I add.

But the creature shakes its head now before skipping all around the courtyard. Or rather, floating with a bizarre little hitch to its movements. Almost like the soul is glitching.

When it leaves the in-between to become corporeal once again, I follow suit, curious.

Then I watch as the being arranges a bunch of bones —branches that have fallen off the skeletal trees—on the ground.

"Pip?" I read, not understanding at all.

The soul points to its chest, then to the word.

"Are you trying to tell me your name?"

Pip nods.

Meanwhile, I blink. "Since when do souls have names?"

The creature makes a chattering sound that almost reminds me of a snort before rearranging the bones again to spell *Sera*.

My brow creases. "Serapina named you Pip?"

The soul nods and does a happy little twirl, one that causes its cloak to swirl around it.

"Why?" I ask, utterly lost now.

Pip does nothing for a moment, just scans the ground and taps its chin. I wait, too intrigued to urge the little creature along. When it picks up a bony branch and starts drawing in the black sand-like dirt, I remain quiet.

The letters form and disappear quickly, the obsidian substance clearly not enjoying this writing game. However, it works as I say, "Friend," once Pip is done drawing the word. "You and Serapina are friends?"

Pip spins in excitement while enthusiastically bobbing its head.

I narrow my gaze. "If that's true, why did she scream?"

Another sigh escapes the soul as its head droops once more. Then Pip starts writing furiously with the skeletal stick. It takes me a few seconds to realize the being is writing a sentence because the word makes no sense. But as Pip finishes, I understand. "You made her breakfast."

Soft chattering teeth answer my comment, the bone digging into the sandy ground again.

"The breakfast caught on fire," I translate after the creature finishes.

Pip continues to write.

"Everything you touch dies," I tell it, already aware of

what the soul is probably going to say. "So when you try to cook, it doesn't go well."

I tilt my head, suddenly realizing the importance of the outfit.

"That's why you're wearing a cloak—so you don't accidentally kill Serapina." A soul's touch can be deadly, especially to a human, but it requires direct contact. "You're dressed like that to protect her from your essence."

Big blue eyes meet mine as the creature nods swiftly, confirming my statement.

"Because Hades asked you to?" I guess.

The soul flinches, then shakes its head and looks around frantically like it did before.

"He's not here," I promise the little troublemaker. "And I'm not going to call for him." Voicing my cousin's name aloud doesn't make him appear, something the beings in this kingdom don't seem to understand. They all refer to Hades as *my lord* or *our lord*. It's ridiculous.

And it's just the way Hades likes it.

He would rather be feared and revered; it means no one will bother him.

I prefer to meddle.

Hence my purpose in this kingdom right now.

"I won't take you to Hades," I add. "And I won't escort you back to the Soul Yards either." Which is what most fae would do in this case, as the creature has clearly escaped. But Serapina wouldn't know or understand that.

And she named it. *Him*, I think. "Do you identify as male?" I ask, just to be sure.

Pip nods.

"Interesting." Most souls don't interact like this. Though, most souls don't escape the Soul Yards to make friends with human females either. Yet here we are. "Well, *Pip*, I think you and I need to be friends, too."

49

The soul looks at me expectantly.

"I assume you're not fond of Maliki since you fled Serapina's house the moment he arrived," I say. "And you don't work for Hades."

Pip shivers visibly but doesn't start glancing all over the place again. Instead, he holds my gaze and waits for me to continue.

It's not exactly a confirmation of my assumptions, but I don't really need him to corroborate my statements. His reaction to Maliki told me everything I needed to know.

So I move on to my next point, which is simply, "I also care about Serapina."

Pip continues to stare.

"So we should protect her together," I inform him.

More silence accompanies my commentary. Silence that appears to be underlined with doubt.

Hmm. I like this soul. He's smart not to trust me. Unfortunately, though, I need to change his mind on that.

"As a show of good faith, how about I make her evening breakfast tomorrow?" I offer. "Then I can mist it into the kitchen for you to present it to her."

Pip considers this, the flames of his eyes narrowing into fiery blue crescents.

"I'm not going to hurt her," I promise. "Our souls are destined." Something Hades refuses to accept, but it's true. Persephone was meant to be my mate, too. Perhaps if he'd listened to me, Omega kind would have survived.

But that's a debate for another day.

However, a history lesson may be appropriate for now. Especially if it helps convince Pip to ally with me.

"How about a story?" I suggest. "After I'm done, you can decide if we're to be friends or not, hmm?"

Pip floats a tad bit closer, his movements slightly less guarded.

"I'm going to interpret that as you being interested in my tale," I muse. "To start, allow me to introduce myself. I'm Morpheus. You probably know me as the God of Dreams."

If that information startles Pip, he doesn't show it.

I smile. "Now that the formalities are done, I'll begin. Many moons ago…"

SERA

HADES.

The name whispers through my mind, both familiar and frightening. "You think I'm engaged to Hades?" I ask Ghost, my voice sounding a million miles away as I try to sort through the confusion in my head. "Is this because of Alina?"

That's the only thing that makes sense. My sister is an Omega. Maybe Hades assumes I'm one, too.

But I'm not.

I'm nothing like Alina.

I don't mean that as an insult or a barb; it's merely the truth.

Alina is fearless. Comfortably mated. Happy.

I've been called timid all my life. Fragile. Malleable. *Naïve*.

None of those adjectives are accurate. But this male—the one who seems to think I'm *engaged*—no doubt has his assumptions.

"I know she's mated to Orcus," I go on, my thoughts spilling out through my mouth. "But that doesn't mean I'm suitable for his brother." My brow furrows. "And besides that, I've never even met Hades. So…" I lift my gaze from Ghost's abs—I didn't even realize that was where I was looking until I went to find his face—and say, "I think you have me confused with someone else."

"You said that last night," he replies, his muscles rippling as he folds his arms. "And as I said then, I know exactly who you are, Persephone."

My jaw clenches. *There's that name again.* "My name is Sera."

"Which you also said last night."

"Then perhaps you should try listening to me," I interject before he can go on or say something else to annoy me. "I've never met Hades. I'm not engaged to him. I'm also not an Omega—hence I'm not like Alina—and I would really like you to go now."

He pops his hip against my counter, his gaze assessing.

"What if I stay and fill you in on what I know instead?" he offers. "Such as the fact that Hades says you possess an Omega's soul, and not just any soul, but the one he was mated to in a past life. And by the way, her name was Persephone. Therefore…" He gestures at me while I gape back at him.

Because that was a lot of information to pass along in the blink of a few words.

"Hmm, I see I've finally made *you* listen," he muses. "Shall I feed you as well?" He glances at my ruined stove. "Or did you have your heart set on charcoaled pancakes?"

"I…" I follow his gaze to the burnt mess as my stomach begins to grumble. I haven't eaten anything since before my shift last night, and now my kitchen is destroyed. My options are pretty limited—walk over to the Bone Shack for a burger or take Ghost up on his offer.

I'm not particularly fond of meat first thing in the morning. So the latter seems more appetizing. Except…

"What kind of breakfast are you going to make?" I ask him, unable to mask the wariness in my tone.

His gaze dances over me, his lips quirking upward into a smirk. "Get dressed, then come over and find out."

My brow furrows, my eyes dropping to the towel I'm still clutching to my chest. "Oh." It feels like an hour has passed since my shower and the whole fiasco in the kitchen.

"And be prepared to tell me who *he* is," Ghost adds.

"He?" I echo, not following at all.

"The *he* who was supposedly making you breakfast," he says.

"Oh," I repeat, my lips twisting. "Pip." I glance around. "Where did he go, anyway?"

"Who the fuck is Pip?" Ghost demands.

"A spirit," I tell him, then shake my head. "Wait, why am I explaining myself to you? It's you who owes me answers, not the other way around."

"I owe you answers?" he asks, sounding incredulous.

"Yeah," I reply, my hands dropping to my hips. "About my supposed *fia*—"

The towel begins to unravel, ending my commentary as I scramble to grab the cotton and hold it against my chest.

"You know what? I'm going to go put on some clothes."

"I did suggest that already," he drawls.

But I ignore him and leave for the small bedroom. It's not a far walk, the door only two paces to my left. Actually, I'm pretty sure the entire space is about fifteen steps or so from the front door to the back wall of my bedroom.

Very different from the room I stayed in at Death's Palace.

Hades's home, I think.

My sister and her mates live in one wing of the massive estate, and I lived there for a year without ever seeing Hades. Yet he seems to think we're engaged.

No, worse than that—*mates*.

"If that's true, then why didn't he ever come to see me?" I mutter aloud as I pull out a pair of jeans and a tank top.

I'm about to put them on when I think better of it and grab some black pants instead. The cotton fabric is a lot softer and meant for sleeping, but I don't care. It's a comfort-first kind of morning. Especially considering all the work I'm going to have to do in the kitchen today.

Stars, what a way to spend my day. Fortunately, I only have the late shift at the Den tonight.

Pip and I are going to have a very long one-sided conversation whenever he returns.

But first, I'm going to get some answers from Ghost. And hopefully eat something edible in the process.

I yank the black tank top on, the built-in sports bra making it a comfortable top to pair with the casual pants. Then I gather my wet hair and tie it up into a messy bun.

Apparently, I'm engaged.

No need to tempt the sexy shirtless fae waiting in my living room, right?

Not that I want to tempt him. Or tempt anyone. Or find a mate. *Or be engaged*.

It feels like I told Ghost and Jack a week ago that I have no interest in the mating games. Yet it's been, like, twelve hours.

Insanity.

Blowing out a breath, I walk back into the kitchen and find Ghost evaluating my stove again. "Yeah, that'll do," he says, causing me to glance around. "Thanks, Jerry."

My brow furrows. "Jerry?"

Ghost turns to point to his rounded ear.

I stare at it for a beat, frowning. *Uh, okay...* If he's on a phone, I don't see it.

"I don't care how many inks, man, just don't involve Bear." He nods to himself. "Good. Two hours, yeah?" Another nod. "I'll pass it along. Thanks again." He taps his head, his eyes on me. "I thought clothes would help curb the temptation. I was wrong."

I frown, but he doesn't give me a chance to reply—not that I know what to say to his commentary anyway—and heads toward the door.

He pauses after stepping through the threshold and looks back at me. "Pip is a Death Fae. That's what you meant by 'spirit,' right?"

"Uh, no. I mean he's a spirit. You know, like a ghost. Only not you, obviously." I meet him in the doorway. "But I think we established that you're answering the questions now, not me."

"I never said anything about answering questions, trouble. I offered to share what I know." He takes a step backward. "And I promised you food. So follow me and I'll feed you something more appetizing than the meal *Pip* prepared."

"He meant well," I mutter as I trail after Ghost to the hut I share a wall with. *Tank's house.*

Only it seems Ghost has been staying here, something he proves by entering without knocking and walking straight to the kitchen. When he pulls out a bunch of items without pause, I know he isn't lying, because he doesn't hesitate in finding what he needs.

I close the door, then join him by sitting at the two-person table. He moves around without comment, clearly focused on his task.

"I'm not a ghost, by the way," he says conversationally. "I'm an abominable mix of several fae, but Death Fae isn't in my monstrous makeup."

I frown at him. "I never called you a ghost. I was referring to your name."

He pauses whatever he's doing with his knife and looks up at me. "My name is Maliki. Ghost is a nickname."

I scrunch my nose. "Oh."

"Not a fan?" he asks, arching a brow.

"Uh, no." I clear my throat, realizing how that sounds. "No, I mean, I… I've just been calling you *Ghost*. So I'm, um, adjusting?" It comes out uncertain because I sound like a babbling idiot.

Which isn't me.

I'm not this nervous, confused, delirious female. I'm… overwhelmed, I guess.

And hungry.

My stomach growls.

Scratch that. I'm *very* hungry.

The sensation seems to be growing by the second as savory aromas start to scent the air. I didn't realize that Ghost—*Maliki*—started something on the stove. But I notice now as he drops whatever he chopped up into it.

He moves around the kitchen like he owns it, which I suppose he does to an extent.

Because Tank is on holiday. That's what Maliki said, anyway.

I frown. "You didn't hurt Tank, right?" I'm not sure why I ask. But something about this male screams danger.

And now I'm a little concerned that a fae was harmed in Maliki's quest to live next door.

For reasons I still don't understand.

"And why are you staying in his place?" I ask before he answers my Tank question. Only, I already know the answer to this query. "To guard me?" I voice that knowledge as a question because I don't understand the reason. "Why?"

Maliki looks up from the counter where he's chopping something else now. His dark hair falls across his forehead in a messy wave, one he seems to ignore even as it grazes his golden eyes.

"Why would I have hurt Tank?" he questions me. "Did he touch you?"

My frown deepens. "What? No. We spoke for, like, thirty seconds. He asked what I was doing here, I told him I just moved in, and he nodded, gave me his name, then went into his house." It was probably the easiest conversation I've had with a fae since moving to this kingdom.

Unfortunately, the interaction set an unfair standard. Tank didn't ask for my mate status or try to flirt with me. That was part of what made him memorable—he treated me like a normal person, not some exotic animal.

"Then why would you think I hurt him?" Maliki asks.

I stare at him. "Because you said he's on an all-expenses-paid holiday..." I trail off, the words leaving my lips slowly as I'm not sure how to complete my thought out loud or how to explain that my mind translated his words to mean something else.

The reply, *You're intimidating,* sits on the edge of my tongue. *And you have a violent aura.*

Yeah, those comments would go over really well, I'm sure.

"I'm not one to mince words, trouble," he informs me. "If I hurt someone in your honor, you would know."

"In my honor?" I repeat. "And why are you calling me trouble?" It's the second time he's said that, but I was too preoccupied to comment on it the first time.

"Because you're trouble," he replies, returning to his task. "And a mystery."

"I'm neither," I promise him. "I'm just a human named Sera."

"You're a human that possesses the soul of a Goddess," he corrects me. "Which is both exhilarating and frustrating. You're powerful, yet ridiculously breakable. An infuriating combination to protect and now guide, apparently."

That last part is muttered under his breath, causing me to ask, "Guide in what way?"

"Toward the altar," he drawls as he drops more items into his pan, causing a sizzle to enter the air. He hums an odd tune under his breath that sounds like a march of some kind before adding, "And I now pronounce you husband and wife. Or is it God and Goddess?" He shrugs. "I guess we'll find out."

I scowl. "I'm not marrying anyone."

"Because you're not an Omega and not Persephone." His sarcastic tone is not appreciated, nor is the slight feminine lilt he attempted to add to the statement. "At least I believe your memory problem now."

"My memory problem?"

He nods. "Hades thinks you're acting." Maliki glances back at me. "If you are, then bravo, because you certainly have me convinced, little mystery."

I stare at his muscular back as he resumes cooking. "He thinks I'm pretending not to remember? That I'm secretly aware of my soul somehow?" Does he hear how insane that sounds?

"Yes, he thinks this is all a game or an act," Maliki confirms. "But it's been thirteen months since you arrived here, and you truly do seem to be clueless to me."

"That doesn't sound like a compliment," I mutter.

"It's probably not." He flips something in the pan, making me wonder what he's making. "That said, I don't mean it as an insult. As I said before, I don't mince words."

He reaches for a cupboard to pull out two plates, then sets them on the counter.

"So to answer your earlier question," he goes on, "no, I didn't hurt Tank. He's in the Midnight Fae Realm with his boyfriend. And I gave him three months of ink coins in exchange for borrowing his place. So he's fine."

He picks up the pan and lets something slide off it onto one of the plates, then the other.

"As to your follow-up question regarding my purpose as your guard, it's because Hades gave me you as an assignment."

Maliki opens a drawer to grab two forks, then turns around to bring the food to the table.

I meet his gaze, my throat struggling to swallow. Not just because of how intense he looks right now or the alluring display of skin, but because of him referring to me as an *assignment*.

"You're valuable," Maliki tells me as he sets the plate down in front of me along with one of the forks. "More than valuable, actually. You're one of a kind. And I'm here to protect you. Although, as of last night, it's also apparently my job to convince you to marry Hades."

I blink at him. "He wants you to make me marry him?" I suppose Maliki did say something about me choosing the *hard way* and not to blame him for our next meeting.

"No, I said *convince*, not *make*," Maliki reiterates. "One suggests persuasion; the other implies force. So we're going to start with me explaining everything and go from there. But first, you should eat. The sounds coming from your stomach are reminding me of the Blood River rapids."

I grimace. "Pretty sure that's not a compliment either."

His lips quirk up as he sits across from me. "You don't need me to compliment you, trouble. In fact, I'd advise against it."

I huff out a breath, then pick up the fork to poke at the yellowish patty on my plate. "Why would you advise against it?" I ask, half aware of my question as I examine the food he's made. "And what is this?"

"You seem fond of asking two questions at once," he muses. "As to what that is, it's similar to an omelet. Regarding why you don't want me to compliment you, it's because I happen to like being among the living."

I blink. "I don't know what an omelet is," I tell him, then look up at him. "And I have no idea what complimenting me has to do with you enjoying life."

He gives me a surprised look. "You're human and you've never had an omelet?"

"No."

He huffs a breath. "I keep forgetting that you grew up in an alternate dimension where humans are stuck in the seventeen or eighteen hundreds. Granted, I'm pretty sure omelets date back to Ancient Persia, but I digress." He gestures to my plate with his fork. "It's basically eggs and vegetables with a pinch of cheese. Try it."

My stomach grumbles again, making him give me a pointed look.

Sighing, I give in and try the *omelet*.

And instantly groan.

Because *wow*. The flavors are so much better than the cereal I usually munch on in the morning. It even beats the pastries I enjoyed at the palace. "This is really good," I say around a mouthful, not caring at all that it's probably impolite.

"You sound surprised," he murmurs in response.

"I am."

"Why?" he asks, arching a brow. "You didn't think an assassin could cook?"

I choke on my food at the term, causing Maliki to push away from the table. I stare at him wide-eyed as he opens the fridge to pull out a pitcher of water that he promptly pours into a glass and hands to me.

I almost don't accept it, but I need to swallow, so I do.

Then I sputter out the word, "Assassin?"

He grunts. "Would you prefer the term *enforcer*? That's a favorite title among the Death Fae."

I just stare at him.

Which earns me a sigh from the *assassin*. "I've already told you I'm here to protect you, Sera. Obviously, that means I'm not going to hurt you."

When I don't reply, he leans back in his chair, his plate as forgotten as mine.

"You don't need to fear me."

"I think I do," I counter. "You're an assassin who is here to *convince* me to marry the God of Death. What happens when I keep refusing?"

He lifts a shoulder. "Then I'll probably be punished for failing, and Hades will come up with a new method to persuade you."

"That sounds ominous," I say, swallowing.

But Maliki just smiles. "Actually, I think he should be

the one explaining himself to you, not me. So it would serve him right to have to change course."

With another shrug, he leans forward again and resumes eating.

I gape at him.

He ignores me for several minutes, then says, "Oh, and the reason compliments would be bad is because they can be construed as flirting. And Hades is a possessive asshole. So flirting with you would equate to a death sentence. Ergo, no compliments. Now eat your omelet, or I'll be forced to feed it to you."

MALIKI

Sᴇʀᴀ sɪᴍᴘʟʏ ᴄᴏɴᴛɪɴᴜᴇs ᴛᴏ sᴛᴀʀᴇ ᴀᴛ ᴍᴇ.

Apparently, I shouldn't have referred to myself as an assassin. But it's not like my profession is a secret. I've also told her several times that I'm here to protect her, not hurt her.

Though, I certainly wouldn't mind reddening her skin a bit. Preferably with clamps. And maybe a little wax play.

Hmm. That's a dangerous thought path to follow. Of course, it's difficult not to consider it after seeing her in that towel and freshly wet from her shower. Her skin still possessed a hint of pink from the heat of the fire, too, telling me exactly what she would look like after being fucked in my bed.

I thought clothes would help with the attraction.

They didn't.

This female is alluring, witty, and a tiny bit rebellious. All traits I adore. Except she's also very much off-limits.

Which marks her as forbidden desire.

I nearly growl in annoyance. Hades told me I could seduce her, but I know him too well to accept that offer. He'll use it against me in the end.

And as I told Sera, I very much enjoy living.

Thus, I have to ignore the temptation and do my job instead.

Which includes seeing to Sera's needs—like her hunger. "I can still hear your stomach rumbling, little mystery," I tell her. "Please eat." Because if I have to feed her, I'll have to touch her. And I'm not sure I can do that without also enjoying it.

Naturally, she continues to ignore me and just stares.

"All right." I push my plate to the side and fold my arms on the table. "Yes, I'm an assassin. But I only kill those who have done something to deserve their fates. And you rejecting the God of Death is certainly not worthy of my lethal skills."

Although, what her soul supposedly did about two thousand years ago might qualify for my brand of punishment.

But I opt not to voice that knowledge out loud.

As far as I'm concerned, Sera is an innocent. Her soul, however, still requires judgment. That obviously complicates the situation, especially since Sera and her soul should join during her first Omega heat.

If that ever happens, I think, recalling what Hades said about the timing of her estrous cycle. It should have already occurred. However, nothing about Sera seems to be going according to plan.

Including right now.

Because she still isn't fucking eating.

"Sera," I say in the softest tone I can muster. "Do you know how precious Omegas are to their Alphas?"

Her brow furrows a little, telling me the words have broken through some sort of barrier. "I've seen how Orcus treats Alina."

I nod. "Then you understand why I won't hurt you."

"Because you're an Alpha?" she asks in a whisper.

A chuckle taunts my chest, one that escapes in a low rumble as I reply, "No. *Styx*, no. I'm a combination of a lot of fae, making me an abomination by many standards. But I don't have any Mythos Fae inside me."

Her brow crinkles. "Oh."

"What I'm trying to say is, Hades is an Alpha. And he's not just any Alpha. He's one who claims to be fated to your Omega soul. And I work for him. So, I can't touch you. I'm also duty-bound to protect you."

She swallows, seemingly unconvinced.

"Consider it from another perspective, mystery," I suggest. "I'm an assassin, and I happen to be very good at my job. Which means you've never been safer than you are right now. Because I will kill anyone who even looks at you the wrong way."

Her pretty blue eyes widen. "What? Why?"

I just stare at her. "I've already explained that." Leaning back in my chair, I add, "I've been guarding you for nearly a year as well. When you first arrived, I was stuck in a hellish interrogation—I pissed off the Hell Fae King by opening an illegal portal, one that led to your old world, actually. Alas, that's a story for another day."

And one I don't feel like elaborating on right now, so I don't.

"But shortly after my release, Hades assigned me to your protective detail, and I've been guarding you ever since." I leave the table to start some coffee. The caffeine doesn't do anything for me; I just enjoy the taste.

When I turn around, I find Sera still watching me. However, the fork is in her hand again. *Good.*

Rather than comment on it—I don't want to scare her off of eating—I continue sharing some history.

"I mostly just hung out in the palace and ensured no one entered that shouldn't be there. I didn't want to intrude on your space. But when you chose to move to the village, I was forced to get closer to you. So I spoke to Tank about renting his place."

It took about a week to work out the details, which left me a little uneasy, as I had to complete perimeter sweeps around the village while she slept each night. Once I moved in, though, things were easier because I was close enough to hear her scream then.

Not that she ever did.

Until this morning, anyway.

I tell her all that, not leaving any details out, and even inform her that I've spent most nights at Death's Den, guarding her from the shadows.

"You probably think I'm some sort of creepy stalker, and I guess I am. But I've done my best not to violate your privacy. The only reason I showed myself at the bar last night was because Hades asked me to escort you back to the palace. Otherwise, I would have just remained in the shadows."

And I would have had a nice little chat with Jack after he left, I think, not wanting to add that part aloud.

Because I've had a lot of *chats* over the last month.

This female is a fucking magnet for flirtatious trouble.

I pause to focus on my coffee—the grinder is a piece of Styx rocks, making me want to throw it out the bloody window. Alas, it's not my grinder. It's Tank's. Though if I have to stay here much longer, I may just buy him a new one as a welcome-home gift.

Once the machine finishes its job of pulverizing the beans, I take out a filter and get the coffee machine ready.

Such a menial thing to do.

But while I possess many intriguing talents, manifestation magic isn't one of them.

Sighing, I turn back toward my little guest and grin when I find the fork in her mouth. "That's my good girl," I praise her. "Your stomach will thank me later by being quiet, I assume."

Her cheeks pinken, causing my smile to widen. She really is stunning. Why Hades chooses to stay away from her is a mystery.

Well, not really.

He thinks she's guilty of betraying him two thousand years ago. And he believes she knows all about that betrayal, too.

I saunter back over to my chair and collapse into it, my gaze on Sera. "Hades told me you were taken by a crazy Alpha in your old world. Is that true?" I know it is, but I'm trying to give her an option as to whether or not she wants to talk about it.

Her lips thin, her gaze seeming to blink into a faraway stare before coming back to me. "I'm not sure if she was crazy or not, and honestly, it all feels like a dream to me. But yes, it's true, I guess. Only, she kind of saved me, too."

"Saved you?" I echo.

"From Monsters Night," she explains.

"Ah, yes, that." I'm familiar with the infamous mating game from her dimension, the one where monsters roam the streets once a year to claim their brides.

Hades once said the annual event reminded him of Halloween. I'm still not quite sure why. Sure, some of the monsters look like they belong in a costume contest, but that's really the only similarity.

"That's how your sister met her mates," I add, causing Sera to nod. "She seems rather pleased by that development."

"She's lucky," Sera tells me. "Her mates respect her and cherish her."

"Just as Hades will do with you," I say, then wonder if I've just lied.

Because he's talked about breaking her on several occasions.

He needs the memories inside her soul. And the only way to free them is to force Sera to merge with the Omega inside her.

Or however that'll work, anyway.

Fortunately, I'm saved from dwelling on it because the coffee maker signals that it's done. *At least the machine works properly*, I think as I go to pour myself a cup.

I offer Sera one, but she scrunches her nose and declines.

So instead I say, "Tell me what questions you have." There's a lot of information I can share. However, I don't want to overwhelm her.

Which I've clearly already done.

Because she says nothing as I start cleaning up the kitchen. I sip my coffee as I work, then head back to the table to claim my empty plate. Hers is mostly clear, causing me to ask, "Are you finished?"

She nods, so I take the dish to the sink.

"Why you?" she inquires, causing my brow to furrow.

I glance back at her. "What do you mean?"

"Why are you here telling me that I'm engaged and not Hades? Why has he avoided me for the last thirteen months? I mean, I lived in his palace for a year. If we're supposedly betrothed, why didn't he come talk to me? Or, I don't know, introduce himself? Or tell me he thinks I'm Persephone, or whatever else he could have said?"

She's doing that thing again where she spews questions at me. I don't comment on it, though. Instead, I try to answer her thoroughly.

But without giving away too much.

Because telling her Hades both loves and hates her... will probably overwhelm her right now.

"As I mentioned, he asked me to convince you to accept the nuptials. He seems to think I'm good with women."

Which I very much am in sexual circumstances.

Unfortunately, that doesn't apply here.

However, I don't comment on that.

Instead, I continue by saying, "He hasn't come to you himself because he's convinced you already know him and remember everything."

"I don't," she interjects. "I don't remember him at all."

"And yet, I know you recognized the name Persephone," I point out. Because I saw the way she reacted to it last night when I called her that. So some part of her knows something.

Her paling complexion now confirms it.

Only, her words that follow are not what I expect. "I hear that name in my dreams."

I blink at her. "Your dreams?"

But in the next breath, I already understand. *Morpheus.* He's the God of Dreams and seems to think he has a claim on Sera as well. *Fucking meddler.*

"Yeah, it's what he..." She trails off and shakes her head. "Never mind that. You said Hades thinks I *remember* everything... everything being what?"

"Your history together," I say vaguely.

70

"As… as this Persephone?"

I nod. "Yes."

She frowns. "But I don't remember anything."

"As I already stated, I suspect that's true."

"There's nothing to suspect. It *is* true," she insists. "You have to tell him that. And tell him I don't want to marry him, too."

"Okay, I don't have to tell him anything," I correct her. "But if you ask me nicely, I will think about sharing those two points with him."

She scowls. "Or you can just tell him to come here so I can inform him to his face." Her cheeks flush a little more, telling me she's getting angry. "Who does this guy think he is, demanding I marry him because he thinks I remember him? Yet he doesn't feel the need to come meet me himself?" She scoffs. "Some Alpha he is."

My eyebrows lift. "Shall I give him that information, too?"

"Sure," she says, all sassy-like. "Maybe it'll make him come talk to me himself instead of sending his *enforcer* to do it all for him." She pushes away from the table, her gaze narrowing. "If he wants me to marry him, he'll have to come to me himself. And even then, I'll still be saying no."

She starts for the door, then pauses as she reaches the threshold.

"Thank you for breakfast." The words sound stilted, but it's kind of cute that she felt the need to say them.

"Anytime, trouble," I tell her. "But, uh, you might want to stay over here for a few—"

She's out the door before I can conclude my statements with *more minutes*.

I sigh and set the dish down that I was in the middle of washing, then trail after her just in time to hear another one of her now-infamous shrieks.

When I meet her at the entrance to her hut, I find Jerry standing with his hands up in the middle of her kitchen. "S-sorry, ma'am." The stutter sounds a little strange given his deep, gravelly voice. "I'm, uh, almost done with the repairs."

"Repairs?" she repeats, gaping at him.

"I asked him to come over and magic up the place," I explain, my shoulder meeting the wall as I casually lean against it and observe her reaction. "I thought it would be faster and easier than trying to replace everything."

She blinks, then gapes as Jerry uses a wand to remove all the scorch marks. The scent disappears next.

"What... what is he?" she asks in a loud whisper.

"A Midnight Fae," I muse. "Well, part Midnight Fae, anyway. The Death Bloods and the Death Fae like to play, hence the reason Tank is off with his lover in the Midnight Fae Realm right now."

Jerry grunts in response, causing my lips to twitch.

"Tank and Jerry have history," I stage-whisper.

"Currently doing you a favor, Ghost," Jerry reminds me. "Could easily charge you more."

"But then I wouldn't pass on your name to Hades," I return. "And that would be a shame, yeah?"

The male glances around nervously, like he expects the God of Death to materialize nearby.

It's a stupid superstition. I fucking wish it worked that way. It would simplify so many of my tasks if he'd just fucking appear at the mention of his name.

Jerry clenches his jaw and quickly finishes his job while Sera observes, her lips parting in awe. Leaning forward, I press my lips near her ear and whisper, "Don't let Hades see you staring at another male like that, or he'll make me kill the poor soul."

She jumps and stares at me. "You will not."

"You're right. I probably won't. But Hades sure as Styx will." I return to my position by the wall as I add, "You've met Reaper, right?"

She nods, then her eyes round as she no doubt understands where I'm going. "He's psychotic."

"He's brilliant," I correct her. "And I'm sure you know what he would do if he caught your sister looking at a male outside of their mate-circle. Or at least what he would do if that male looked back."

"He'd make a bouquet out of their bones," Sera mutters, shuddering.

I don't have the same reaction, as I find the gift more amusing and appropriate than grotesque. "That would be one hell of a present."

She gives me a look. "You Death Fae are strange."

"Not a Death Fae," I inform her. "My mom is a Corpse Fae Royal. My father is the mixed one, but no Death Fae in him as far as I know." Not that I know him well. And he's not exactly around for me to question, either. "Anyway, I need to get some things done before your shift later. You good?"

Her long lashes flutter. "You're coming with me to work?" It's voiced as a question, but the wary resignation tells me she already knows the answer.

Which means she was listening to me earlier.

Good girl, I think.

Out loud, I say, "I wouldn't miss it." I take a step back toward my temporary home and pause. "Actually, I can't miss it, and not just because I'm on guard duty, but because the nuptial invitations are going out today. You're going to be a popular female tonight, Serapina Everheart." I smile. "Good luck, trouble."

Her lips part, her eyebrows hitting her hairline.

So, naturally, I shadow back to my kitchen instead of walking.

And smirk when I hear her growl, "*Thorns.*"

It's such a cute little curse.

Perhaps one of these days, I'll give her a rose just for fun. Hades can't fault me for a gift, right?

Oh, who am I kidding? Of course he can. He's a God. He can do whatever the fuck he wants.

Including breaking Sera, I think, frowning.

It's a thought I've had often over the last few months, and it's grown increasingly troubling.

Because I don't think Sera has earned his wrath. Yet whenever I broach the topic of her innocence, he scoffs.

I shake my head, clearing it.

Not my fate. Not my business. Not my female.

I'll guard her.

Convince her to go willingly to Hades.

And be done with this task.

For good.

HADES

"WHAT THE FUCK IS THIS?" MY LITTLE BROTHER DEMANDS as he shadows into my office and slams his fist onto my desk.

I know what has him interrupting my day without even looking at the fiery paper in his hand.

"An invitation to my nuptials," I say, feigning boredom. "Which reminds me, I need you to be my witness."

"Your witness," he repeats, sounding incredulous.

I minimize the message I was working on when my brother arrived and look up from my translucent screen to meet his dark gaze.

"That is what I said, little brother," I tell him flatly. "If you're not up for the task, I'll ask Maliki."

Orcus stares down at me. "Hades, you're lucky I found this before Alina did." He holds up the invitation when he says "this," causing me to arch a brow.

"I'm lucky?" I repeat, not following his logic.

"You can't possibly think she'll allow this, let alone approve of it," he says, leaving the fiery paper on my desk before collapsing into the chair across from me. "Hades—"

"Why would your mate have any say in my dealings?" I ask, cutting him off. "And why would she even care? Surely this won't be a surprise to her?"

The look he gives me is not one I want to see on his face right now.

Because it suggests regret. Remorse. And perhaps a hint of guilt.

I huff a humorless laugh when I realize the cause of that expression. "You've not told her about our history."

"Have you told Sera?"

My gaze narrows. "Her name is Persephone. And she is fully aware of our history."

"Persephone, yes," Orcus says. "But Sera doesn't. Not unless you've actually spoken to her, which I'm guessing you haven't."

"Why would I waste my time by speaking with her?" I ask him, deflecting.

Because I don't want to admit that, yes, I have spoken to her. Once. And she pretended not to know me.

Her innocence during that meeting still grates on my nerves. It felt genuine. *Too* genuine.

"Hades, I know you sense Persephone inside of Sera, but all I've felt from her is a hum of potential. And all I've observed is innocence. She… she's very human."

I grunt at that.

Maliki feels similarly, his claims of Serapina Everheart's ignorance ones he voices almost every time we discuss her.

And it seems Persephone has manipulated Orcus as well.

But I know my mate.

She's devious to her core. An actress of supreme

caliber. *A temptress who manipulates everyone and everything around her.*

With a snap of my fingers, I call for the Netherworld Fae Registry, the netherite-encased book mine to command, as I manifested it long ago.

When the book arrives, it drops with a thud that has Orcus's brow furrowing.

I ignore him and flip to the page he needs to see. *Four thousand and seven.* Then I spin it around for him to read the words for himself.

"If my devious little mate wants to play this game, then so be it," I tell him. "We'll see what she has to say after I claim her in front of the entire fucking kingdom."

Orcus gives me a look, one that borders on pity as his eyes return to their usual obsidian color. "She's not playing a game, Hades. Sera has no idea who you are. And she *is* single. She's very human."

"On the outside, yes," I agree. "But her soul is all Omega."

"While I agree on her soul—because I sense it, too—don't you find it strange that she hasn't shown any outward signs of her Omega heritage?"

"It's all part of her game."

He snorts. "Hades, Omegas can't hide their heats. You know this as well as I do. I mean, fuck, she's not even nesting."

"Probably because she's taken some sort of suppressant," I say.

"That she got from where?"

"Her mother, obviously," I tell him. "She spent two years with that wretched bitch. Who knows what she did to help Persephone mask her true nature?" It's a thought I've had several times over the last thirteen months.

Because it's the only thing that makes sense.

Demeter did something to her daughter.

And I'm going to undo it with my knot, as well as my bite.

"The nuptials will go forward as expected in eleven days' time," I go on. "You can be there in support, or you can hear about it afterward. But I've made up my mind, and I won't be changing it."

Orcus stares me down, his Alpha energy pulsing around him. But I'm older and stronger, and he knows it.

There is no fighting me on this.

"She's not yours to protect," I remind him, my tone carrying a soft warning. "I respect that you've mated a woman who considers Persephone to be her sister, but we both know they're not truly related. Not like you and me. And blood claims are everything in our world."

What's left of it, anyway, I think, my fingers threatening to curl into fists.

Because Persephone and her Alpha mother left our kind in ruins.

Destroyed an entire realm.

And all for what?

To hide the Omegas from their Alphas.

The thought of it still infuriates me, perhaps even more so now than it did then. Because I've had two thousand years to foster my fury. To consider the aftermath. To realize exactly what happened and how Persephone played me.

No, I will never trust her again. Not even in this form that everyone else feels is innocent.

Oh, she may still be mine to adore and worship. But she's also mine to punish.

And punish her, I shall.

With reverence and patience.

In a manner only an Alpha and his Omega can understand.

She's mine to love for always. In happiness and betrayal. And my darling little mate is going to understand exactly what that means. *Soon.*

"Before you do something I know you're going to regret, try talking to her," Orcus says, his tone underlined with a dominance I can almost taste. "Omegas are not meant to be disrespected like this, Hades."

"Claiming her before the kingdom isn't a disrespectful act, brother."

"It is when the Omega bride isn't willing."

I wince, not liking the implication in his words. "She's already consented to being my mate."

"No, Persephone consented. Sera did not."

"They're the same being."

"They're not," my brother stresses. "And if you spent more than a handful of seconds with her, you would know it, too."

I narrow my gaze, wondering if he knows about the brief meeting we shared over a year ago, during her first night here.

I let her think it was a dream.

It wasn't.

But I wanted to see how long this game would go on, and it seems my mate is as stubborn as she is clever. Two traits I didn't realize Persephone possessed until after she turned my world upside down.

Unfortunately, there's a lot I've learned about my cruel little mate since that fated event.

Orcus sighs. "I implore you to at least consider an audience with her before the nuptials. If you force her down that aisle, it'll be the biggest mistake of your life.

Now, if you'll excuse me, I need to go inform my mate that you're about to break her heart."

With those ominous words and a lasting look, my brother vanishes, leaving me to mull over his commentary.

Maliki has voiced similar concerns over the last few weeks, his attachment to my mate seeming to grow with each passing day.

It's intriguing.

Infuriating.

Arousing.

I drum my fingers along my mahogany desk, considering my options.

I chose the nuptial event with a purpose in mind. Persephone used to speak of our nuptial day all the time, saying it was the best moment of her life. I thought perhaps we could re-create it and try to reignite our old flame.

Forcing her to participate, though, defeats the purpose. Which is why I requested that Maliki convince her to attend voluntarily.

But maybe I am going about this all the wrong way.

Maybe it's time I try to talk to the female masquerading as a fragile human.

I hum, my fingers still tapping my desk.

Or maybe she'll come to me willingly, just like I desire.

Because the invitations are officially out.

Once she sees one, she'll know I'm onto her little game. And she'll be forced to face me on her own terms, thus coming to me willingly.

Yes.

This will work.

However, if it doesn't, I'll go to her.

And then I'll remind her what it means to be my mate…

SERA

THE MOMENT I WALK INTO DEATH'S DEN, I KNOW Maliki's warning was real.

Because *everyone* is staring at me.

It's like the first day I stepped behind the bar, only this is worse because the den is packed full of fae.

I average maybe thirty to forty patrons a shift. And that's on a busy night.

But this? Right now? Yeah, there have to be at least a hundred fae in here.

And none of them are speaking. Just gawking.

Thorns.

At least there's music playing. Otherwise, it would be eerily quiet in here.

Gritting my teeth, I head toward the bar and startle when Gnarls's red head pops up from behind it. His green eyes go wide as he takes me in. "Sera," he mouths, his gaze darting behind me and then all around to take in the gawkers at my back.

"Gnarls," I greet, forcing a smile. "I didn't expect you to be here tonight."

"I should be saying that to you," he replies. "Er, Your Majesty?"

I frown. "What?"

"My lady?" he tries again. "Or, or... I'm sorry, but I'm not sure how to refer to the God of Death's chosen mate." His eyes round. "Oh, cherries, I'm fudging this up, aren't I?"

I blink at him, his word choices... strange. "Uh, well, no. You're fine. And I'm not his chosen mate. There's been a mistake."

Gnarls's red lashes flutter along his pale cheekbones. "Er, no, I've seen the invitation." He scrambles around while I join him behind the bar, seemingly oblivious to our audience as he searches for something.

When a parchment edged in fire appears, I take a step back, but he thrusts it in my direction, which causes a flurry of golden leaves to sprout—literally, *sprout*—up from the page. I gape at the magic, then start to read the writing beneath the growing stem of leaves.

Or is it a flower? I wonder as glittering petals bloom at the end of the stalk. *Wow, that's pretty.* I almost reach out to touch it, but my gaze snags on my name written in black ink.

> *You're Cordially Invited to the Nuptial Day Event*
> *between*
> *Hades C. Netherworld*
> *and*
> *Serapina P. Everheart*

My brow furrows. "I don't have a middle name." But I

can guess what the *P* stands for. "And this is all just a big misunderstanding. I'm not mating Hades."

Gasps answer my proclamation, reminding me of our audience.

"Sera," Gnarls whispers, his voice underlined in warning. "If you say his name, he'll appear."

"Oh?" I ask, feigning intrigue. "Well then, *Hades. Hades. Hades!*" I glance around, waiting for someone to either appear or step forward.

The problem is, even if the God of Death revealed himself, I wouldn't recognize him.

Because we have never even met!

I nearly scream those words aloud but instead allow them to echo loudly in my head before stealing a deep breath and facing Gnarls. "Well, he's not here. So let me set the record straight—I'm not engaged. The invitations were sent in error. I'm just a human girl trying to survive in the Netherworld Kingdom, okay?"

His expression is underlined in incredulity, making it clear that he doesn't believe me.

I sigh. "Look, just let me work my shift tonight, okay? Then I'll go… sort this out."

A snort from my left has me glancing at Maliki just as he settles at the bar.

Gnarls visibly pales and says, "I was just about to tell our queen that we appreciate all she's done to get to know us, but we obviously don't expect her to work anymore."

I steal a deep breath, my nerves suddenly frayed. "Gnarls, please don't—"

"She likes fixing drinks and talking to fae," Maliki interjects. "Should I tell Hades you're taking away her enjoyment, Gnarls?"

My manager's eyes widen. "No, I—"

"And further, I think Hades owns this place, yeah?" He glances back at the entrance. "I mean, there's not a sign outside, I guess, but it is called *Death's Den*, is it not?"

"It is. It's his. I know th—"

"So if his fiancée wants to work here," Maliki interrupts again, "then I think it might be wise to let her, yeah?"

Gnarls is whiter than Pip's bony face now, his green eyes even less vibrant than before. "Of course," he says, sounding ill. "I would never tell her not to do something, especially if she enjoys it."

Maliki nods, then focuses on me. "Are you in the mood to fix me a spider ale tonight, or should I do it myself?"

I grit my teeth, irritated by him inserting himself into this discussion.

Yeah, okay, he helped.

But I could have handled this without his involvement. "You can get your own drink," I tell him.

His lips quirk. "Sure, trouble."

He disappears, and I don't bother to look behind me because I already know he's standing right there.

I feel his warm breath on my neck as he adds, "I'll be hanging out in the shadows tonight, like I usually do. So try not to flirt with your patrons, trouble. Unless you want a bloody wedding, of course."

I spin as I feel his lips ghost over my pulse.

But he's several feet back and already pouring himself a drink, making me wonder if I imagined the caress.

When he winks at me, I narrow my gaze.

And he vanishes.

Only, unlike last night, he doesn't shadow back to his stool. Instead, he remains hidden. Yet I can almost feel him looking at me.

Or maybe it's everyone else in the den.

Because yeah, they're all still staring.

"I'm not marrying Hades!" I shout at all of them, but the words are especially dedicated to Maliki. "This is all a giant misunderstanding," I go on. "But if you would like a drink, come place your order. I'll be working at the bar."

Several fae exchange glances, then advance on me as a group, causing me to take a step backward in alarm.

Orders start coming in rapid fire, causing my eyes to widen in alarm while I try to keep up.

It's as though everyone accepted my invitation and they haven't had a drink in years.

"Need help?" Gnarls inquires, his voice holding a touch of uncertainty.

"Yes," I tell him, surprised he even had to ask. "You handle that side"—I gesture to the right—"and I'll take the left."

"Of course, Your Ladyship," he replies with a slight bow.

"No, don't do that," I snap. "I'm just Sera. Not your queen or whatever else you want to call me. Sera. Got it?"

"Y-yes, my, um, er, Sera."

I roll my eyes. "Just help me with these drinks, Gnarls."

He nods eagerly and gets to work.

I'm not sure when I became the boss and he became the subordinate, but I'll evaluate that later. *When I'm done taking all these drink orders…*

Which is apparently never going to end.

Just as one group finishes, another pops up.

And I swear there are more than a hundred patrons now in the den. It's like the entire village has arrived and all of them are thirsty.

I glance at the bone clock, shocked to see two hours

have passed in what feels like minutes. Though, my feet and hands are certainly feeling the ache of time.

That ache only worsens with each order, to the point that my fingers begin to cramp from pouring so many types of ales and shots.

"Uh, we'll take three spider ales?" a fae with dreadlocks tells me, his request sounding like a question more than an order.

"Are you sure?" I ask in return.

"Er, no. Five. We want... we want five?"

I stare at him. "Didn't you just have a dozen web shots?"

His eyebrows lift. "Should we order more of those instead?"

I blink. "I don't..." My brow furrows. "Do you even want drinks?"

"Probably not," Maliki drawls as he appears beside me, making me jump from his sudden presence. "But you told them all to order drinks, so they're ordering drinks."

My frown deepens as I look at him. However, he's not paying me any mind—he's just refilling his drink again. I've not bumped into him at all, but I suspect this isn't the first time he's refilled his cup tonight.

"I didn't tell them to do anything," I say to Maliki.

"Not true, trouble," he murmurs, swirling his glass to hold all the smoky substance inside of it. "You told them to come place their orders. Thus..." He gestures to the fae swarm at the bar.

I stare at him. "That's ridiculous."

"Oh, I agree, but I'm not the one who issued the command."

"I didn't command anyone."

His features crinkle as he replies, "Yeah, you did. And as the Bride of Death, they all jumped to obey you."

My eyes widen. "They didn't."

His eyebrow arches, then he cocks his head toward the crowd while giving me a look that says, *But didn't they?*

"Oh, thorns," I breathe, realizing that he's right. "They're drinking themselves into a stupor!"

"That they are," he drawls, his lips quirking up at the sides. "Good thing they're all immortal and can handle it."

With that profound statement, he disappears again.

I growl.

It's a guttural sound, one that has a few fae nearby taking a step backward. And for once, I just do not care.

Because this has gotten out of control.

"Gnarls," I hiss.

He instantly stops what he's doing and is at my side in a blink. "Yes, my, er." He clears his throat. "How can I help you, Sera?"

I bite my cheek, my patience nonexistent. But I can tell he's trying.

Because he thinks I'm engaged to a God.

And not just any God, but *his* God.

How is this my life? I marvel, the urge to pinch the bridge of my nose overwhelming my thoughts.

Yet somehow I maintain a calm I don't feel and politely say, "I would like the rest of the evening off."

"Oh, of course, Sera. You've worked very hard tonight."

I actually have worked pretty hard tonight, so I decide to just accept his words and not question if he means them or if he's just saying them to appease me. "Thank you," I tell him before looking at the crowd. "Please enjoy your evening and do whatever you, um, like to do." It's the dumbest statement I've probably ever made. However, the relief in the bar is palpable.

Because they no longer feel compelled to order drinks.

Stars, this is insane. Utter madness. I just…
I can't even finish the thought. I simply need to leave.
And I know just where I want to go, too.
Later, though.
After the village is asleep…

MORPHEUS

I stand on the village path, watching as Serapina opens her door and looks left, then right.

My eyebrow inches upward. *You should be in bed, sweetheart.*

Yet she appears to be sneaking out.

Mmm, naughty little dreamer.

My power instantly scans the perimeter, touching on several sleeping minds. But none of them belong to Maliki.

Because he's wide awake.

And likely very aware of Serapina's action.

Well, I can fix that, I decide, my gift swirling around the lethal assassin and dragging him into my realm.

I work slowly at first, careful not to alert him of my presence.

Only, he's infuriatingly powerful and senses me within seconds. Because of course he does.

Hades chose well with you, I think before hitting him with a heavy sleeping charm.

He fights it, his growl of annoyance one I hear and feel within my soul.

Shadows seep into my vision as he engages me in a rare mental battle, one that has me both intrigued and irritated.

Fae usually can't fight my influence.

But Maliki is no ordinary adversary.

If I didn't know better, I would say Hades has charmed him in some way.

However, my cousin only has one mate connection in this existence, and it's to Persephone.

Which suggests Serapina is fair game since she's not the Omega he once mated. She just possesses the soul of his past.

Perhaps that's a stretch in the truth, but I adore a good technicality.

And this situation is riddled with them.

A surge of power wraps around my throat, distracting me from my Serapina as I'm forcefully yanked into the dream world.

I stumble, caught off guard, then narrowly miss being punched in the face.

"What the fuck are you doing?" Maliki demands, shocking the nightmares out of me. Because that question is one I should be asking of him.

Or rather, *How the fuck are you doing this?*

Because this is my world. My power. *My existence.*

And he just wrenched me out of reality and into the dream I crafted for him.

Fascinating.

Except being here means there is no one actively

protecting Serapina in the waking world, which means I can't stay. "We'll chat soon," I promise Maliki.

Or perhaps it's a threat.

That remains to be seen as I blast him with a heavy dose of my gift and send him flying backward into a sea of black moss.

The seaweed-like texture grabs him on my command, pulling him under in a wave of fiery fury.

His responding growl echoes throughout the dark landscape, telling me there will be hell to pay whenever I release him. But truly, this was his fault more than mine. Had he simply slept, I wouldn't have needed to resort to these methods.

Alas, powerful fae are countered with powerful dreams.

"I'll be back at some point," I tell him, then blink back into the Netherworld Village to hunt down my Omega.

It's not a difficult task, her aroma one that calls to me on a feral level. So sweet. So sinful. *So addictive.*

I've not allowed myself to truly indulge in her yet, mostly because I've wanted to give her time to settle into this reality while I observed from afar.

But marking herself as single changed everything.

I no longer desired to *watch.* I wanted to *claim.* Yet I gave my cousin a forty-five-day warning.

And he responded by spreading word of his pending nuptials to Serapina Everheart.

I told him to *fix this*, not *force her*.

The bastard hasn't even tried to talk to her, outside of that initial meeting where he threatened to become her worst nightmare.

Such a cruel thing to say.

He's angry, yes. Rightfully so. But is Serapina to blame for her soul's sins? I think not.

Just as I think he should knot up and talk to his betrothed, not send Maliki to seduce her for him.

Oh, I'm sure his pet assassin will do an amazing job pleasing our intended, and I certainly wouldn't mind watching it happen. However, Hades needs to earn her, too. And if he's not willing to fight for her, then he's going to lose her.

To me.

I smile as her fragrance grows stronger, the perfume beckoning me forward. But I don't want to scare her, so I slow my steps and observe her like I usually do—from the mist. It's similar to Maliki's ability to lurk in the shadows, only mine functions as more of a fog.

A fog that very much blends into the Netherworld Courtyard as I follow her down the black cobblestone trail. The sound of creaking echoes all around us as a gust blows through the skeleton trees, the bones rattling in response.

Serapina seems unbothered, her sight set on something ahead.

Her fists clench at the sides as she comes to a halt by a tree. "How in the thorns is that even possible?" she demands, piquing my interest.

She can't possibly be talking to me. And there's no one else around for her to speak to. Not even Pip.

So she's obviously voicing a rhetorical question, yet she kneels and grabs a handful of charcoal-colored dirt.

I creep closer, trying to understand what she's doing, when she releases an adorable little growl and throws the sandy soil back down with a "Hmph."

Narrowing my gaze, I lean over her shoulder to look at the clump she just discarded. It resembles standard Netherworld dirt.

Why has it offended her? I wonder. *Because it's cold?*

Serapina fishes something out of her pocket, her gaze

attempting to scan the label on the bag. I read it easily even though we're shrouded in the shadows cast by a nearby skeleton tree.

Red Roses, the label says.

I arch a brow. "Those seeds will do absolutely nothing because this kingdom is about death, not life."

Serapina shrieks and stands, then spins around in a complete circle, her gaze scanning the courtyard.

Ah, right, I'm still in the mist.

I reveal myself to her, which has her backpedaling quickly into the bony stump of the tree.

"Oh!" she gasps, her heart singing an unsteady beat— one I listen to for a moment before lifting my palms in a gesture of innocence.

Scaring her isn't my intent.

Though, I should have remembered that before I spoke. However, seeing her gardening project inspired me to comment.

"I mean you no harm, little dreamer," I promise her.

She swallows a few times, her palm sliding up to her slender throat in a nervous gesture, one that makes me want to reach for her and offer comfort.

Fae, I would never hurt her. But I would absolutely hurt *for* her.

I'd lie on a thousand burning coals and let her walk across my bare skin if it meant securing her safety. And I'd suffer dozens of Strigoi bites and let Ghouls feast upon my dreams if it gave her pleasure.

She's an Omega.

I live to serve her as an Alpha, even if she chooses another mate.

It's simply the nature of who we are as Mythos Fae.

"I'm sorry for startling you," I add, lowering my hands. "I just wanted to offer some advice."

Her gaze narrows. "What kind of advice?" she asks slowly, suspicion coloring her features. Fortunately, she doesn't seem to fear me. But she clearly doesn't trust me either.

That's fair. We've never met, and she has no idea who or what I am.

"Well, for starters, you're wasting your time on those seeds," I inform her conversationally. "They're meant for the Human Realm, not the Netherworld Kingdom."

"I know. I bought them from one of the swap stores," she tells me, referring to the shops in the Netherworld Village that sell wares from around the realms. "But the storekeeper promised me the roses would grow here."

"The storekeeper lied," I say flatly. "Which one did you speak to?" I don't voice it as a polite inquiry, but as a demand. Because I will absolutely be having a stern word with that individual for tricking my intended.

Serapina mutters a name, one I commit to memory. Then she bends to start digging in the black dirt. I wince as she yanks her hands away on a hiss, the ground likely having gone cold beneath her touch.

"If you planted your seeds there, they're long dead," I tell her softly. "But I can help you acquire new ones."

She looks me over, but she can't see me well in the shadows. I can tell because she keeps squinting. *So very human.*

"Why would you help me at all?" she asks, then places her hands on her hips. "Actually, no, let me guess."

"Please do," I interject, intrigued.

"It's because you felt compelled to, right? Because of the nuptials thing?"

"Hmm, no," I tell her. "I certainly don't feel compelled to as a result of any nuptials."

Though, perhaps I feel compelled to because she's

mine to cherish. However, that wasn't her guess. So I let her continue.

"Oh, okay. So you're helping me like all the other fae males do at the Den, and next you're going to offer to mate me to protect me." She rolls her eyes—an action I see clearly because the shadows can't hide her beautiful features from my immortal gaze. "Yeah, no, thanks."

My lips curl at her easy dismissal. "I'll admit, I'm not used to females turning me down so quickly, especially before I've even offered my knot."

She starts to turn away, but stops, her brow furrowing. "Knot?"

"Mmm," I hum, enjoying that word on her tongue. If only she followed it up with *me*. "Shall we begin anew?" I suggest, stepping out of the shadows cast by the nearby skeleton trees and into a beam of moonlight. "I'm Morpheus."

Her eyes grow round upon seeing me—truly seeing me —and her full lips part. "M-Morpheus?"

"Just Morpheus," I tell her. "One *M*."

She blinks several times. "Like the God…" She pauses on a swallow. "God of Dreams."

"One and the same, I'm afraid." I cant my head and give her my best smile. "Don't worry, little dreamer. You're very much awake." It's the question I'm asked most often when I appear—*Is this a dream?*

"Why are you here?" she whispers.

"To meet you," I tell her honestly.

She stares for a beat and frowns. "You said you weren't talking to me because of the nuptials."

"No, I said I didn't feel compelled to help you because of the nuptials," I correct her. "But I'm also not conversing with you as a result of them, either. I'm simply here for you."

Her frown deepens. "Because you think I'm an Omega."

"I don't think you are; I know you are."

Twin blonde eyebrows lift. "Except I'm not one. I'm a human."

"One who possesses an Omega's soul, yes," I agree.

She heaves a sigh, her irritation palpable. "So I keep hearing."

"Because it's true."

"Hmm." She looks at me. "Okay. So what happens next?"

My brow pinches downward. "Tonight?" I ask her.

"No. I mean with my supposed soul. Is it supposed to take over at some point? Turn me into an Omega? Give me all her previous memories?" She scowls. "Do I just die in the process?"

"I certainly hope not," I reply. "Your sister didn't."

"My sister didn't possess a specific soul like I apparently do," she snaps. "One that makes Hades think I belong to him without ever actually talking to me."

"Ah, yes, that. He's stubborn. Which is probably the understatement of the millennia."

"And I'm guessing he sent you here to talk to me?" she goes on like I haven't spoken. "If that's the case, tell him I'm not interested in fae who send messengers on their behalves. A real God would talk to me."

I smile. "I agree entirely."

"And a real God would—wait, what?" She blinks at me like she just remembered my presence. "You... you agree?"

"Absolutely. A real God would talk to his Omega. A God with, say, long silver hair, perhaps? Blue-green eyes. The kind of face one fantasizes about in the midnight hours?"

She glances over me, then gives me a skeptical look. "A real God named Morpheus?"

"Some call him quite dreamy, you know," I murmur, amused.

"I bet they do," she deadpans, her sassiness thrilling me. "But I'm not an Omega."

"So you've claimed."

"And you haven't helped me at all," she mutters back, causing one of my eyebrows to arch upward.

"Would you like me to help you, Serapina?"

"I'd just like someone to explain to me how and why Hades thinks I'm his Omega. He hasn't even spoken to me. So is he just making assumptions because I'm Alina's sister? Or is there more to it?"

"There's more to it," I tell her. "So much more to it."

She sighs. "Of course there is. Too bad Hades won't share his madness with me."

"It's not madness so much as obsession." *A dangerous one.* But I don't add that part out loud. Instead, I focus on what we were discussing before talking about real Gods. "As for Alina, would you say she's changed?"

Serapina looks at me, obviously startled by my return to this topic. However, it's with a purpose.

I don't want her fearing her soul or what might happen when she embraces her inner Omega. But I also can't fault her skepticism.

"Does she possess any memories of the past?" I press. "Any hints as to her soul's previous life?"

She swallows and looks away. "I don't know."

"You've not talked to her about it?"

Serapina shakes her head. "Not really. Just… just about her link to creationism and power. But I've not wanted to pry."

I nod, understanding a bit. "An Omega's nest with her

mates is sacred," I murmur. "It's instinctual for you to not ask a lot of questions. Though, I suspect your sister would guide you, if you desired it."

I've not met Alina, but I know Omegas well. Familial relationships are intrinsically important to them. And while Serapina may not be related to her by blood, she likely still views her as part of her inner circle.

"That said, if you would like to learn more about Mythos Fae from someone else, I would be happy to share some history with you. I can even tell you about Persephone."

Shadows creep into my vision while I speak, telling me Maliki has mastered his dream faster than I anticipated.

I nearly sigh. The assassin is as alluring as he is irritating.

My vision blacks out for a blink, surprising me.

It seems Maliki was quietly working his way out of his mossy trap, and now he's on the attack.

Fine. I'll wrap this up, I think at him, ensuring the words travel into his dream and echo through his mind.

His responding mental snarl informs me that the message has been received and rejected.

"You don't need to decide now," I say, focusing on Serapina while mentally wrangling Maliki. "But if you do want more information, then I'll be here again tomorrow night. Same time. Exact same place. If you appear, I'll know you're interested."

I take a step back and wince when Maliki lands a blow to my temple. It's not real. It's in my head. But it hurts nonetheless.

Gritting my teeth, I send a paralyzing spell through his dream and take a deep breath to settle my tone before speaking again.

98

"Oh, and please bring Pip. He's quite enjoyable." I just met the little soul earlier in the evening, but our brief introduction endeared him to me instantly. It was too bad he didn't accompany her on this walk through the courtyard.

Alas, I don't have time to tell her any of that.

So I just give her a little bow and conclude with "Until next time, little dreamer."

It takes significant willpower to leave her, but Maliki isn't giving me much of a choice. His persistence is admirable and infuriating.

I mist to his room and introduce my fist to his face just as he wakes up.

Then I teleport to the street outside. I know better than to fight an assassin in his home quarters.

Besides, Serapina lives next door. Can't risk damaging her place.

Tucking my hands behind my back, I begin to pace.

And wait for Maliki to come out to play.

"Are you trying to get me killed?" he demands the moment he appears, his disheveled hair reminding me of a time when I entertained men in the bedroom.

Hmm.

I cock my head. "Definitely not," I tell him, referring to his question more than the entertaining notion of sensual play. Serapina owns my heart and soul. If she wanted me to put on a show for her with Maliki… I wouldn't be opposed.

"I'm actually quite fond of you, Maliki. There are not many souls ballsy enough to fight a Mythos Fae, let alone me."

"You trapped me in a fucking dream."

"I did." No point in denying it. "Would you prefer a more amusing fantasy next time? Perhaps one involving a certain blonde Omega? Because that can be arranged, so long as I get to watch."

Maliki takes a menacing step forward. However, I stand my ground.

He's lethality incarnate, but I'm a God. And I've gone easy on him thus far.

"Careful, Ghost," I murmur, using his infamous nickname. "I'm in a good mood. You don't want to ruin it by picking a fight you can't win."

"I won't exactly lose either," he returns.

"Perhaps not," I agree. "But I think we make better friends than enemies."

"Then stay the fuck out of my head," he tells me.

I smile. "I'm not one for making promises, particularly those I have no intention of keeping."

His gold eyes flash.

Then he sighs and runs his fingers through his unruly strands. He's dressed in sweatpants and nothing else. Not even shoes. "You realize I have to tell Hades about this, yeah?" he asks me, sounding resigned.

"Is that the part that truly annoys you?" I counter, curious. "More than me playing in your mind?"

The look he gives me is underlined with violent intent. "She's not yours, Morpheus."

"Not yet, no," I agree. "But she's not exactly Hades's yet either, is she?"

Maliki doesn't reply.

I wouldn't be surprised if he agreed with me. Hades has sent him here to do all the hard work of wooing the Omega, and Maliki isn't even allowed to taste her.

"For the record, I would share her with you, if that's what she desired," I inform him. "Because unlike your master, I believe in mate-circles, not single pairings."

Maliki grunts. "He's not my master."

"Those are the words you choose to focus on?" I ask, amused. "So be it, then, little pet. But don't worry about reporting back to Hades. I'll talk to him myself."

Since Maliki doesn't appear to be in the mood to play, I'll go pick a fight with a true rival.

"Hades needs to know that I'm done waiting," I tell Maliki. "See you soon."

MALIKI

I PACE THE SMALL LIVING SPACE, TOO AGITATED TO SLEEP. Especially after Morpheus mindfucked me with that dream.

Bloody God.

I don't know him well, our interactions having always been brief. And he's never drowned me in his power before.

Until tonight.

I shiver, the sensation of sharp vines still slithering along my skin. The hour-long shower I took didn't help. Neither did the jog I just went on around the village. And the ice bath I took after also did nothing to rid me of the discomfort left behind by his nightmare.

Growling, I rub my hand over my face and resume pacing.

I could try to drink myself into a stupor, but that would leave Sera unguarded.

Not an option.

I heard her calling for "Pip" shortly after returning to her hut. And I'm still waiting for that bastard fae to arrive so I can have some words.

Thus far, nothing.

And Sera is now asleep.

I only know that because I popped over to check on her when things went silent—I expected to find this infamous "Pip." Then I stayed to ensure Morpheus wasn't fucking with her dreams. Only after I was sure did I go on my jog.

But now I can't rest.

Between this "Pip" fucker and Morpheus, I have my hands full with babysitting my little mystery.

I palm the back of my neck and give it a squeeze, my muscles tight with irritation.

That fucking feeling of knives against my skin makes me twitch, too.

I've tortured a lot of fae. Maybe Morpheus assumed this was my due. Or perhaps he dug that trap up from some dark place in my mind.

Regardless, I hate this experience.

And I fucking loathe Morpheus.

"You look ready to spar," a deep voice muses, preceding Hades's arrival in my personal space.

I turn toward him. "If you've come to chastise me, save it. I'm not in the mood."

He arches a brow. "No, you appear to be in a very different kind of mood. One that usually leads to dark decisions and delicious dealings."

"I'm not fucking anyone for you tonight," I tell him through my teeth. "If you want to get off, go find another *pet* to play with."

"My, but it seems my cousin has thoroughly infuriated you."

I glare at him. "I mean it, Hades. Fuck. Off." I know better than to disrespect a God, let alone *the* God of my kingdom, but I've had a really long bloody night, my skin is still stinging with the memories of that dream, and I've been stuck babysitting a forbidden fruit for the better part of a year.

Yeah, I'm in a bad mood.

And I'm really fucking tired of being treated like a minion. A toy. A fae to be ordered about and discarded without a care.

I resume my pacing, ignoring Hades as he sits on Tank's couch. It's a tiny love seat made of faux leather. The God of Death probably looks ridiculous on it, his six-foot-four height and muscular form no doubt overtaking the small furniture. I barely fit on it at six foot two, and I'm a little less bulky than him.

Hopefully, he's uncomfortable.

Though, I doubt it's anything like that fucking seaweed moss Morpheus threw me into.

"Maliki," Hades says calmly.

I grunt. I told him to leave. Not my fault he chose to stay.

"I'm not going to chastise you," he adds.

I snort. Because I don't give a Styx, not with the electric currents traveling up my arms. It's like getting zapped by eels. That, coupled with the leftover knife-prick sensations, and I'm just living the dream over here.

Fucking literally.

After several moments of silence—whereby I stalk back and forth while Hades watches—he finally says, "I have something that can help remove the rest of Morpheus's spell. Would you like it?"

I slowly pause, then rotate toward him. "Is there a reason you didn't lead with that upon arrival?"

"I was enjoying this edgy side of you. It's not every day a Netherworld Fae talks to me like I'm an equal."

My gaze narrows at his term. *Netherworld Fae* encompasses all of the kingdom, including Death Fae and Corpse Fae. It's a locational term more than a species term.

And he knows full well I'm a combination of several breeds. At least on my father's side.

"I'm not your *ordinary* Netherworld Fae," I tell him.

He smiles. "No, you're not. You're quite extraordinary, Maliki." He holds up his hand. "Here."

I stare as he reveals a plain gold coin in his palm. "Am I supposed to eat that?"

A mirthless chuckle leaves him. "No. Just set it on your wrist."

My gaze narrows. "This feels like a trap."

"Because you know me well. But I promise this will dispel Morpheus's touch and keep him from bothering you again."

I study him for a long moment.

"It's not like you to turn down a daring opportunity," he murmurs.

He's not wrong. But I'm not exactly feeling like my usual self right now.

Though, maybe this is the pick-me-up that I need.

Or perhaps it'll make it worse.

Styx it, I think, grabbing the coin.

Energy instantly hums across my skin, canceling out the residual irritation left behind by Morpheus's mindfuck.

Only it comes at a clear price as the gold coin dissolves into my skin, just like my tattoos often do when I use them to manifest shadows.

My jaw ticks as my blood heats, Hades's presence surrounding me in an invisible fog that I can sense with every fiber of my being.

I sigh as I look into his fathomless dark eyes. "Do I even want to know what you just did to me?"

He shrugs. "Probably not."

I shake my head. "How much is this going to cost me?"

"Nothing but loyalty," he says. "Which I don't foresee as being a problem." He pushes up off the couch.

I don't move out of his way, so we end up chest to chest. Bowing to him is a natural response for most fae. But not for me. "Do you want me to thank you?"

"No."

"Good. Because I wouldn't have needed whatever antidote you just gave me if you would handle your own mate."

He nods. "A fair assessment."

I arch a brow. "Oh? Does that mean you're finally going to talk to her?"

"That does seem to be the advice of everyone in my life. You, Orcus, Morpheus." He grimaces. "Do you have any idea what he did to her?"

I assume he's referring to Morpheus and Sera, as Orcus hasn't been anywhere near here since helping Sera move into her hut. "I'm not sure what they discussed, but from what I could tell, all they did was meet in the courtyard."

Hades hums. "You know, he didn't say much to me during his visit tonight. A strange thing for Morpheus, as he loves to chat. But he told me three things."

I stare at him, waiting for him to elaborate.

"First, he informed me that he'd introduced himself to my bride. Then he stated that he's done waiting for me to grow a knot. And before I could even begin to react to that insult, he told me not to kill you because you're perfect for our mate-circle."

His dark eyes burn into mine, his dominance an aura that threatens to force me into submission.

I didn't miss the hint of fury that entered his tone and expression as he uttered the third item. I'm familiar with mate-circles. Many fae have them, including Hades's brother Orcus.

It's not uncommon for a male mate-circle to form around a single female. There are just more men than women in our world.

But Hades is too possessive to form a mate-circle. He's been devoted to Persephone and only Persephone for over two thousand years.

Oh, he'll watch me play, his voyeuristic tendencies enough to satisfy his needs. But he never touches. Nor does he ever engage. Which is fine with me. I tend to prefer women. And I happen to enjoy putting on performances for others, too. It works for us.

However, I sense the possessiveness pouring off him in waves. He doesn't like the suggestion of me being in his mate-circle.

Or perhaps it's the use of the word *our* from Morpheus, indicating that not only does one already exist, but that Morpheus is involved as well.

"Is there something you want to ask me, Hades?"

"No. My coin told me all I need to know," he answers cryptically.

My eyes narrow a bit. "So that was a loyalty test?"

"More like a reward for loyalty," he murmurs while fixing his suit jacket. We're standing so close that his knuckles brush my chest.

Normally, I would step backward. But I'm not yielding to him.

Not today, anyway.

"It's an ancient relic, one that I should have given you a long time ago," he adds, still as cryptic as ever. Then he promptly changes the topic by saying, "When you see Morpheus again, remind him that Persephone is mine."

"I don't think he cares about your claim."

"Tell him anyway."

I shrug. "Fine."

He stares down at me, gaze intense. "Is there anything you want to say to me, Maliki?" he asks after a long beat of silence.

"Would it matter if I did?" I counter. "I've mentioned my thoughts on Serapina several times, yet you've made it clear that my opinion doesn't matter. She's your mate. You'll handle the situation however you see fit."

"I will," he agrees. "But you're wrong about your opinions. They matter a great deal to me."

I scoff at that. "If that were true, then this wouldn't be your first time visiting me here in the Netherworld Village."

One dark eyebrow wings upward. "Who says this is the first time?" He glances around. "Besides, there isn't much to see here. The accommodations are rather drab."

"Tank isn't fond of interior decorating," I deadpan.

"Tank?"

"The Death Fae I had to bribe so I could watch your mate," I mutter, finally taking a step away from him as exhaustion starts to creep in. I won't be able to sleep— *thanks, Morpheus*—but I can at least relax.

Stepping around him, I take over the love seat.

Hades remains standing but rotates toward me, his gaze assessing. "Are you disliking this assignment?" he asks after another beat of silence.

I pick up the controller from the table beside me and

aim it at the painting across from the couch. The flowery façade melts away to reveal a screen that has access to channels in various realms throughout the universe.

Naturally, I select the Human Realm. Their assassin movies are the best in all the worlds, mostly because they don't shy away from the blood and gore.

Hades shifts again, glancing at the screen and rolling his eyes. "Can you at least answer my question before the shooting starts?"

"I'm still considering my answer," I tell him, my focus going to the screen as the movie opens. "I like Sera." That's an understatement. I'm pretty sure I more than like her, but I don't really want to get into that right now. "Protecting her isn't an issue."

"Then what is the issue?" he presses.

"You already know the answer to that, *my lord*." Well-timed bullets are fired from a gun while I utter that formal address, making my lips curl a bit.

Fitting, I think.

Then, out loud, I add, "If you want to marry her, you're going to have to put forth more effort. If you don't believe me, ask me what happened in the Den tonight."

I doubt he's heard the news yet; he rarely converses with anyone outside of his palace walls.

An explosion sounds from the speakers embedded in the wall, causing me to turn the volume down. I don't want to risk startling Sera with my movie obsession.

"Tell me," Hades demands.

I meet his simmering gaze and say, "She announced to the entire Den that she is not mating you. When she used your name, they warned her you might appear, so she started shouting it." Which I found hilarious as fuck. But I don't add that part out loud. It's not needed. My enjoyment is absolutely evident in my tone.

I go on to tell him how the patrons drank themselves into a stupor because she insisted on working and demanded they all order drinks, not realizing they would take her words as an order, not a request.

And how she eventually released the poor sods from their plight once she understood what she'd done.

"Did she see the invitation?" he asks quietly, causing me to arch a brow.

"Yes. Why?"

"How did she react to it?" His soft tone suggests this question is important to him.

So I answer him bluntly. "By stating that she doesn't have a middle name and telling everyone she's not mating you."

His lips curl down. "No hint of recognition?"

"Well, I think she recognized your name, if that's what you mean. But otherwise, no. She was... I think she was mad. Or maybe fed up?" I shrug, my attention drifting back to the screen. "Whatever the emotion, it was hot. She certainly reminded me of a queen." Which Gnarls called her at one point—yet another amusing moment from the night.

"You're enjoying this," Hades remarks.

"I told you, I like Sera. So the assignment of guarding her is fine. The task of convincing her to marry you, though, fucking sucks."

Hades falls silent.

Then he begins moving around my space.

I finally glance his way when I hear the fridge open.

"There's a pack of blood ale on the bottom shelf," I tell him, aware that's his favorite beverage. I bought it when I first moved in, guessing that he might visit.

He grabs one, as well as a spider ale for me, then takes over the tiny recliner to my right.

Neither of us speaks; we just watch the film.

Our friendship, or whatever this is called, is abnormal. But he's one of the few fae I allow into my personal space. He's typically respectful of my need for quiet.

It isn't until the end of the movie that he finally says, "That was dreadful."

I huff out a laugh. "You wanted more of them to die, didn't you?"

"Yes." A flat answer.

I shake my head, still laughing. "The sequel is better."

"I doubt it."

My shoulder lifts into a partial shrug. "To each his own, my lord."

"Stop calling me that."

I take a page out of his book and simply reply, "No."

His jaw clenches, his indignation painting a humorous picture, especially as he's still all buttoned up in that suit while looking ridiculously large in that tiny recliner. "I'll talk to her," he says.

"Her who?" I ask, playing dumb.

The look he casts my way would cause most men to shrivel in place.

I merely smile. "About fucking time, *my lord*. Please tell me it'll be soon."

He casts me a withering look and stands. "Good night, Maliki."

He disappears before I can reply.

"So it won't be tonight," I mutter. "Great."

I pull up the sequel I mentioned and hit Play.

Nothing like a bloodbath to calm my soul…

SERA

Pip appears to my right as I enter my hut, his cloak swishing as he twirls in a circle of excitement.

I haven't seen him since I snuck out last night. I'd asked him to stay here, mostly because I didn't want to risk him touching my seeds—something that apparently wouldn't have mattered.

Because the roses can't grow here like the shopkeeper said they could.

I narrow my gaze in annoyance. I've been trying to create a rose for weeks. They were my favorite back home, and I miss the sweet fragrance that accompanies them, particularly when paired with the cold of a winter's night.

So strange how specific that is. Yet I grew so many of them in the greenhouse, and every winter, I stepped outside to enjoy the scent when mixed with the crisp air that often coincided with an alluring snowfall.

I thought, perhaps, I could re-create it here since the Netherworld Kingdom is often chilly.

No snow, though.

At least not in the year I've been here.

Unfortunately, it's impossible since the ground is apparently dead.

At least according to Morpheus, the God of Dreams.

Fae, when he appeared last night, I just about swallowed my tongue. All the beings of this kingdom are good-looking, but Morpheus took the standards to a whole new level.

I could see why he was in charge of a fantasy realm. He really shouldn't exist at all. Not with those incredible blue-green eyes, perfect lips, and defined cheekbones.

With a sigh—one that sounds a bit too dreamy to my ears—I kick off my shoes and head toward Pip.

He's currently hovering in the kitchen, making me a little nervous. I want to ask him how he knows Morpheus, as it's been on my mind since last night. But Pip was gone when I returned home, and I hadn't seen him at all today.

Until now, anyway.

However, the anxious little dance he's doing has me preoccupied with a new concern. "Please tell me you didn't try to cook again."

He shakes his head in his cloak, then bounces.

I narrow my gaze, afraid of what I'm going to find.

When all I see is a pot, I carefully lean toward it. "Did you plant something in there?" I ask warily, noting the brown dirt.

Pip shakes his head with vigor, causing his hood to nearly fall off his head. He quickly fixes it, the blue flames of his eyes going wide.

I don't exactly know why he's obsessed with that cloak, but I've gathered it has something to do with protecting me. Because every time it's almost fallen off, he checks me over like he's making sure I'm okay. Just as he does right now despite being several feet away.

"So it's just dirt?" I inquire, my brow crinkling.

He nods.

Then disappears through the wall.

I frown after him. "Hey, we still haven't talked about the kitchen episode from yesterday, and I have some questions for you about Mor—"

A knock at the door cuts me off.

My gaze narrows. No one ever visits me.

Not until the last few days, anyway.

"Maliki," I mutter, leaving the pot on the ground to go see what my stalker neighbor wants from me. But when I open the door, it's not Maliki standing there. It's the fae from the swap store I bought the roses from.

Sweat beads across his forehead as he holds out a bag for me.

"I... I'm sorry, Your Majesty," he stammers. "I... I didn't realize. I mean, I just, well, I." He bows his head. "I've brought you more seeds. Every color I could find. And he told me you already have the dirt you need. But I'll find you more. I can. I promise. I'll go to the Human Realm myself to procure it. Just for you. If you'll... if you'll..."

I gape at him as he visibly shakes. "Are you okay?" I ask him, concerned.

He nods. "Yes, Y-Your Majesty." He glances up at me and then away like he's not allowed to look at me. "I'm so very sorry, Your—"

"Sera," I interject, not wanting to hear that *Your Majesty* phrase again. "I'm just Sera. And thank you for the, er, seeds. But what do you mean about dirt?"

He looks at me. "I'll go to the Human Realm and—"

"No, sorry, you said I have what I need, as in the dirt?"

"Yes." His eyes widen. "Wait, you do have it, right? He told me you did. I offered to get some, but he said it was already handled."

"He who?" I ask.

He glances around and leans toward me. "You know. *Him*."

"I… No. I don't know who you mean. Maliki?"

He shakes his head. "No, no. *Him*. He said… he said a courier was bringing you the dirt in a pot. Did it arrive?"

"A courier…" I repeat slowly, then glance back at my kitchen. "I, uh, yeah. I do have a pot…"

"Oh, good," the swap store fae says, sounding relieved. "Good, good. I'll bring you more. I promise, Your Majesty. As much Human Realm dirt as you need." He bows. "Every day until you forgive me. I vow it."

"That really won't be necessary," I tell him.

Sure, I was annoyed before.

But now, well, I'm annoyed for different reasons.

"It's very necessary," he says, backing away from my door. "I must repent for upsetting the Gods."

"Gods?" I echo, my brow furrowing. Then I realize what must have happened.

A courier—*Pip*—brought me the dirt.

He knows Morpheus.

And Morpheus knew about the shopkeeper telling me the roses would grow here.

"The God of Dreams came to talk to you," I say, unable to hold the note of disbelief in my voice.

But the swap store fae disappears before I finish my statement, like I've scared him off by the title alone.

"I did," a deep voice informs me as Morpheus materializes a few feet away. "I requested he make amends for lying to you. That sort of behavior isn't tolerated among Mythos Fae. Omegas are meant to be worshipped and praised, not deceived or tormented."

The door to Maliki's—*er, Tank's*—home opens. "I'm supposed to remind you that Persephone belongs to Hades," Maliki drawls. "And now that I've completed my task, I can do this."

My eyes widen as a blade sails through the air, only to be caught by Morpheus in a blink. He examines the silver, tilting it this way and that. "You shouldn't waste such fine craftsmanship, Maliki."

"I didn't."

Morpheus frowns, then hisses and drops the blade.

"Slug venom is very useful," Maliki adds conversationally. "Don't worry, though. The sensation isn't permanent. Just like your fucking dream moss."

I gape at him and then at Morpheus as his knees give out, sending him to the ground in what appears to be a very expensive suit.

Or it would have been expensive in my home realm, anyway. Though, it's a bit sleeker and sexier than the fashion I'm used to.

Not that his suit matters.

The Alpha God is shaking, his silver head bowed. "What did you do?" I ask in a whisper, the bag falling from my fingers as I dart toward Morpheus.

Maliki appears in front of me in a shadowy flash, his big body resembling a ton of bricks as I accidentally run right into him.

His hands catch my hips when I bounce backward, my bare feet tripping over themselves and tipping me off-balance.

But I don't fall.

Because Maliki is holding me against him.

And I'm suddenly surrounded by the scent of leather

and smoke. Masculine intoxication. Strength personified. *Delectable male.*

I nearly nuzzle into his chest, which I now realize is bare.

So warm. I startle at the thought, my eyes blinking rapidly. *Why do I feel so dazed?*

"Are you all right?" Maliki asks, his lips close to my ear.

"I…" I don't understand what just happened.

"You were about to touch Morpheus," Maliki tells me, making me wonder if I voiced my confusion out loud. I thought I'd kept it to myself, but now I'm not sure. "The slug venom spreads."

"S-slug venom?"

"It's from the Creek of the Dead," he tells me. "The slugs live in the decaying skulls and leave behind a sludge that basically electrocutes anyone who touches it. Kind of like a poisonous caterpillar, if you've ever seen one of those in your home world."

I nod.

Because I am familiar with those colorful creatures and their spiky hairs.

"Caterpillars don't leave sludge in skulls," I reply, frowning and tilting my head back to look up at him.

Maliki smiles. "No, but some species of them leave behind a stinging or electrifying sensation if you touch them. Slug venom is kind of like that, but on the scale of being stung by a million jellyfish."

He releases me, just to wrap an arm around my shoulders to guide me back toward my home.

"Morpheus will recover soon. In the interim, show me what's in the bag." He picks up said bag before pulling me through the open entryway.

The door seems to magically close behind us. But I

barely notice it because I'm replaying the last however many minutes in my head.

Maliki's warmth slowly leaves me, and I realize he wasn't just touching me with his hands, but with his... his whatever the fae those tattoos are called, too. I watch them unravel from my body and seep back into his skin, the thick bands of energy leaving my skin tingling in their wake.

"Do you hypnotize your victims?" I ask slowly, trying to understand what just happened. Because I still feel dazed and I don't understand why.

"No. But I do enjoy paralyzing them."

My eyes widen. "Is that what this was?"

His brow furrows as he stares down at me. "What what was?"

"That," I say, gesturing to the inky smoke crawling over his skin to form new tattoos.

He glances down, his frown seeming to deepen. "You felt paralyzed by my shadows?"

"That's what they're called?"

"Yes. To some. To most." He shakes his head. "You felt paralyzed by them?" he repeats.

"No, just... just out of it? Like I was hypnotized."

He stares at me and then at his arms. "I told them to soothe you. Maybe it worked too well?"

"Soothe me?"

"Yeah. They..." He trails off and palms the back of his neck. "Have you seen what Reaper can do with his shadows?"

"Not personally, no, but I've heard he makes weapons. You do, too?"

He shakes his head again. "No. But my shadows function similarly in that I have a unique power tied to them, too. They basically operate as an extension of my mind and can manipulate things around me. They can also influence sensations, like calming effects… or pain."

My eyebrows lift. "That's quite a spectrum."

He shrugs, the last of his inky strands disappearing into his arm. "It's who I am, mystery. I've not lied to you. I'm an assassin. But I'm currently *your* assassin. Which makes you the safest human in all the realms. Now, are we going to talk about what's in the bag?" He holds it up for me to see and gives it a little rattle.

"Seeds," I reply. "For roses."

He arches a brow. "Like the flower with the thorns?"

"Yes."

"And where are we planting them?" he asks.

I scowl. "*We*"—I take the bag from him—"are not planting anything." I stalk off toward the kitchen, which is unfortunately only a few feet away, and bend to grab the pot Pip left for me. He's nowhere to be seen again, naturally.

Setting the pot and bag on the counter, I go to find a fork, then return to carefully draw it through the soil. Pip handled this, which means it's likely hazardous.

However, as I dig through the pot, all I find is fresh dirt. It's even a little moist, and the scent coming from it suggests it's been recently fertilized, too.

Smiling, I grab the bag from the swap store fae and start going through the seed options. When I find seeds for Autumn Damask roses, I smile. "I used to maintain some of these in our village gardens," I say, aware that Maliki is still here. "I think they were sent to the Elite City to be used in various perfumes. Or perhaps as decorations."

I don't actually know, as I never visited the Elite City. I grew up in Nightingale Village, left on a train for Monsters Night, and then ended up in a dream.

Or a greenhouse, I suppose.

"The Elite City is like Chicago, right?" Maliki asks.

I shrug. "It's not a city name I'm familiar with, but that's what Alina's mates told her, yes." I don't look at Maliki while I talk, my focus on the small pot and counting the appropriate number of seeds. "I'm going to need a much bigger plot once this starts growing."

"Death's Palace has miles of gardens for you to play within," he tells me.

I snort at that. "I won't be living there again." I already stayed in Orcus's wing for a year and barely saw ten percent of the massive residence. "I'm not mating Hades."

"So you've said," a deep voice replies, one that sends a chill down my spine.

Because it doesn't belong to Maliki.

It belongs to the man from my dreams.

Dreams that have haunted me for my entire existence.

Dreams that could never be a reality.

Yet, I just heard him…

And Maliki is still here, standing on the opposite side of the counter, his gaze on something behind me.

No, not something.

Someone.

I spin around, my eyes widening at the tall figment of my imagination.

His intensely dark irises burn into mine, his dominant aura surrounding me in an all-too-familiar embrace.

Yet his cruel smile now isn't familiar at all as he murmurs, "Hello, Persephone."

My mate stares at me like she can't believe I'm here. "Hades," she breathes.

I smile. "So you're not going to pretend I'm a stranger this time?"

She swallows, her blue eyes captivating me just as much as her former brown ones. Both versions of my mate are beautiful, but in entirely different ways.

Even her scent is unique in this form, yet exquisitely captivating nonetheless. *Like a bouquet of blooming fire lilies*, I muse, inhaling deeply.

"The dream was real," she whispers, causing my eyebrow to lift. "You came to me my first night here and told me your name was Hades. I... I thought it was a dream. Why did you let me think it was a dream?"

Her voice gains power as she speaks, her pretty eyes sparking with a blue flame that excites my inner Alpha. I rather like this feisty energy. It's a new trait, one that's unexpectedly arousing.

"So you're Hades." She utters the words like she's evaluating me. Her gaze runs over me, her lips pursing. "Hmm."

She turns around to focus on something on the counter, effectively dismissing me.

Maliki shoots me an amused look before disappearing. I didn't exactly expect him to stay, but I'm a little surprised he didn't comment before leaving.

Regardless, this is my task now.

"You're going back to pretending we don't know each other, then?" I guess, her words about the dream a not-so-clever way of explaining how she knew my name. "Haven't you grown tired of this game, Persephone?"

"My name is Sera," she replies without looking at me. "And I'm not the one who pretended to be a dream, so don't accuse me of playing games."

"I didn't pretend anything, little mate. You made an assumption, and I chose not to correct it." And that's assuming I even believe her.

Which I don't.

When she continues to give the counter more attention than me, I move around to her side and arch a brow at the pot of soil she's tending to.

Picking up the packet beside it, I read the rose breed and scoff. "If you're going to pretend you don't know me or our history, then perhaps you shouldn't pick a flower that's so much like your favorite one from our home realm."

Her hands still. "What flower?"

I study her profile, noting the way she's stopped blinking. "Fire lilies, like the ones our nuptial invitations created." Which I assume is why she's suddenly wanting to groom a similar plant to life.

That explains the scent, I think.

It's everywhere here.

And it's obviously not just coming from her.

Though, I don't see any other flowers in her little hut. A strange development, as Persephone always needed life blooming around her in our Mythos Fae palace.

Her vines and flowers died shortly after her disappearance.

Despite her betrayal, I did try to care for them. But I'm death, while she's life. Living objects tend to wilt beneath my attention as a result.

And they did horribly after she left.

Pretty sure my heart shriveled up and died right along with all her precious lilies.

"This is an Autumn Damask rose, not a lily," she tells me. "Very different species."

"Perhaps," I agree. "But the scent of that particular rose is the same as a fire lily, telling me you chose it with a purpose."

Maliki reappears, carrying the scent of butter with him.

Rather than comment, he simply takes a seat on a creaky old wooden chair at the small dining table just off the kitchen and begins munching on his treat.

"Is that popcorn?" I ask him.

"It is indeed," he drawls before taking a mouthful. "Please continue and act like I'm not here."

Loud crunching follows, making that an impossible task. "Fuck off, Maliki."

"Excuse me," Persephone interjects before the male in question can respond. "This is *my* home. You do not come in here uninvited and then tell my guest to leave."

Maliki grins and gives me a cocky look.

My gaze narrows. "I was invited when you called for me at the Den." I didn't hear her, of course. But Maliki told me about it—the knowledge of which I am more than happy to use now.

Some of his smugness leaves his expression, no doubt aware of what I'm doing.

"Just as I was *invited* when you publicly denounced my claim." *More than once*, I nearly add, that damn registry floating through my mind. Her *single status* was the catalyst that forced my hand.

I was enjoying watching her until she lied to the kingdom by declaring herself as *unmated*.

"Further, you are mine," I remind her. "Therefore, I am *always* invited into your personal quarters."

Maliki is no longer smiling. Instead, he appears nervous.

I have no idea why. It's not like I intend to hurt Persephone. She's mine to cherish and adore. And also to punish, yes. But my brand of punishment isn't cruel. If anything, it can be quite pleasurable.

"I am not yours," Persephone fires at me with so much venom I nearly take a step back. I've never seen her like this. She's always so meek and soft, her anger practically nonexistent.

But she's mad now.

I daresay she may even be furious.

Yet I have no idea why. Nothing I've said is incorrect. She is the one who is mistaken by claiming not to be mine.

"Do you have any idea how it feels to know you've rejected my claim in front of hundreds of fae?" I ask her, my voice soft despite the pain and fury the words awaken within me. "I stayed faithful despite your betrayal, yet you have the audacity to treat your Alpha this way?"

"I don't even know you!" she snaps. "Outside of the dreams, anyway. Which don't count since they're not real. I don't even know what they mean or what they are, just that… that *you* took advantage of me when I first arrived by allowing me to think you were a figment."

Dreams, I think, eyes narrowing.

She mentioned that during our first meeting, suggesting she *dreams* of me. As she should. I've dreamt of her nonstop since the moment we met. And that never stopped, despite the two thousand years we've been apart.

I'm also not fond of her accusation that I took advantage of her. "I didn't even touch you." Apart from a soft kiss to her forehead after she fell asleep. *Does she know I did that?*

"And what *betrayal?*" she goes on, acting as though I haven't spoken. "I would have to *know* you to *betray* you, and if anyone has betrayed anyone, *you* betrayed *me* by announcing our supposed engagement to the entire kingdom without my permission or acceptance."

The munching of popcorn intensifies, distracting me for a moment and making me want to smite Maliki. Helpful, he might be, but he's being intentionally obnoxious right now. His gold eyes practically glitter with amusement when I look at him.

Most fae know not to push me.

Alas, Maliki is not most fae.

"Do you know what happened in the Den last night?" my mate continues. "The fae nearly drank themselves into an early grave because they translated my request to order drinks as a demand. And they kept calling me *Your Majesty*. One even called me his queen." She folds her arms, causing my gaze to drift down to her chest.

It's an automatic response.

One that has me regretting my instincts instantly, as

125

I'm already aroused by her anger, and now I'm enjoying the view of her breasts being pumped up in that tight tank top of hers.

"Are you even listening to me?" she demands.

"It would be impossible not to hear you, darling," I murmur. "I'm fairly certain everyone in the village is listening to you right now."

Not that I care. She's my Omega. If she wants to yell, then so be it. Though, I'm not quite sure what I've done to deserve such ire. Nor did I know my mate was capable of such fury.

She scowls, the expression more adorable than it should be. "You're infuriating."

I arch a brow. "I've barely spoken."

"I know!" she snaps back at me. "Yet you assume I'm yours because of some soul bond?" She huffs at the question she's voiced. "I don't know you, Hades. Nor have you tried to get to know me. So I will not be marrying you."

"The nuptials are a formality to inform the kingdom that you're mine," I tell her. "But we are, in fact, already wed, *wife*."

"In another life," she replies. "A life I don't remember."

"So we're back to this game again?" I ask with a sigh. "All right, darling."

She throws up her hands and looks at Maliki. "Is he always this impossible?"

"Yep," he says without hesitation. "Popcorn?" He offers it to her without looking at me.

My jaw ticks. "Why do I feel ganged up on?"

"No idea," the male I often think of as my *best friend* drawls. "Did you want popcorn, too?"

I close my eyes and take a deep breath. Maliki wanted

me to talk to Persephone, as did everyone else. And now he's going to make me feel like a fool for doing so?

"I don't know you, Hades," Persephone repeats, the words sounding far too genuine. Too practiced. Too *real*.

"I love you, Persephone, but I don't believe you," I admit, my eyes opening once more to meet her new-to-me gaze. Everything about her is physically different. Yet I can sense her soul. The one that hurt me. Nearly destroyed me. And ruined all of Mythos Fae kind.

She has to be punished for her sins. It's unfortunately my job to carry that sentence out, and I absolutely hate that I have to potentially hurt her.

"You love a soul that supposedly exists inside me," she replies, her voice shifting to a softer tone, one that almost sounds defeated.

I'm not sure I care for it. Though, it does remind me of the Persephone I once knew. *Did she use this tone to manipulate me then?* I wonder. *Is she doing it again now?*

I've spent millennia trying to understand how I miscalculated my mate's intentions, how I missed her motives and devious acts.

But I'm paying attention now.

Because I won't be tricked again.

"My sister doesn't remember any specifics from the past," she goes on. "If you don't believe me, ask Orcus."

"She's not your sister," I tell her. "Not even in human form." Their biological parents were different; they were just raised by the same assigned mother and father.

Her version of the Human Realm is unique, her experience there *dark*.

Children of her home world are produced to mate monsters. To do that, many human offspring are genetically created in a clinical setting.

It's not well known to the mortals of that world, but I know Persephone is aware.

Because Alina knows the truth.

The two of them grew up in a contrived household with a pair of humans designed as their caregivers. They thought they were their parents.

Until recently.

When Alina learned that everything she knew was a lie.

The Elite City controls reproduction of humans and disperses them to the villages.

My mate and her "sister" were among that operation.

"You already know this," I go on. "Aside from that, it should be obvious with your pale features and her darker ones."

Persephone's eyes narrow. "All the more reason for you to know that this is just a giant misunderstanding. Alina's a real Omega. I'm not."

I arch a brow. "That's an interesting evaluation. Explain."

"Explain?" she parrots back at me. "Explain what? That I'm just a human? That you've mistaken me for someone else?"

"I don't make mistakes. You know this."

"No, I don't," she tells me, her impatience another new trait. My Persephone is patience personified. As evidenced by her miraculous deception. "I. Don't. Know. You." She utters the repeated words with a slow precision, like she's talking to a muttonhead.

Maliki is no longer grinning or eating his popcorn. He actually looks a bit concerned. Maybe because he noticed my hand clenching into a fist.

It's not out of anger, but another emotion. One that tightens my chest. A sensation I refuse to identify.

"Look, I'm not even an Omega. And as you pointed out, Alina isn't my blood sister. So this is all just some sort of misunderstanding." She unfolds her arms, her expression suddenly exuding an unnatural amount of exhaustion. Or is it sadness I'm witnessing? Maybe a hint of jealousy?

I don't understand it.

Nor do I understand her proclamation. "You possess an Omega's soul. Specifically, Persephone's soul."

"Then why haven't I gone into heat?" she asks me, her eyebrows rising. "I may not know a lot about Mythos Fae, but Alina has taught me some of the basics. And I've not experienced anything like her. So maybe you're wrong."

"I'm not."

She just stares at me, then shakes her head. "You're like a brick wall."

I frown, not following the strange comment. "Meaning?"

She snorts and turns away from me to resume fussing with her plant. "Never mind. It's not worth trying. Just know that I am not marrying you."

My frown deepens. "You're already married to me, so I hardly see how a simple ceremony will be an issue for you."

She doesn't deign to respond. Instead, she picks up her pot and carries it into the living room to set it by the solitary window. I watch as she arranges the curtains, then frowns when she looks outside. "There's no sun here."

"That's by design," I tell her, pleased with myself. "This kingdom embraces death." I should know, as I influenced various features after its creation.

All with Persephone in mind.

Because I wanted her to be miserable here.

It seemed appropriate for her impending imprisonment.

Many Alphas believe that Omegas are lost forever. I've never agreed with that theory because I could sense not only Persephone's soul but my mother's as well.

So rather than wallow like many of my brethren, I chose to search. And while I searched, I found a new home for my darling wife.

One that would make her feel bereft.

Alone.

Cold.

Just like I've felt since the moment she left.

Loving and hating someone is complex. But with Persephone, I've mastered the conflicting emotions.

Because I adore her as much as I despise her.

Desire to both worship and destroy her.

Cherish her and punish her.

Kiss her and bite her.

So many convoluted needs that I've not even begun to bestow upon her.

Ignoring what I've said, she merely sighs and places her plant beneath a dull light bulb. "I'll need to find a heat lamp," she mutters.

I smile. "Good luck." This kingdom is chilled to the bone for a reason. She can't escape it. I've made certain of that.

Her shoulders slump a little, the action killing my mounting amusement.

I don't want to hurt her. Not really. But she needs to repent for her wrongdoings, to acknowledge the past, to *apologize.*

Yet instead of owning her sins, she continues to claim she has no memory of them.

My jaw ticks again as I consider what it means if she's telling the truth.

But I can't embrace even the concept of it. *Persephone lied to me. She broke my heart. She destroyed our world.*

To give her even a speck of faith would be naïve on my part.

No. I can't entertain the notion that she's truly without her memories. I simply can't.

This is my Persephone.

My mate.

My wife.

"You will walk down that aisle next week," I tell her. "You owe me at least that much after everything you've done to me and our kind."

Her shoulders stiffen, which is an improvement from the way they caved a moment ago. The relit fire in her eyes is even more enthralling.

"And stay away from Morpheus," I go on, aware that he was here recently. I could feel his residual presence in the air, his scent one that made my nose curl. But he left before I could catch him in the act of talking to my mate.

A shame.

I would have enjoyed making him appear inferior in front of *my* Persephone.

"Don't talk to him again," I add, feeling the need to ensure she knows all my rules. I'm her Alpha. Her *husband*. "You disrespected me in a way that's unforgivable, Persephone. Don't earn a worse punishment for yourself by making poor decisions."

Her lips part. "*Excuse me?*"

"No," I tell her, walking up to where she stands in the living area. "I won't excuse anything you've done. Especially when you pretend not to remember a thing.

This game ends now." I take a final step to invade her personal space, but I don't touch her.

Because if I do, I don't think I'll be able to stop.

However, I do let her feel the weight of my dominance.

I'm an Alpha.

She's an Omega.

Therefore, she *will* submit.

Her nostrils flare, her eyes widening in a way that confirms everything I know about her. She claims not to be an Omega, but it's written into her every reaction. The way she inhales, the shudder that follows, the dilation of her pupils, and the sweet scent strengthening with every passing second.

"You're mine to own," I whisper to her. "Mine to claim. Mine to knot. *Mine.*"

"You're a monster," she breathes.

"I am," I agree. "But I'm your monster, *wife.*"

And I'll do anything you desire of me except let you go, I think, my gaze holding hers as I consider the words I long to say out loud yet can't. *I'll even forgive you, darling. In fact, part of me already has.*

Otherwise, I wouldn't be going out of my way to try to re-create what we once had.

Every detail of the nuptials has been completed with her in mind. I want to remind her of our love, of the day we first spoke our vows, and show her how an Alpha cares for his Omega.

Even an Omega who destroyed her Alpha's heart.

I love you, I long to tell her. *I love you more than you'll ever comprehend. And I hate you for what you've done. But I'll help you fix it… if you'll let me.*

My palm itches to caress her cheek, to pull her into a kiss and forgive her with my tongue.

But instead of giving in to my urge, I simply say, "I'll see you next week, Persephone. At our nuptials."

Then I disappear.

And ignore the startled gasp that chases me all the way back to my palace.

I have a wedding to plan.

One where I will win my mate back.

Even if I have to fucking crawl.

SERA

It takes me a moment to remember how to breathe.

Hades's aura, his *presence*, was so intense, it was suffocating.

So unlike the male from my dreams, the one who holds me and kisses me in places I've never experienced before.

How is this possible? I swallow. *How do I even begin to reconcile my fantasies with the reality that is Hades?*

"Sera," Maliki murmurs, reminding me that he's still here. That he witnessed everything. That he was eating *popcorn* while Hades dominated me with his existence alone.

But as I look at the assassin now, I don't see his popcorn anywhere. Nor do I see any traces of amusement in his features.

"Are you all right?" The soft words sound genuine. Caring, even.

However, everything I know about Maliki makes him

untrustworthy in this experience. He's here to force me to marry Hades. To escort me. *Whatever.*

He works for the monster that just threatened to punish me for my soul's betrayal. "I don't even know what Persephone did to make him so angry," I whisper, more to myself than to Maliki. "I don't understand what's happening. Why does he hate me so much? I don't... *I don't even know him.*"

Not outside of my dreams, anyway.

Yet it doesn't matter how many times I say it. Hades didn't believe me at all. He just kept accusing me of playing a game.

"What did she do?" I say again, only voicing it as a question. "What did Persephone do?"

"Don't ask me for details, as I don't know them. However, I know..." Maliki trails off for a moment, his gold eyes seeming to lose some of their light. "I just know that Persephone helped her mother annihilate all of Omega kind. And how she did that had something to do with using and betraying Hades."

I gape at him. "*What?*"

He shrugs. "As I said, I don't know more than that."

"But I do," an accented voice murmurs from several paces away.

An accent that sounds like Hades's, only more regal somehow. Less deep, yet still very much in charge.

"Morpheus," I whisper.

"In the flesh," the God of Dreams replies, his shoulder bracing against my front entry as the door hangs open. He clearly let himself in yet hasn't stepped over the threshold. "After I'm done handling Maliki, I would be more than happy to elaborate on exactly what Persephone did to Hades."

My eyes widen. I almost completely forgot what Maliki had done to Morpheus with the slug venom outside.

It's like Hades wiped my memory the moment he arrived, grounding me solely in the reality of his dominance and commanding presence.

One of the final things he told me was to stay away from Morpheus.

"Don't earn a worse punishment for yourself by making poor decisions."

I shiver, Hades's threat haunting my mind. He was angry. So, *so* angry. I could feel it in every breath I took in his presence, the fury pouring off him in hot waves that threatened to drown me.

"Sera," Maliki says, his serious tone pulling me from my thoughts. "As furious as Hades may be at your soul, he will never hurt you."

I swallow, unnerved by how well he seems to have read my mind.

Or maybe his comment is a response to my trembling.

I… I can't seem to stop.

Actually, I'm pretty sure it's getting worse.

My soul helped someone annihilate all of Omega kind.

How does one reconcile that?

Can I even proclaim my innocence? I wasn't there. I didn't do it. And yet, I possess the spirit responsible for the crime.

Which is why Hades plans to punish me.

How? What will he do?

"Serapina," Morpheus murmurs, a strange sort of vibration underlining his accented voice. It continues long after he speaks, the sound seeming to seep into my skin to soothe my quivering.

It's… it's so hypnotic. Strangely comforting. A rhythmic hum I feel through every inch of my being.

My eyes begin to close, only to open when I feel a hand on my arm. Maliki stares down at me, concern etched into his features. "Hades is a stubborn asshole," he tells me. "But I meant what I said—he won't hurt you. It's not in his nature to do so."

"He's right," Morpheus says, that alluring vibration growing as he nears me. "Alphas are driven to comfort and protect Omegas, not harm them."

The reverberations seem to be emanating from his chest. "What is that humming noise?" I ask, a bit dazed by the conflicting sensations rolling through me.

I'm horrified by what Maliki told me about Persephone.

Terrified by what Hades intends to do to me.

And comforted by that hypnotic rumble.

"It's an Alpha purr," Morpheus replies. "Omegas are innately calmed by it."

I shudder as the hum intensifies, his nearness making my knees weak.

Or maybe that's Maliki's hand rubbing up and down my arm.

He's still shirtless. And Morpheus is wearing what appears to be a freshly pressed suit, suggesting he changed after the whole slug venom incident.

Regardless, their wardrobe choices are not helping my nerves. Nor is their close proximity.

Something about their nearness is making me... hot.

Only, that purr is calming me down, too.

It leaves me conflicted. Dizzy. Disoriented. And strangely secure.

I feel safe.

Which is insane given what I've learned tonight. *Who* I've met.

Hades.

The figment from my dreams.

The only man to ever truly touch me. And it wasn't even real. Just a series of dreams.

Dreams that I wonder now if he somehow manifested.

Or did he ask Morpheus to do it for him? I wonder, blinking. *Is that why he doesn't want me talking to the God of Dreams?*

A chill runs down my spine, only to be chased away by the Alpha purr emanating all around me.

But the thought remains, the realization that I can't trust anyone pulling me out of this false comfort. "Do you manipulate my dreams?" I ask Morpheus, my voice drowsier than I desire. But at least the question came out clearly.

"Manipulate?" Morpheus repeats, his silver eyebrows angling downward. "In what way?"

"To make me dream of Hades," I say.

He scoffs. "I would never make you dream of Hades unless it was a fantasy about stabbing him." His arms cross. "Did he accuse me of playing in your mind, Serapina? Because I can promise that if I had, you would have recognized more than just my name yesterday."

Heat creeps up my neck at the insinuation in his tone. "Have you seen my dreams?" It's a question I meant to think mentally, yet the words sort of trip out of my mouth.

Because if he's watched my dreams, then he knows how intimate I've been with Hades in them.

Morpheus studies me for a moment, his blue-green eyes glinting in the low lighting of my home. "I've witnessed pieces of them, yes. I'm always aware when you dream because our souls are connected, similar to how you are linked to Hades. However, I try to respect your privacy by not prying and leaving the moment I'm pulled to you."

I stare at him, unsure if I can believe anything he's telling me.

But that purr makes me want to trust every word.

It's a dangerous vibration, one that lulls me into an artificial state of comfort. I can see through it, yet I can't seem to truly battle the need to simply relax. "Your Alpha purr is hypnotizing me, just like Maliki's tattoos."

Morpheus glances at the other man, his eyebrow lifting. "You've introduced her to your smoky tendrils? And you didn't invite me to watch?" He tsks. "I thought we were friends, Maliki."

The assassin grunts. "Did you think that when torturing me in that dream yesterday?"

My brow furrows. "What dream?"

"The one he yanked me into so he could frolic with you in the park."

"We did not frolic," Morpheus interjects. "We simply discussed Human Realm roses. Which reminds me"—his focus returns to me—"I see you received the pot from Pip. Good. I'll have a proper lamp brought in tomorrow."

"Who is Pip?" Maliki demands before I can even reply. "Is he one of your Ghouls or Strigoi? Is that why I don't recognize the name?"

Morpheus chuckles. "No, he's not part of my kingdom. He's very much a Netherworld creature."

Maliki frowns.

Clearing my throat, I say, "Thank you for the pot. And the seeds. But please don't scare shopkeepers on my behalf again."

The God of Dreams gives me a smile that befits his title. "As you wish, little dreamer. Any other requests?"

"Can you stop purring?" I ask.

His smile slips a little, but the vibrations instantly cease. "Better?"

No, I think, immediately missing the soothing sound. Yet I force myself to nod because I want my brain back.

These two males are distracting me. And I'm liking it a little too much.

I take a step back from them, causing Maliki's hand to drop.

Unfortunately, the action does nothing to dispel the dizzy sensation in my head. If anything, it gets worse as both men stare at me intently.

"What else do you desire?" Morpheus asks me. "More information on Persephone? Answers to other questions? Perhaps a lesson on Mythos Fae?"

I consider the options he's just provided. For some reason, that last offer feels the safest. I already know a lot about Mythos Fae from Alina. So this could be a nice way to test Morpheus's sincerity. If I catch him in a lie, then I'll know everything else he's said can't be trusted.

And besides, Hades told me not to talk to Morpheus.

Doing the opposite feels like a good way to rebel.

"A lesson on Mythos Fae would be nice," I tell him.

His lips curl. "All right." He looks at Maliki. "Are you tagging along or staying here?"

"Tagging along to where?" Maliki asks, suspicion lacing his tone.

The God of Dreams shrugs. "Does it matter? Either you maintain your protective detail, or you don't. The choice is yours."

Maliki narrows his gaze. "You are not—"

"Five seconds," Morpheus interjects.

"Um," I start.

But Maliki growls, "No, Morpheus."

"Four seconds," the God of Dreams returns. "You may want to grab a shirt and shoes. Three seconds."

Maliki grabs Morpheus by the throat.

And the God of Dreams takes hold of my hand. "Excellent choice, Enforcer," he mouths.

Maliki's eyes widen at the same time mine do, and the world begins to spin.

Oh, fae…

Maybe I should have gone with another option after all.

MORPHEUS

MALIKI'S PALM BURNS AROUND MY THROAT, ALERTING ME TO Hades's power rolling over his skin.

It's about fucking time my cousin claimed Maliki as his own.

Though, I wonder if Maliki even knows.

Hmm. Not my place to tell him.

It is my place, though, to punch him in the face after that slug venom incident. However, it was clever. Which, naturally, amused me once the electrifying sensation wore off.

I can't remember the last time someone got the best of me like that. Maybe four or five hundred years ago when sparring with Ares.

There's a reason I don't accept his challenges anymore. His fondness for strategy marks him as a worthy adversary. But his violent temper makes him unpredictable and therefore dangerous. Hence, no more playing with Ares.

Maliki, though, I'll play with again.

But not here.

I need him alert and ready to kill.

Because we're about to enter a dying world—the Mythos Fae Realm.

Which is why I slow our journey down long enough to grab Sera's boots before completely leaving her hut, and take us to my palace.

We arrive in my former bedroom, where Maliki instantly pins me against a wall, his golden eyes glowing with rage. "Have you completely lost your fucking mind?"

"Possibly," I wheeze, his palm constricting my airflow.

Misting out of his hold, I teleport to my closet.

It's just as I last saw it a few years ago, thanks to Beta Abigail maintaining my rooms. A dozen Betas live in my palace, their sole responsibilities built around general upkeep. As payment, I allow them to reside here behind my enchanted gates.

I only visit when there's an issue—something my magic alerts me to.

Or on the rare occasion that I'm craving a visit. Such as today.

Not many Alphas reside in this realm now. It's mostly Betas trying to survive the dystopian landscape.

But my palace is built on dreams. Thus, it's a literal utopia when compared to the fields outside the gates.

Thumbing through my suits, I move on to my sweaters and select a black one for Maliki. Then I grab a pair of socks and some boots.

Hades will absolutely loathe knowing that I dressed Maliki in my clothes, a fact that makes me smile as I walk through the bathroom connected to my closet.

When I step through the door into my suite, I find Maliki pacing near the four-poster bed.

Meanwhile, Sera is staring around with a bewildered expression. Her shoes are on the floor, their haphazard placement a result of me dropping them when Maliki shoved me up against the wall moments ago.

Seeing me again, he comes charging, so I mist to his back, only to take a blow to the head.

Because he followed my movements.

"Impressive," I mutter before misting ten feet away from him. "And stupid," I add. "Do you want me to drop you in the middle of Hades's old palace? Because I can. And I'll leave you there."

Where we both know you'll be trapped, I don't add out loud. Because I don't need to. He knows trying to shadow in this realm would be dangerous for him. He's not a Mythos Fae. Our magic works very differently here.

Though, Hades's subtle claim might be enough to protect his pet assassin.

Fortunately, Maliki doesn't know that. Which explains his irritated growl now.

I respond by tossing him the boots and socks.

He catches them before they can hit him.

"Be nice and I'll give you this sweater, too," I tell him.

His jaw clenches in response, then he searches the room like he's looking for a weapon.

"No slug venom here, I'm afraid," I drawl. "But there are a lot of other deadly creatures to play with in this realm, myself included, if you fancy a fight."

I wouldn't mind showing off for my intended. It would help me redeem myself for that embarrassing display Maliki made of me outside of her hut.

Alas, the assassin stalks over to the bench at the foot of

my bed, drops the footwear to the floor, and sits to pull on the socks.

"The boots might be a bit big," I say, wanting to goad him. "I'd apologize, but I'm rather fond of my Alpha characteristics."

His gold eyes flash up to mine as he slides his foot into a boot. "They're actually a tad snug."

I smile. "I suppose one would need to be a decent liar to work for someone like Hades."

Maliki grunts at that, though I notice that the footwear does seem to fit him perfectly. Not surprising, honestly. We're nearly the same height and stature, which suggests other parts of us may be similar as well.

However, I'm the one with a knot.

Something Serapina will hopefully benefit from someday soon. Maybe while Maliki is inside her, too. *Hmm.* That would be fun.

The glare he shoots my way only makes me desire that outcome even more. He will be ever so fun to share a female with, as he'll probably try to kill me while we fuck her.

Delicious, I decide, my focus returning to Serapina. She's moved toward the balcony doors, her hands cupping the glass as she tries to see through the blue tint. "I'll take you outside to explore after you've put on your shoes," I promise her. "And also after we've discussed the rules."

She turns around, her beautiful face taking my breath away even as her eyes narrow into a distrusting stare. "I said I wanted a Mythos Fae lesson, not to be kidnapped to… Where are we?"

"The Mythos Fae Realm," I answer without hesitation. "Where I intended to provide a Mythos Fae lesson."

Suspicion colors her features. "You tricked me."

"I didn't," I reply. "Not intentionally, anyway. I offered

you choices on what you wanted to learn more about, and you chose the Mythos Fae, so I misted us to my palace. I want to ensure I tell you everything and show you anything you might not believe."

I'm very aware that she has no reason to trust me. And her commentary on her dreams made that even more evident. She probably doesn't have faith in anyone right now, and I can't really blame her for that.

Hades, of course, has only worsened the situation, too.

I'm not sure what he said to her while I was healing from the slug venom, but her broken expression when I arrived told me it wasn't anything good.

If he weren't mated to her soul, I would consider killing him for hurting her. Though, he would just regenerate since our kind can't really die. So I suppose that's an option to consider later.

"This is your palace? As in, where you live?" she asks me slowly.

"Yes and no. This is my palace, but I live in the Morpheus Kingdom."

"Oh. So you just have... two palaces."

I smile. "Yes. Does that impress you?"

"Not really," she says, causing my smile to grow wider.

"Maliki has been teaching you how to lie. That's cute," I murmur, looking back at the assassin. He's standing now, still shirtless, with his arms folded over his chest. His tattoos begin to writhe, exciting my inner Alpha. He's just spoiling for a fight. I may provide him with one before our tour is through. "Catch," I tell him, tossing him the sweater.

He obeys.

"Good boy," I add.

He rolls his eyes. "I hope Hades kills you for this."

"He'll likely try," I admit with a shrug. "Should be fun." I look at Serapina and watch as she zips up her footwear. "You're stunning, little dreamer," I murmur when she straightens, thus revealing her long legs in those tight black pants and calf-hugging boots. "Thank you for putting on your shoes."

Her cheeks pinken a little, confirming my suspicions that she enjoys praise. She probably doesn't understand why, but it's only natural for an Omega to react favorably to compliments from an Alpha.

Just as it's my innate need to ensure she feels adored.

"So I suppose we can start with a tour of my palace, as it represents some of what the Mythos Fae used to be," I say, then pause to look at Maliki. "Sorry, I should have asked—have you ever visited this realm?"

"Only Pandora's Box," he replies, referring to our infamous prison.

"Well, that sounds like a story I would like to hear later," I admit.

"It's not mine to share," he answers cryptically.

"Ah, then I'll need to ask Hades." Which I won't, as it'll just be a waste of my time. "I assume he's provided ample history to you on Mythos Fae, so I'll be directing most of this lesson toward Serapina."

Maliki simply waves a hand in response as if to say, *Well, go on, then*.

Returning my attention to her, I add, "I'm not sure how much your sister has taught you, so I apologize if I repeat some information."

She just dips her chin once in acceptance, her eyes betraying her interest. She may not have appreciated our field trip, but she's intrigued.

And that pleases me.

I want to fascinate her. Tell her everything. Make her comfortable. Please her. *Claim* her.

Which I'm sure will feel very intense to her if I share

that up front, but her soul sings to mine. Her scent is a beacon for my knot, making it pulse even from several feet away.

I just want to chase her, prove that I'm worthy, and bury myself inside her.

But that's… too fast.

She needs to know me. To see me as a worthy mate.

Thus, I'll do whatever she desires to become hers.

And I don't just mean Persephone; I mean Serapina.

That's what Hades fails to understand—Serapina is the entity in charge now. Persephone's essence may be a part of her, but she's still her own person. Which means she needs to be wooed and worshipped, too.

"To understand Mythos Fae," I begin, "you need to know the history of our creation."

It's a long story, one I relay as I lead Maliki and Serapina out of my suite and down a long corridor.

I start by explaining where all fae come from—the collapse of the Virtuous Fae Source. "Basically, a significant betrayal led to the explosion of power, and pieces from that detonation created all the various faedoms we know of today. Except for Mythos Fae."

Serapina's brow furrowed. "So you're saying all fae species are related?"

"Not exactly. But their Sources—also known as the beacons of power that support each fae realm—all came from the Virtuous Fae Source."

"Except for the Mythos Fae," she parrots back at me.

"Precisely," I tell her. "Because we don't have a Source."

"Oh. Is that… normal?"

"No," Maliki answers for me. "All faedoms have Sources. But Mythos Fae are not really fae."

"I think that's up for debate," I tell him.

"There's a reason you're seen as Gods and not fae," he returns. "You're literally walking beacons of power."

I nod. "True."

"And many of you have your own worlds," he adds.

"Also true," I concede. "I own the dream world. Hades maintains the world of the dead. Ares manages Pandora's Box. We all have our own realms, some of which we share. Such as Hades and Orcus, though Hades is the more powerful of the pair."

Serapina swallows, then freezes when she spies something—or rather, *someone*—ahead.

I smile. "Abigail, darling, thank you for ensuring my suite was ready for my arrival."

The Beta does her best to mask her shock, but I see it in her reddish-brown eyes as she forces them to stop rounding. "Y-yes, Alpha. Of course. Shall I… ready any guest rooms?"

I shake my head. "No, we won't be staying long."

"Thank fuck for that," Maliki mutters.

Ignoring him, I look at Serapina. "This is Beta Abigail. She helps maintain my palace in exchange for my protection." Refocusing on the Beta, I add, "Abigail, this is Serapina. And the surly one is Maliki."

Abigail nods her head, then curtsies toward me. "It's a pleasure to see you again, my lord."

It's a title I don't particularly care for, but I nod in acknowledgment. Then wait to see if she notices what Serapina is. The scent seems obvious to me, but I'm also tied to Serapina in a unique way. Just like Hades.

When all Abigail does is curtsy once more and excuse herself, I frown a bit to myself.

There's something not quite right about Serapina's Omega status. I've known this since she arrived in the Netherworld, and confirmed it when she never went into

149

heat. But the fact that Abigail couldn't even sense a whiff of it suggests the issue runs deeper than Serapina's lack of an estrous cycle.

What did you do to your daughter, Demeter? I wonder as I force myself to resume walking. "You may meet a few other Betas," I tell Serapina, then go on to explain how I've offered them safe haven here in exchange for maintaining the palace.

She nods in understanding while taking in the painted ceilings of the hallway. They're reminiscent of some famous art from the Vatican in the Human Realm, though I don't tell her that, as she's never been. Instead, I just let her marvel at the pastel angels and golden adornments.

It's all rather mystical, which is intentional, as I enjoy fantasy elements and color.

While she admires the designs, I continue our discussion on fae Sources and how our kind are living beings of power.

"Specifically Alphas," I inform her. "Alphas are therefore protectors as well."

I elaborate by explaining the hierarchy, how Alphas are revered among the Betas.

"They're born powerless," I tell her. "It's what marks them as Betas. Now, I don't mean they're mortal or on par with a human in regard to strength or ability. I just mean they have no inner Source. So they pledge fealty to an Alpha in exchange for mythical energy."

All my Betas can access the dream world, something I tell Serapina now.

Then I go on to talk about the final type of Mythos Fae. The most important type. The type that ceased to exist many moons ago. *Omegas.*

SERA

"Omegas are creation Goddesses," Morpheus says as we reach a colossal entrance hall that seems to stretch up into the sky above. Literally. The ceiling is adorned with decorative clouds that *move*.

Nothing about this palace seems real. It's all so dreamlike. Which makes sense given that we're in Morpheus's palace.

In the Mythos Fae Realm.

Which is… I don't know where. I'm pretty sure Alina hasn't even been here.

I should be scared. Nervous. *Something*. But all I feel is intrigued.

This place has *sun*. I can see it streaming through the frosted windows. And now we appear to be heading for the doors.

I can't wait to go outside. To feel the warmth on my skin. To revel in the burn that follows. *It'll be like home.*

"That's what makes Alphas and Omegas so exquisitely paired," Morpheus goes on. "Alphas are beacons of energy, and Omegas manifest energy. They create *life*, and Alphas guard that precious gift. It's a symbiotic marriage between souls, a balance that helps Mythos Fae thrive."

He pauses by a set of massive doors, his palm resting on an ornate gold handle.

"Is it safe out there?" Maliki asks, his tone holding an undeniably serious quality to it.

"No." Morpheus opens the door. "It hasn't been safe here for a very long time."

With that ominous pronouncement, he steps through the threshold.

Maliki glances at me. "If I grab your hand, don't let go."

I swallow. "Okay."

He nods once and follows Morpheus.

I squint before joining them, the abundance of sunlight brighter than I anticipated. It seemed natural through the tinted windows. Now I realize that tint serves a grander purpose.

Shielding my eyes, I move outside and gasp as intense heat bathes my exposed shoulders.

Yet in a second, that heat shifts into icy pricks.

I frown, not understanding what I'm feeling.

It should be warm. The sun is too bright to be this cold. But my teeth begin to chatter.

Until suddenly I'm swathed in a thick wool coat. *Morpheus's suit jacket.* I can't see it, but I feel it.

And I'm suddenly engulfed in his scent.

Fae. He smells like fresh cotton sheets. Or maybe that's simply his detergent. It's just so clean. Silky. With a hint of… of lavender.

I inhale deeply, my shoulders loosening beneath the jacket as every part of me relaxes.

"As I said, Alphas and Omegas create a utopian harmony, one that benefits all of Mythos Fae kind," Morpheus says softly. "But Omegas haven't existed for quite some time. Without a nurturing counterpart to steady the Alpha intensity of our world, our realm has become severely imbalanced."

A flash of light nearly blinds me despite my still-closed eyes.

And suddenly, everything goes dark.

"Fuck," Maliki breathes.

My nose scrunches as the stench of decay overwhelms my previous blanket of gentle scents, and my eyes open on instinct.

The sun is gone, the sky littered with fragmented lights.

And all around us are piles of dead earth. Rubble. Bones. Unspeakable remains.

When one of those lumps moves in the distance, I jump, and Maliki instantly pulls me into his side with one hand while brandishing a fiery purple sword with the other.

"Paradox Fae?" Morpheus asks, sounding impressed.

"One of the many gifts I received from my father," Maliki mutters, his focus on the shifting ground ahead.

It's black soot mixed with rock and what appears to be charcoaled roots.

"How is this real?" I whisper, confused by the juxtaposition between the palace we just left and *this*. "I don't understand."

"We're outside my gates," Morpheus murmurs. "Now you see why those Betas prefer maintaining my estate in return for protection."

A growl echoes on the wind, the sound making my knees weak. Maliki's arm tightens around me, his gaze still on our surroundings.

"When the Omegas disappeared, their souls could no longer be felt or sensed. Which should be impossible, as Mythos Fae cannot die. But their loss could be felt by everyone in this realm, especially all of Alpha kind. Many of those Alphas have gone mad. And with them, their Betas."

Another growl accompanies Morpheus's words, adding an ominous undertone to what he's telling me.

"The realm is now a wasteland of violence. There are no nurturers here. No life. No love. No pleasure. No joy. Our heart is quite literally dead. So all the Alphas can do is try to survive. Feral needs take over. Dominance wars become a trivial playtime." He shrugs. "The sun no longer has a need to even shine."

"Then why does it glow outside your palace?" I whisper, my pulse thudding loudly in my ears.

"Because I live in a world of dreams," he murmurs. "I manifest fantasies, and the fantasy of my Betas revolved around what used to be."

It's such a sad answer. So disappointing. So *heartbreaking.*

"And how did this happen?" I ask, afraid that I already know the answer based on what little I've learned about Persephone.

"No one really knows," he says, surprising me. "But it's believed that an Omega betrayed her Alpha by mating him for the sole desire of stealing his energy. And she used his energy to suffocate Omega souls once and for all."

I stare at him, no longer seeing or hearing anything else around us. "How is that possible?"

"Because that Alpha is the God of Death. His power revolves around ending life for good. Freeing souls to a world no one else can find or feel. And it's assumed that his Omega tapped into that power to end all of Omega kind."

I've forgotten how to swallow.

Because that Omega is Persephone. *My soul.*

And the God is Hades.

No wonder he hates me…

It's a miracle he hasn't tried to kill me for what my soul did to him.

"What is lesser understood, though, is her mother's involvement," Morpheus goes on. "Persephone and Demeter were very close. And Demeter was an Alpha renowned for hating many of her kind. What I wonder is if Persephone helped her willingly or if Demeter forced——"

A screech cuts him off as an animal comes from the sky and strikes a creature just as it appears within inches of Morpheus's back.

Maliki shifts, his sword angled toward the two tussling beasts, a shock of silver and gray feathers whirling in a pile of… of… *Is that dirt?*

I can't figure out what I'm seeing. It's like a glob of skeletal remains made of charcoal.

And it appears to be fighting an owl.

Morpheus growls at it, the low rumble of sound underlined with power.

Power that's unlike anything I've ever felt.

Power that makes my knees give out beneath me.

But Malaki catches me with his arm, his body holding mine as every part of me longs to supplicate.

Only for Morpheus's purr to rumble through me in the next breath as a cloud of mist overtakes my vision.

In seconds, we're back in the room we originally arrived in.

Except that feathery beast has followed us. Its orange beak releases a hiss that has Morpheus chuckling. "Sorry,

Athena. I know how you feel about getting your feathers dirty, sweet girl." He coos at the thing that's too massive to be a bird.

However, it looks like an owl.

A really big owl.

Like the size of a large dog. But with feathers. Huge wings. Talons. *And stars for eyes.*

Literal stars.

I blink at it, convinced I've lost my mind.

Maybe all of this is a wicked dream. That would make sense. God of Dreams. Mythos Fae Realm. *Dirt zombies fighting oversized owls.*

I shake my head and curl into Maliki's chest.

Which is when I realize he's holding me in his arms. In the air.

I blink again, not sure when he picked me up. And I'm suddenly not all that eager for him to put me down.

Yep. I've definitely lost my mind.

"I think she's had enough of a lesson for today, Morpheus."

The God of Dreams nods. "Yes, I agree." He's not looking at us but at his massive owl. I'm pretty sure he's giving the beast a treat.

I have no idea where he found the item in his hand, nor do I know what it is. But Athena is staring at it with a greedy expression.

When he releases it into the air, the item flaps once before Athena catches it with her talons.

And promptly disappears.

Yep. Not even going to ask. I'm just going to close my eyes and try to wake up now.

I hold on to that hope as Maliki and Morpheus discuss returning to the Netherworld Village.

And I feel as though I'm manifesting my dream—

156

whereby I wake up and none of this is real—until I hear Hades's cold tone say, "Welcome back."

Oh, fae.

This isn't a dream. It's a nightmare.

And it's never going to end.

MALIKI

FUCKING MYTHOS FAE.

First, Hades upsets Sera and leaves me to fix it.

Then Morpheus mists Sera and me off to a dystopian Styx hole, knowing full well I couldn't just shadow out of that realm without risking some serious consequences.

Shadowing to and from the Human Realm? Fine. Midnight Fae Realm? Cool. Pretty much all other Faedoms? Yep.

But the Mythos Fae Realm? The land without a Source? The fucking epitome of "should not exist"? Nope. No. Absolutely not.

I probably would have ended up in a fire geyser had I tried.

And now Hades has the fucking audacity to show up again. He's had thirteen months to get to know his mate.

Yet he chooses twice in the same day? When she's already clearly traumatized?

"No," I say before he can even utter another word. "Fuck off." I look at Hades and then at Morpheus. "Both of you."

Hades simply arches one of his fucking brows, his expression saying, *Excuse me? Do you know who you're talking to?*

Yeah, I fucking do.

The God of Idiocy. The God Who Fucked Up. The God Who Doesn't Understand Women At Fucking All.

I mean, Styx. I know it's been a long time for him. But the way he spoke to Sera today was absolutely asinine. He's lucky she didn't slap him.

All that possessive Alpha shit.

Mine. Mine. Mine.

Well, not tonight.

"Go home," I growl at him and Morpheus. "Sera needs food and sleep. Because apparently you've both forgotten that she's a *fucking human*."

I'm usually the chill one who doesn't give a Styx about much. But seeing the light dim in Sera's eyes tonight did something to me.

She went from my feisty little mystery to a docile, broken lamb.

I'm not tolerating it.

And my expression must convey that because both Morpheus and Hades take a step back.

"We should talk," Hades says, his words for the God of Dreams. And it's not an offer so much as a demand.

"Oh, now you want to chat? After thirteen months of telling me to leave?" Morpheus grins. "How about no?" He looks at me. "Take care of our mate, Enforcer."

He disappears before I can reply, the word *our* seeming to echo in the air.

Hades narrows his gaze, making me sigh.

Apparently, Morpheus wants to imply that I've formed an alliance with him. And that Sera is the center of that relationship.

Or maybe he meant "our," as in "Morpheus and Hades." I have no clue. And it's not really my riddle to solve.

"We will be discussing this," Hades warns me.

"I'll pencil it into my calendar," I deadpan.

He isn't amused by my sarcasm. In fact, I suspect he's furious.

And that anger is only going to grow when he finds out where Morpheus took us. Though, the dangerous glint in his fathomless eyes suggests he already knows.

He glances down at Sera, some of the ire seeming to dissipate as he studies her shaking form.

She's awake and silent, her nerves obviously shot by everything she's seen and heard tonight.

I tighten my hold, something Hades notices because he stares at my arms. "That sweater looks awful on you. Burn it," he demands. Then vanishes without another word.

But his residual ire is a chill in the air I feel all around us.

Sera must sense it as well because she shudders.

"I'm going to give you ten minutes to recover in peace," I murmur, carrying her into her room to her bed. "While you do that, I'll fix something up in the kitchen. Then we will talk while we eat."

Because I assume by then she's going to have a thousand questions or comments to voice.

I gently set her on the bed, only to find her hand knotted in the sweater I'm wearing. When I try to pry her fingers off the thick wool, she winces.

Frowning, I ask, "Do you want me to hold you for a little bit?"

Her head barely moves in a nod, but it's the most noteworthy reaction I've ever seen from her.

Because she's asking for comfort.

This strong, resilient woman who has verbally sparred with countless fae at the bar… needs to be cuddled.

Although, I suppose those obnoxious males pale in comparison to learning one's soul caused the downfall of an entire realm.

"Okay, trouble," I murmur. "But let me take off my shoes first."

I should probably remove hers as well.

It takes a moment for her to release the sweater, but once she does, I run my hand along her calf and slowly unzip her boots. She seems to relax as I do so, her body enjoying my touch. Or perhaps she's just pleased to be free of her shoes.

I pull off her socks next, then work on my own footwear.

Once my feet are bare, I consider her and her bed. She looks so soft and vulnerable. But the way she's watching me is intense. It's like she plans to come after me if I walk away.

I almost wish I could read her mind. Though, something tells me that would be dangerous.

Yet probably enlightening, too.

And absolutely none of my business.

With a resigned sigh, I slip into her bed and instantly note how hard the mattress is. If she were in any other mood, I would ask her how she sleeps on this every day.

But since she's not in a teasing headspace, I simply pull her into me.

She nuzzles my chest as she curls herself against me,

her legs tangling with mine. It says a lot that she's doing this with someone she hardly knows.

Has anyone ever held you like this? I wonder. It starts as a sad question in my mind but quickly morphs into a true concern. *Have you ever been touched?*

I realize she belongs to Hades. And maybe Morpheus. That's fine.

But the notion of anyone coming before us, er, *them*, is maddening.

She's not meant for others.

I frown. If anyone else has held her like this, I'll kill them.

Unless it was Alina. I can understand that. But that's it. Only sisters. No other men. *Never another man.*

Only I can touch her like this. Well, Morpheus and Hades, too.

Sera releases a deep exhale, her body seeming to melt into mine like she's agreeing with my inane thoughts.

Because they are inane.

I shouldn't care if anyone else has touched her. She's not mine in that way. Nor should I be thinking about how this is okay or how it feels right.

She's not mine. She's forbidden. *Hades will fucking kill me for this.*

A small part of me—a clearly suicidal part—whispers that it doesn't care. Just holding her is worth the pain.

Is it, though? I counter. *Is it?*

My teeth grind together in irritation.

This is ridiculous.

She merely needs a little comfort. That's all I'm providing. It's fine.

I close my eyes and will myself to stop thinking. To shut it all off. And just breathe.

In ten minutes, I'll sneak out and cook for Sera. Then

I'll let her lead our dinner conversation, and afterward, I'll go back to Tank's place to sleep in the tiny fucking bed.

I failed to rest last night after Morpheus's antics.

Something tells me that won't be an issue tonight.

I'm too exhausted to fight it.

Which is probably something I should have considered before lying down and wrapping myself around a warm, pliable female.

I yawn.

I also should have remembered my exhaustion before closing my eyes.

Yeah. Yeah, there are a lot of things I probably should have done.

But I've never been the kind of fae who plays the "should have" game.

Mistakes happen every day. Mistakes like... falling asleep... with the Bride of Death.

SERA

SCENTS SURROUND ME. HEAVENLY ONES.

Silky cotton.

Leather and smoke.

A hint of crisp, wintry air.

Mmm. I nuzzle into the source of the alluring aroma and inhale deeply. Fae, it feels warm. Safe. Hard, yet soft. Like muscle.

Sculpted muscle.

Abs.

My brow furrows as my fingers skim the ridges of a masculine torso.

Am I dreaming? It feels hotter than usual. Even more defined, too.

Hades is always tense, his abdomen a playground for my hands.

But this landscape is slightly different. There's no thin trail of hair beneath the belly button to tempt my fingertips downward. Instead, it's all smooth, toned skin.

"Sera," a deep, growly voice rumbles against my ear. "If you go any lower, I cannot be held accountable for my response."

I slowly lift my head away from the pillow—er, *masculine chest*—and gape up at Maliki. "Oh!" I yank my hand away, and he visibly shudders.

Which isn't just visible, actually. I feel it against my leg.

Because my thigh is wedged between his.

My eyes widen as I try to untangle our limbs.

He grabs my hip just before I tip backward off the bed.

Because yeah, I overcompensated and nearly sent myself to the floor.

I wince, then go to bury myself in my pillow.

Which is just Maliki's chest.

"Thorns," I breathe.

"No, just Maliki," he returns. "In a very itchy sweater."

I peek up at him and realize said sweater is pushed up all the way to his neck. Because I apparently made a bed out of his bare chest.

My eyes close, and I slowly roll away from him this time. Cloth whispers beside me, likely a result of him fixing his sweater. After a beat of silence follows, I open my eyes again, as I assume it's safe.

And find him now shirtless in the bed.

I gape at the delicious display of muscle before forcing myself to look up at his face. "Do shirts just offend you or something?" I blurt out. "You never seem to wear them."

One dark brow inches upward. "I've been in that itchy sweater for far longer than I care to admit, all because I didn't want to wake you. So yeah, that sweater does offend me. Particularly as I've been choking on it since you tried to push it over my head while sleeping on me."

My cheeks burn in response to everything he just said. "Oh. Um. Sorry?"

He grasps my chin between his thumb and finger, his gaze intent as he stares down at me. "Don't ever apologize for trying to disrobe me, trouble. I really don't mind."

With that unexpected pronouncement, he releases me and rolls off the bed to his feet in a deft motion that makes me a little jealous. "I'm going to make breakfast. How do you feel about crepes?"

"Breakfast?" I repeat, feeling dumb. Or just confused. Yeah, I prefer confused.

"You slept for over twelve hours," he murmurs. "So yes, breakfast. Crepes?"

I don't know what crepes are, but I nod anyway. Because my stomach is growling. I'm warm and tingly everywhere. And I'm feeling a bit bewildered.

So breakfast would be good.

Because it would mean Maliki is giving me some space to process what just happened.

"Thank you," I whisper. I voice the gratitude in response to him leaving me alone for a minute, but the words feel weighted, like I mean them for so much more.

And I realize I do.

Because I asked him to stay for a few minutes, my need to just be held overriding my pride.

My soul is evil. It destroyed an entire realm. I… I don't know how to reconcile that.

"Hey," Maliki says, grabbing my chin again. Only, he's towering over me this time, as he walked over to my side of the bed.

I stare up into his gold eyes, my throat working to swallow.

"Don't thank me for giving you what you need, Sera. While I appreciate the acknowledgment, I don't want you to ever feel like you owe me something in return. Okay?"

I finally get my throat to function properly, but now my mouth feels dry. "Okay," I manage to reply.

"Good girl," he murmurs, his thumb brushing my lower lip and leaving a foreign warmth behind. "I need to grab some things from Tank's place so I can cook here. While I'm doing that, why don't you take a shower and try to relax?"

I nod because I don't think I can speak anymore.

He gives me a small smile. "Everything is going to be all right."

Are you sure about that? I want to ask. *Because I feel like I'm about to catch on fire.*

He gives my chin a little squeeze, then releases me again. "I'll start your shower for you," he says. "Then I'll head over to find what I need to make crepes."

I gape at his muscular back as he wanders into my bathroom to do exactly what he just said. When he doesn't return, I frown.

The water is running. I can hear it. So why didn't he come back out?

My eyes widen. *Did he decide to shower first? With the door wide open?*

For whatever reason, that thought has me slipping out of bed, curiosity guiding my actions.

I shouldn't go look. I really shouldn't. But a naked Maliki might be in my shower right now.

And I... I find myself very interested in seeing that.

Only, my bathroom is empty when I arrive.

Because he said he was going to start the shower and then make the crepes.

He shadowed back to Tank's place, I realize, my eyes closing at my own idiocy. *Wow, Sera. Wow.*

I... I really need to just stand under the water until I find my brain again.

So I do. I take probably the longest shower of my life. Which is impressive considering how chilly the water is here.

By the time I surface, I'm basically an ice cube. But some part of me recognizes that I probably deserve to feel cold given what my soul did in a past life.

I wince. *Why did you pick me as your host?* I want to demand. *Why did you hurt all those fae?*

I grab the sink counter and close my eyes, my towel loosely wrapped around my torso.

What happens if I become an Omega like Alina? I asked this before, wondering if I would lose who I am in favor of my soul.

But as Morpheus pointed out, Alina is still herself. Maybe I'll remain the same, too.

Only, Alina didn't possess a spirit with a known identity. So what does that mean for me?

Swallowing, I force myself to focus on finding clothes. Except my heart isn't really in it, so I end up pulling on some black shorts and pairing them with a long-sleeved top.

It's a weird combination, but I don't care. I want to be comfortable. So no jeans. And the blouse-like top has a low V-neck that makes me feel like I can breathe.

Maliki's gaze runs over me when I enter my kitchen, a towel in my hand as I try to dry my hair. He doesn't say anything, so I assume that means my outfit is fine.

Instead, he returns his focus to the stove—which doesn't look repaired so much as brand-new. I don't know what his magic-wielding friend did, but I swear he upgraded my entire kitchen after the Pip incident.

I take a seat at my small kitchen table and watch Maliki work. He's put on a long-sleeved shirt and changed into a dark pair of pants. There are little droplets of water clinging to his unruly hair, suggesting he may have just taken a shower, too.

Naturally, my mind conjures up an image of him bathing.

Naked.

All those tattoos on display.

Do they move when he's wet? I wonder, then shiver as I think about what that looks like.

"Do you prefer sweet or savory for breakfast?" Maliki asks, interrupting my fantasy.

"Savory," I say, admiring him again. His outfit is all black, the fabric clinging to him in a way that accentuates his muscular physique.

I snuggled that body all night, I think, shivering. I've never shared a bed with a male before. I've never desired to, either. But I rather liked the warmth Maliki provided.

And his scent.

I inhale now and nearly flutter my lashes at the fragrances blossoming to life in my kitchen. I smell his leathery cologne. I smell fruit. I smell something buttery.

So many alluring aromas.

So many alluring sights.

Fae, what is wrong with me? I took a long, cold shower, yet I feel overly warm.

Maybe I should have worn a tank top with my shorts instead of long sleeves.

I tug at my low neckline, my chest feeling a little funny.

The last few days have been intense.

Thorns, the last several *years* have been intense.

I just... I don't know how to reconcile any of this. *My soul is evil.*

But there's so much I don't understand.

Morpheus said the Omegas disappeared and are believed to be dead. Yet he worded it in a way that suggested he didn't believe that. Which makes sense—Alina is an Omega. And she's very much alive.

"So were the Omegas reincarnated?" I wonder out loud, causing Maliki to glance back at me.

"That's the theory," he answers, making me frown. "Hades found traces of an Omega's essence—his mother's, actually—in your home world. That's why he had me open a portal to the infamous Monsters Night; he wanted to give Orcus a proper cover story for exploring the alternate dimension."

Maliki returns to his task while I consider what he just told me. "That means the Omegas might be... alive, right?" I'm not sure if *alive* is the right term. *Maybe...* "Like they survived after all?"

"Hades never thought they were dead, just hidden away somewhere. That's why he's been hunting for them all this time." He flips something onto a plate and sets it to the side. "But Alina's existence, as well as yours, suggests that the souls were hidden in new forms of life in alternate dimensions."

He repeats the action with a second plate, then turns off the stove and rotates toward me.

"So, yes, it seems that at least some of them were reincarnated. Unfortunately, there are only two souls who know the truth. One is currently imprisoned in Pandora's Box, where she's refusing to speak. And the other..."

"Is Persephone," I whisper, finishing the sentence for him.

He nods.

"But Alina doesn't remember anything about a past life," I tell him. "She has a deep understanding of what it means to be an Omega, but not exact experiences." Or that's how she's explained it to me, anyway. "Is that because she didn't have a specific spirit inside her?"

Maliki walks over with the two plates, setting one in front of me and the other near his own seat. But rather than sit, he returns to the kitchen and starts up the coffee. As that's not my machine, I assume he brought it from Tank's place.

"I'm not sure," Maliki replies while fixing a mug. He doesn't ask if I want one today. Instead, he brings me a glass of juice. "Freshly squeezed oranges. Let me know if it's too tart." He settles across from me and sips his coffee before adding, "Hades is under the impression that you remember everything."

Yeah, I've gathered that, I think. Out loud, all I say is "I don't."

"I know," Maliki murmurs. "But the fact that he thinks you do suggests you may acquire those memories someday."

My stomach churns at that logical assertion. "I don't want to remember." The words are more for myself than for him.

But in the next beat, I retract the statement.

"Actually, no. I do want to remember. Because then I might be able to help somehow." It's… it's an insane notion. Yet now that I've thought about it, I doubt I'll ever let it go.

Persephone deserves to rot on a thorn for the rest of her existence.

However, if I can somehow fix what she's done…

Is that really my responsibility, though? I wonder, my brow furrowing. *Maybe not, but if I can help…*

I swallow.

If I can help find those Omegas, I will.

It's not about responsibility or answering for the sins of my soul. It's simply the right thing to do. "How can I try to remember?"

"Best guess?" Maliki replies, his tone and expression telling me I'm not going to like his suggestion. "By embracing your Omega half."

I stare at him. "Yeah, sure, okay. And how do I do that, again?" Because it's not like I haven't spent the last thirteen months waiting for something like that to happen to me. Given my links to Alina, and the fact that an Alpha kidnapped me for two years whilst claiming me to be her daughter—

My eyes widen.

"Demeter."

Maliki arches a brow. "What about her?"

"She claimed to be my mother." I knew this already. But I just… I just remembered something else. Something I should have recalled before, yet it's all so murky. "She called me Persephone."

"Yeah…" He draws it out like he's not following. Or maybe he doesn't understand why this is a surprise to me.

"My time with her feels like a dream. I struggle to know what really happened. But she's the one in Pandora's Box—my supposed mother."

He nods. "That's my understanding, yes. Alpha Ares is guarding her."

"And who is Ares?"

"Another Mythos Fae," he answers vaguely. "Like Morpheus said, Alphas maintain their own worlds. Ares's world is Pandora's Box."

"Oh." My nose scrunches at the idea of being in charge of a prison-like universe.

Though, I suppose Hades owning the land of the dead isn't much better.

Granted, I like the Netherworld Kingdom. A lot of the fae here are beings of death, yet they all seem friendly enough. Sometimes a little too friendly.

Shaking my head, I try to focus on eating because I need some energy to think through everything.

My memories. My dreams. My... my reality?

It's all such a convoluted mix of truth and fiction.

Did Demeter call me Persephone in the garden? Or is that from a past life?

I can't remember, but I can distinctly hear her saying it now in my head.

Closing my eyes, I force myself to concentrate on the flavors bursting across my tongue. I understand now why Maliki asked if I preferred savory or sweet. Because mine is cheesy with some sort of salty meat. Peeking through my lashes, I see that his crepe is stuffed full of fruit.

"Want to try a bite?" he asks, his voice soft.

"Yes," I admit.

He cuts a piece off and offers it to me with his fork.

Rather than take it from him, I just lean in and accept the piece directly into my mouth.

His golden irises burn as he watches me, some foreign emotion darkening his features.

I swallow slowly, then groan at the taste as it finally registers. "Wow," I say, surprised. "I don't normally enjoy sweets in the morning, but that's really good."

"I know," he answers, cocky as ever.

My lips twitch. Arrogance isn't usually a trait I find endearing, but it seems appropriate on Maliki.

He offers me another bite without comment, and I accept it into my mouth like the last one.

Then I return to my own food, and we finish our meal in silence.

When we're both done, I stand to clean up, but Maliki ushers me back to my seat and takes over my kitchen again. I watch him work and let his fluid movements distract me from thinking about everything I've learned.

For the most part, I'm successful in forgetting everything else.

At least until a shadow appears to my left.

A shadow that slowly turns into an ominous presence.

Hades.

His gaze finds mine, his cold, dark orbs conveying so much meaning that I nearly stop breathing.

Because I can see his hatred now.

And not only that, but I can understand it also.

He has every right to wish me dead. Persephone used him for his power and hurt so many others in the process.

I'm honestly lucky he hasn't imprisoned me in Pandora's Box next to Demeter.

It's probably what my spirit deserves.

So why hasn't he done that? I wonder, frowning at him. "Why in all the realms would you want to marry me?" I ask him, so utterly confounded by that desire that I don't even bother with formalities or greetings. Just bluntly add, "My soul doesn't deserve a nuptial event. It deserves to be punished. So why would you make me your bride? How could you possibly want me by your side?"

HADES

My mate's words are so unexpected that I simply stare for a moment.

Then I say the first response that comes to mind. "I don't want you by my side, pet. I want you kneeling at my feet." *Preferably with my knot in your fucking throat*, I nearly add aloud, but manage to stop myself from continuing when Maliki slams down a pot in the sink.

"I respect you. I do," Maliki says in a slow, measured tone. "But speak to Sera like that again and I will fucking deck you."

One of my eyebrows wings upward. "First of all, how very human of you to use that ridiculous phrase. Perhaps you should consider cutting back on the assassin flicks; they're not meant to be educational. Secondly, how I speak to my mate isn't your concern."

"It is when you put me in charge of protecting her," he counters, grabbing a rag to dry his hands. "It's also my concern because you tasked me with convincing her to marry you. And you're making my job that much fucking harder."

He stalks toward me, his height rivaling my own.

But my gaze is on my wife.

Her eyes widened with the latter half of Maliki's commentary. "You're trying to convince me to marry him?" she asks, sounding... well, I'm not quite sure. She sounds surprised, but also a bit upset. "I don't..." She trails off, her shoulders falling. "Oh."

She looks defeated somehow, and I have no idea why.

This meek side of her—which I first witnessed upon her return from our home realm and again now—is much more like the Persephone I know. Except I don't remember her ever being this sad.

I don't care for it.

"Why are you upset?" I demand, needing to fix it.

She simply huffs in response.

"That's not an answer, Persephone. Tell me what's troubling you so I can solve it."

The look she gives me is equal parts confused and annoyed. "What?"

Maliki steps between us, cutting off my view and irritating me greatly.

But his expression is dark as he says, "I know I suggested that you talk to Sera, but I didn't mean like this. You should knock and let her invite you in, not just show up unannounced. And do not spout that bullshit again about having free access to her space because she's yours. That is not going to fly with me in my current mood."

"But she is my mate."

"Her soul mated yours over two thousand years ago, yes. However, *Sera,* the *human,* is not yours."

I take a step back, mostly because his words are delivered like a blow to the chest. "They are the same."

"Yeah?" He folds his arms across his chest. "Then why is Sera asking me about how to access her memories? Oh, and would you like to know why she asked me how to do that?" He doesn't even give me a second to reply before saying, "Because she wants to *help*."

"I can speak for myself," my mate says quietly.

"Oh, I'm aware that you can," Maliki replies. "I'm just trying to help Hades keep his foot out of his mouth this time."

"He put his foot in his mouth?" she asks, sounding confused.

Despite the irritation pouring off Maliki, his lips twitch in amusement. "It's a saying, trouble."

"I don't understand it," she tells him.

"It means he's trying to prevent me from saying things I shouldn't," I explain, still looking at Maliki. "You've completely fallen for her game, haven't you?" My question is obviously for my enforcer.

He sighs and runs his hand over his face. "If she's playing a game, then why is she asking about how to awaken her memories?"

"To trick you into a false state of comfort." That's exactly what she did to me with her innocence and soft coos of affection. None of it was real. Yet she snagged my heart for eternity and still owns it today. "She's very clever."

"I wish I could take that as a compliment," my mate mutters. "However, I'm not nearly as *clever* as you want to believe. I don't know what Persephone did in a past life outside of what Morpheus and Maliki explained yesterday. But I'm willing to do whatever you need me to do to unlock the memories inside me. If you really think that's possible."

She's standing now, her blonde head barely reaching Maliki's shoulder as she steps around him and into view.

The resignation in her features sends a pang through my chest. I'm not fond of this side of my mate. It's new. And so very different from the feisty emotions I saw yesterday. While that was arousing, this is... upsetting.

"Maliki says I need to embrace my inner Omega. So. How do I do that?" Her direct stare is at odds with her defeated posture.

It's an interesting disparity, one I contemplate for a moment too long.

Or maybe it's her eyes that render me silent.

So incredibly blue. So beautiful.

I used to think Persephone's brown eyes were the most beautiful color in all the realms. Yet I find myself conflicted now. Because these new irises of hers are simply exquisite.

"I know you think I remember everything and I'm tricking you," she goes on with a sigh. "Given what little I've learned about my soul, you're justified in that feeling. I won't fault you for it. But I need guidance, my... my lord. Alina seems to have naturally turned into an Omega. I have not. Can you tell me what I have to do?"

Her stammering over my title pulls me under her spell even more.

Persephone has *never* referred to me as *my lord*. Always *my love*. Or simply, *Hades*.

"Please?" she adds. "I understand you hate me... or my soul... or..." She clears her throat. "It doesn't matter. But if all this is true, then I need someone to help me figure out how to activate my inner Omega. Can you see past the hatred enough to help me do that? So I can try to access the memories of what really happened?"

I… I'm so astounded by everything she's saying that all I can do is blink before looking at Maliki. "What exactly has she been told?"

"That my soul is responsible for what happened to your realm," she says before Maliki can reply. "And while I understand now why you haven't wanted to talk to me at all over the last thirteen months, I would appreciate not being treated as invisible. I would also really like an answer to my question, please."

There are a thousand inquiries boiling in my head, starting with *Who made you think I hate you?* But rather than voice them, I focus on the need my mate just mentioned. "Which question?" I ask her, unsure of what she's referring to.

"Why do you want to marry me? My soul is responsible for a sin I can barely even understand. Your hatred is justified. But I don't understand the point of the nuptials. Is it to inspire my Omega to come out?"

I search her features, the sincerity doing something to me.

Is it possible…?

No. No, it can't be possible. She's playing me.

But then why ask me such innocent questions?

And she keeps telling me I hate her. I… I do. But I love her as well. As my wife, she should understand that.

She blows out a breath when I don't reply, her gaze finally leaving mine. "Never mind. I'll do whatever you want, my lord. Just… I only ask that you guide me. Please. I want to remember… to… to help."

Maliki wraps his arm around her, the move startling me. "It's not your responsibility, Sera."

"Maybe not," she replies, giving him her gaze—something that makes me narrow my own. "But if I can access the memories like you all seem to think I can, then it's worth taking on that responsibility, don't you agree?"

"Actually, no, I don't. I prefer delivering justice to those who deserve it, not to innocent parties. I've also never been into the martyr role. Executioner, assassin, enforcer, all fine. Martyr? No, thank you."

She just shakes her head, though I catch the hint of a smile on her lips.

Because of Maliki.

My gaze narrows even more.

I told him to convince her to marry me, and it seems he's done too good a job. Not only does she seem ready to do whatever I ask, but she also appears to be falling for my best friend.

Hmm.

This game no longer makes any sense.

I thought Persephone might try to use me again, perhaps to free her mother from Pandora's Box. Maliki can't help with that. Morpheus could, though. Yet her adoring focus is on Maliki.

So what's your goal, darling mate? I wonder. *What will you use Maliki for? His protection?*

That's almost laughable.

Persephone would know that very few can fight me and win.

And while Maliki may have gotten between us today, as well as last night, he didn't exactly challenge me.

Which brings me back to pondering Persephone's desires.

"I'm not a martyr," she tells Maliki. "Or I don't mean to be. But knowing my soul is evil has me… conflicted about right and wrong."

"Your soul is not evil," I interject, disliking that term in relation to my mate. "Troubled, perhaps. But certainly not evil."

I refuse to believe that.

Persephone betrayed me. Hurt me and countless others. But she… she never possessed evil tendencies.

Hence the reason I've been so at odds over her intentions these last two thousand years.

It didn't make sense then, and it certainly doesn't now.

Is it because I took you from Demeter? I long to ask.

Her mother always did favor Persephone. Though, my mate often said she felt stifled by her mother's influence. She wanted to be free.

That's why we mated.

So I could take her to my palace and give her a new life.

Only, my world is shrouded in death, thus making it hard for her to thrive—a fact Demeter always blamed me for.

That's why we struck a deal, one whereby Persephone left every spring to help prepare the fields for future harvest.

She was always so relieved to return to me.

Truth or a lie? I wonder, still staring at the embodiment of my mate. She looks nothing like my Persephone. Nor does she act like her.

My lord.

Calling her soul evil.

Looking at Maliki with hearts in her beautiful eyes.

My jaw clenches. "If you mean what you say about being willing to do whatever it takes, then I need you to return to my palace and take over the accommodations I've created for you." Okay, none of that is actually *required* to free her Omega. But it may help. Close proximity to an Alpha should inspire her estrus.

Except, she spent a year near me, and nothing.

Perhaps being in my quarters will help.

The magic in the walls guards my privacy. Maybe that enchantment worked a little too well and shadowed her from my Alpha influence.

"Further, we will wed again to try to re-create the bond," I go on. This should awaken her inner Omega.

It will also, at the very least, confirm my suspicions that Persephone has been lying since she arrived.

Or prove she's been telling the truth and doesn't remember anything at all, a small voice whispers in my head as I watch her slender throat bob on a swallow.

I don't like that voice, so I ignore the mental whisper.

"We will also have dinner," I add. "Tonight." I glance at Maliki, then back at her. "*Alone.*"

Maybe being around just me will allow the real Persephone to come out and play. She won't have to put on an act for anyone else. And then we can have a real conversation.

"Okay," she says, her voice soft. She swallows again. "Anything else, my lord?"

I narrow my gaze again. "Yes. You can stop calling me *my lord.*"

With that, I disappear and leave Maliki to handle her move.

It's the least he can do after seducing my female.

I may have taunted him with that concept, but I didn't anticipate him rolling all over her and drenching the female in his scent.

My chest rumbles with a mixture of disapproval and need.

Because part of me likes their combined scents. *Like a bouquet of fire lilies tied up in a leathery ribbon.*

Ridiculous.

Insane.

Fucking hot.

I shake my head. If Maliki were here, I would seek him out for a sparring match, as I'm suddenly in the mood to hit something. Or someone.

The problem is *he's* the one I want to hurt.

Energy swarms around me as soon as I enter my office, the signature one I recognize instantly.

I turn to face my cousin as he says, "You're welcome."

I have no idea what Morpheus is talking about.

And I don't fucking care.

I simply reply, "Yeah, you'll do." And introduce my fist to his face.

MORPHEUS

My jaw smarts from Hades's abrupt hit, my smile disappearing in a flash.

Alpha aggression is dangerous. It easily escalates into feral territory.

So when he attempts to land another blow, I wrap my arms around him and mist us to a deserted field in our home realm.

It's more desolate than the Barren Lands of the Hell Fae Realm.

It's simply nothing apart from scorched dirt, making it the perfect place for whatever Hades has in mind.

He yanks off his jacket and drops it onto the charcoaled ground. I follow suit.

His button-down shirt is next, the buttons scattering as he all but rips it off.

I do the same, though I'm a bit more careful with my fingers and manage to disrobe without destroying my shirt.

He paces around me, his dark eyes glittering with barely restrained power. I'm surprised his wings haven't appeared, his black plumes an ominous flurry of feathers that he rarely displays.

But anger is usually a catalyst for his beast to come out. Interesting that he's holding that part of him back. For now, anyway.

I match him step for step, my energy building in cadence with his own.

If he wants a fight, I'll give him one. But he should know there will be consequences.

Such as other Alphas potentially joining the fray.

Alphas like Ares.

Violence calls to him. And I'm sure he's spoiling for a good battle right about now.

A chill sweeps through the air as Hades engages his gifts, the death world responding to his call and coming right for me.

I deflect with an illusion of sunshine, bursting from the murky sky above and angling right at Hades's eyes. He holds up a hand to deflect the intense light, giving me just enough time to mist to him and deliver a punch to his nose.

He curses.

I grin.

And then the real fight begins.

Lightning strikes the charcoaled ground as we slam into each other, our powers mounting with each hefty blow.

Hades strikes my arm, causing it to go temporarily numb—like it's dead—and I respond by shoving him into another reality.

One filled with a million of those moss plants that Maliki loved so much.

A roar comes from the dream as Hades fights his way out of the illusion and back into reality, just as my limb begins to recover.

Only, he's not alone as he resurfaces.

He brings the hounds of death with him.

I sigh. "You really want to do this?"

The growls coming from his three-headed creature tell me oh, yeah, he absolutely does.

So I whistle for Athena.

But she's already on her way, her link to my mind informing me that she heard the call before I even finished thinking about it.

Howl—or is that Mort?—looks up right as my owl appears above. A loud growl leaves the hellhound-like creature's snout, alerting the other two heads to follow his gaze.

And the animals go sprawling across the vacant landscape.

I smirk, only to find my neck in a twist, courtesy of Hades.

"Bastard," I snarl, realizing he used our familiars as a distraction.

"Why did you bring her here?" he demands.

I assume *her* is Serapina. "To teach her," I ground out as he starts trying to twist my head off. I mist out of his hold, only to lose feeling in my legs.

Glancing down, I curse at the deadly trap Hades has left for me here.

It's worse than the slug venom on Maliki's blade.

This... this is true *death*.

A pit of souls like Pip, only these beings are not wearing cloaks.

And they're *all* touching me.

I can survive this. But it still smarts like a son of a fae.

"What did you think she needed to be taught?" Hades asks, his silky voice near my ear as he crouches behind me.

"Everything, you imbecile," I hiss at him. "She knows *nothing*. Not about Persephone. Not about mating an Alpha. Not about our world. She's utterly lost, with only her sister's words to guide her. And she thinks she's not an Omega."

That last line is delivered with such rage that I can't control my tone. Because I'm furious that he let it get this far.

"You're her Alpha, yet you've left her woefully unprepared for our life," I accuse, my voice growing hoarse from all the deadly toxins flowing through my veins. I would mist if I could, but the damn souls neutralized that ability the moment my feet touched this pit.

Well played, I would normally tell Hades.

But I'm not in much of a praising mood right now. I'm too irritated with him to be commending his sparring choices.

"You do not tell me what I have and have not done for *my mate*," Hades replies, his voice reverberating through his deadly minions.

"If Serapina is your mate, then you've already failed her," I return, hating how weak I sound. "She doesn't understand or know you at all, as evidenced by her thinking you hate her when we both know you could never truly hate your Omega. And she thinks marrying you will help her Omega side take over."

I grunt after that last sentence, still irritated by the conversation I overheard.

Because yes, I was lurking in the mist. I probably

should have made my presence known, but I wanted to give Hades a chance to properly woo Serapina.

But his own stubborn nature took over. He's hurt from a betrayal that happened two thousand years ago. I understand. We're all *hurt* by what happened.

However, his pain blinds him to what everyone else can plainly see—that Serapina *is not* Persephone. She's a separate entity. A human. A beautiful mortal who has been paired with a turbulent soul.

That's not her fault.

She shouldn't be punished for another being's sins.

Yet the beautiful individual that Serapina is came out on full display as she offered to do whatever was necessary to try to access the memories buried deep inside her spirit.

"What are you going to do on your nuptial night, Hades?" I ask, my vision starting to go black. "Continue to assume it's Persephone, thereby justifying your growl? Seduce the Omega into taking your knot when she doesn't even bloody know what a knot is?"

"And how do you know *that?*" His fury underlines that last word, making me sigh.

Because I'm about to lose consciousness.

And he's probably going to leave me here to suffer until Ares comes along.

Or maybe Athena will pull me out. But only if she's careful. I would die a thousand deaths before letting any ill fate befall my precious owl.

"Because I made an offhanded comment the other night," I tell him, my voice barely audible. "She repeated the term like a question."

I don't hear his reply.

Not even sure he makes one.

But I really only have one last thing to say to him anyway. "All I've ever wanted was to share her, Hades. Not take her. Not claim her as my own. *Share*. Alas, it's something you'll never understand. Not even for Maliki."

Because I know that's what set him off—his possessive jealousy.

He took it out on me. Which is fine. I can handle his fury.

Yet I'm so bloody tired of this fight.

Maybe he'll finally hear me.

Maybe he won't.

With one last breath, I simply fall deeper into the pit.

And give his minions what they crave. *My life*.

SERA

"Are you sure you're okay?" Maliki asks me for the third time in the last thirty minutes.

And I…

I simply can't take hearing this question again.

Because… "*No.* I'm not okay. But I don't really have a choice, do I?"

"You always have a choice, Sera."

"Oh?" I drop the clothes I'm holding onto the bed and rotate to face him. "What happened to you telling me I would be going about this the hard way if I refused the God of Death's proposal? Where was my choice then?"

"If I recall correctly, you chose to tell him to go to Styx and didn't agree to relocate to your new accommodations," he reminds me.

"I don't even know where Styx is," I gripe back at him. But the second part of that statement is true—I refused.

"It's an infamous river in the Mythos Fae Realm that

has since dried up. But I actually first learned about it in Greek mythology."

I blink at him. "Greek mythology?" I shake my head because I don't even think I want to know. "Never mind. My point is, no, I'm not okay. And I need you to stop asking."

His expression turns solemn as he nods. "Okay, Sera. What else do you need me to do?"

I consider my hut.

My things.

What little I own.

The closet is not even a quarter of the way full. I have very little in my dressers. The pots and pans and eatery items all came with my kitchen.

I guess I have the plant I only just started to nurture. Though, I don't think there is much of a point in that hobby anymore.

There's really nothing I care about here.

Except Pip.

And I haven't seen him since he gave me the pot.

"Do you think Hades will let me take Pip with me?" I ask Maliki, feeling more dejected than I can ever remember in my life.

This isn't the Sera I want to be, I think, disappointed. *I guess I'll just go back to being Serapina until Persephone takes over.*

"No, I don't think the obsessive-possessive God named Hades is going to let you bring a male fae to live in the palace with you," Maliki says slowly. "How could you even ask that? And for the last time, *who the fuck is Pip?*"

I gape at him. "What male fae?" I ask, utterly lost as to where he even came up with that idea. "And I've told you —Pip is a spirit."

"A Death Fae," he says.

I just look at him. "What Death Fae?"

"Pip."

"What?" I blink. "You're not making any sense."

"You keep calling Pip a spirit. You mean Death Fae."

"Uh, no, I mean *spirit*. He's about this tall"—I place my palm around my belly button—"he floats around in a pretty blue cloak, and he has fiery sapphire eyes that glow in the dark." Which scared the thorns out of me the first time I saw him. But that's a story for another day.

"I have no idea what you're talking about right now," Maliki says.

"Well, that makes two of us. Now, which male fae did you think I wanted to bring with me to live in the palace?" I inquire, still confused about that. And a whole lot of other things, actually.

"Pip."

"Pip isn't a Death Fae," I tell him, exasperated. "*He's a spirit.* He brings me dead flowers and tries to cook for me but fails. And he has big hollows where his eyes go." I point at my own features so he knows what I mean. "Oh, and his face is a skull. But his nose is pretty cute. Like an upside-down heart."

Maliki looks at me like I've lost my mind. "Are you sure you're okay?"

"Oh my fae!" I shout, throwing my arms up in the air. "We've already been over that. *No.* I am *not* okay. Why do you keep changing the subject back to that?"

I'm ready to go pick up the pot in the other room and throw it at his ridiculously handsome head.

In fact, maybe I will.

I start to walk that way, only to find my hip trapped by one of his hands as he grasps my chin with the other.

My stomach flips as he walks me backward into the wall, his large frame towering over me as he stares down into my eyes. "I'm sorry I asked that again," he says slowly. "I'm just very confused by your fae friend Pip."

"He's not a fae."

"So you keep saying." His brow furrows. "His face is covered in skull paint?"

"No, it's a literal skull. Because he's a spirit. Like he's *dead*."

Maliki's lips part. "You mean a *soul*."

"That is the same as a spirit," I tell him as I try to ignore the tingles erupting across my jaw from his touch on my chin.

"It's not, well, yes, it is, but a soul is very different in this kingdom. It's a literal soul."

"Also known as a spirit," I mutter.

He presses his forehead to mine and chuckles. "You're adorable, trouble."

I stop breathing, his nearness stirring feelings inside me that I've never experienced before. Not in reality, anyway.

Only ever in my dreams.

But the way my heart races now is so much more intense than anything my mind has ever been able to fabricate.

My lungs force me to inhale, which has my eyes threatening to close.

Because fae, he smells good.

I just want to lose myself in his scent. His touch. His *warmth*.

Does he even realize what he's doing to me? Does he feel it, too?

I can't tell. He's staring down at me like he's trying to memorize my features. Our foreheads are no longer touching, but he's still so close.

"Fuck, you're beautiful," he tells me, his voice so soft I almost wonder if I imagined hearing those words.

"Thank you," I reply, swallowing. "And thank you for being here for..." The words trail off as I suddenly recall *why* he's here.

"It's also my concern because you tasked me with convincing her to marry you."

That's what he said to Hades.

I press my palm to Maliki's chest and nudge him back. "That's why you've been so nice to me—because of your job." I shake my head, a humorless laugh falling from my lips. "To convince me to marry Hades."

Stars, I... I almost thought this was something else.

He's an attractive fae. Thorns, he's more than attractive. He's one of the sexiest men I've ever seen.

And he held me all night.

It's only natural for me to feel interested in him. But it's one-sided.

"I'm sorry," I say, laughing again at my own expense. "I... I don't even know what we're doing here. I'm just a task that needs to be finished. So I... I guess we need to... wrap this up." Because I'm supposed to be packing.

Yet I have nothing of worth to take with me except the flowerpot and Pip.

I don't even want my clothes. They were given to me by Alina.

In fact, nothing here is mine. Not even my own choices.

I was brought to this kingdom by my sister and her mates. For my protection. But now I suspect it was so much more than that.

Orcus has to know the truth about my soul. He's Hades's brother. Surely they've spoken.

So does Alina know?

No. She... she would tell me, right?

Unless she was trying to protect me.

"Ugh." Of course she was protecting me. That's what she's done our entire lives. Why would it be any different now?

This whole experience with my independence was just some idiotic experiment.

And now I have to go right back to where I was a month ago.

A very bratty, very frustrated part of me longs to scream.

But what good would that do?

"Sera," Maliki says, and something in his tone suggests it's not the first time he's said my name.

He's still touching my chin, too, which I realize now as he forces me to meet his gaze. His other hand burns on my hip as he holds me against the wall.

"You are the most infuriating assignment Hades has ever given to me."

I wince, his words a slap to the face. I definitely don't want to hear this. "You—

"No, Sera, let me finish," he says, his thumb sliding up to press against my lips. "I've been tasked with watching you for nearly a year. At first, it was fine. You stayed in the palace, and I barely saw you. But once you moved here, I spent every day getting to know you. Which makes me sound like a stalker."

"It's—

"Not done, trouble," he murmurs, cutting me off again. "I've never hated a task as much as this one."

I wince again, my eyes closing.

"Because I've never been tempted as much as you tempt me," he says, his forehead touching mine again. "You're not mine to want, sweet mystery. And I've been good. So fucking good. Even with Hades's goading, I've kept my hands to myself. I haven't touched you. Not until..."

I peek at him through my lashes, noting the pain in his features.

"Now that I've touched you, Sera, I don't think I want to stop," he tells me. "So hate me if you need to, but I need you to know that this is so much more than an assignment to me. You're absolutely forbidden to me. The female I'm not allowed to crave."

I shudder, his words undoing something inside me. "Maliki..."

His lashes flutter, his forehead still pressed against mine. "Fuck, Sera, you have me wondering if tasting you is worth the wrath of a possessive God." His soft words are a breath against my lips. Then he pushes himself away from me and turns toward my bed, his breathing echoing through the small room.

Or maybe that's my breathing.

I... I feel like I've run a marathon.

Pressing my palm to my chest, I try to still my beating heart. But it's impossible, because I can see Maliki struggling to control himself.

Except his comment about wondering if it's worth the wrath of Hades...

It's not. *I'm* not worth that. Not for Maliki.

My soul...

My head falls back, my mind vacillating between guilt and fury. I don't deserve to be punished. *I* did nothing wrong.

But how can that be true when my very essence is riddled with evil?

Hades might have said otherwise, but how can I believe him?

Persephone destroyed a realm.

My gaze falls to the floor.

It might not be my burden to carry, but fate paired us for a reason.

And I'm determined to find out why.

Which means I need to unlock my inner Omega.

"We should go," I tell Maliki softly. "The only items I want to take with me are my flower and Pip."

His shoulders visibly tighten. "I'm not sure Hades will let you have Pip in the palace."

I narrow my gaze. "You know what? Given everything? I'm not sure I care." Because I'm literally about to give up my life for this Alpha so he can trigger the memories buried deep within my soul.

If I want a ghost friend, I can have a ghost friend.

Besides, maybe Pip will follow me into the afterlife when all this is done.

There's a morbid thought, I think, laughing to myself. *Fae, maybe I have lost my mind*.

Well, I blame Persephone.

And Hades.

And fate.

"Let's go find Pip," I say to Maliki. "He can decide if he wants to come with me or not."

HADES

I SIT IN THE DIRT, MY GAZE ON THE SKY WHILE I WAIT FOR Morpheus to return to the land of the living.

Some of my ire has melted. Not all of it, but enough.

And all because of a knot.

I nearly laugh at the insanity of it all.

However, Morpheus's statements were truthful. Everyone's always are when faced with the pit of death. That's what makes it such an effective tool for eternal judgment.

"All I've ever wanted was to share her, Hades. Not take her. Not claim her as my own. Share. Alas, it's something you'll never understand. Not even for Maliki."

Morpheus's dying proclamation plays through my mind, the words ones I struggle to accept.

Only, I know he meant each and every statement.

"How could Persephone not know what a knot is?" I

ask his corpse. "I've knotted that Omega thousands of times. Trust me, *she knows what a knot is*."

Yet I heard the truth in his commentary then, too. *"She repeated the term like a question."*

I grunt. "That doesn't sound like my Persephone at all," I tell him, aware he can't hear a word I'm saying. "You need to regenerate faster, Morpheus. This one-sided conversation is boring me."

The irony of the situation is not lost on me.

Usually, I can't wait for him to shut the fuck up.

Yet right now, all I want is for him to answer me.

I shake my head. "Everything is twisted. Nothing is right. And Persephone... She doesn't know what a knot is?" I can't help but voice the question aloud for what's probably the third or fourth time. "I don't understand. She's not..." I trail off, my mind struggling with the logical assessment that's so blatantly obvious I want to disregard it.

Because I can't trust her.

Except, what if it's not her? What if Morpheus and Maliki are right? Orcus, too...

They've all said Serapina is her own individual.

I've not wanted to believe it.

Maybe that's the true reason I avoided her for the last thirteen months—I didn't want to be proved wrong.

My jaw clenches at the very real likelihood of that scenario.

"Am I just being stubborn?" I ask myself.

"Fucking... always," a hoarse voice answers from beside me.

"Oh." I look down at Morpheus. "Good. You're up. We need to talk."

The corpse-like version of my cousin sputters out a sound that might be a laugh. Or maybe a curse. I'm not sure. Nor do I care.

"What did you mean, *not even for Maliki*?" I ask my cousin. "Are you suggesting I share him as an enforcer?"

The look Morpheus gives me tells me that's too complex a question for his waking brain.

Or maybe he's trying to convey irritation with his gaze.

"You're going to need to rouse faster," I tell him. "I have a date with my Omega tonight, and I don't want to be late."

I think he tries to shake his head. It's hard to say.

"Your hair is white, by the way," I muse. "I wonder if that'll be permanent or if you'll revive it?"

Now my cousin looks like he wants to kill me.

Can't say I blame him. I often feel that way about him, too.

Though, his commentary about *sharing* has me... conflicted.

I've never desired to share my Persephone. He knows this. He's simply refused to accept it. He's even gone as far as to blame me for her betrayal, saying that had she been surrounded by a mate-circle, it would never have happened.

I hate that I've wondered if he's right.

Just as I hate that I'm considering the option of allying with him now.

"I don't want to share her with you," I murmur.

He rolls his eyes. "Shocking." His voice still resembles a rasp, which has me sighing.

"When was the last time you sparred, Cousin? I fear you've gotten weak."

An invisible force meets my jaw, sending me backward into the ground.

I grunt, not pleased at all when I hear the telltale sign of my jacket ripping.

I should have known better than to put it back on while waiting for my cousin to rejoin the living.

"Arse," I mutter, sitting up again.

Only for that invisible fist to try to hit me again. I catch it this time with my hand and block the follow-up coming from my left.

It's dream energy, making it impossible to see. However, I can *feel* it.

"*Enough*," I tell Morpheus. "I want to talk."

"You've had months to talk to me," he says, his voice completely normal now.

I glance at where he's lying to find him no longer there. Instead, he's standing a dozen feet away, completely dressed and appearing as pressed as ever.

My eyes narrow. "Did you create a mirage of yourself?"

His lips simply curl.

I scoff. I should have seen that coming. The moment his power regenerated, he no doubt crafted this entire scene and secretly pulled me into an illusion whereby I've been talking to a fake corpse. "How long were you listening?" I ask, resigned.

"Long enough," he replies. "Serapina isn't Persephone, Hades. That's why she doesn't know what a knot is. She doesn't have any of her memories. But I know my word isn't good enough for you, so I have a suggestion instead."

I almost correct him on that last part regarding his word. I actually do trust him. I trust him a great deal. More than I care to admit.

So rather than comment on it, I say, "I'm listening."

"Kiss her." Two very simple words and yet they absolutely floor me.

"I beg your pardon?"

"You heard me—*kiss her*. I realize it's been a while, but

I'm sure you remember exactly what Persephone is like in the nest. So ask Serapina for a kiss and see if it's anything like your soulmate's." He slides his hands into his slacks and shrugs. "An Omega can't deny her Alpha's growl. Either she'll react the way you're used to, or she won't."

I frown, not sure if I like this notion. "If she truly is a separate entity like you all claim, then wouldn't that make her despise me more than she probably already does?" I really hate voicing that question aloud, but it's worth a conversation.

"I don't think Serapina despises you, Hades. She just doesn't understand you. Not yet. But she's trying. And that's more than I can say about your efforts in learning about her."

My teeth clench, my gaze narrowing. "I've spent the last thirteen months studying her."

"No, you've spent the last thirteen months waiting for her to go into heat so you would have a reasonable excuse to knot her," he counters.

"I've been waiting for this game to cease."

He nods. "Yes, and your ideal end is between her legs in her nest with your knot buried deep inside her."

"Stop talking about my mate's nest."

He rolls his eyes. "Is she even your mate, Cousin? Her soul might be, but is Serapina?" he stresses. "You asked if you're being stubborn, and the answer is yes, Hades. Yes, you are. You're always stubborn. And I've tolerated it for far too long. But I'm starting to think I was wrong about our compatibility."

I snort at that.

While I could say a lot of derogatory things about Morpheus, claiming a lack of compatibility isn't one of them.

We're insufferably well matched, a fact I've loathed his entire existence.

"Maybe I need to create my own mate-circle," he goes on. "And you know the first fae I'm recruiting? *Maliki.*"

"Are you intentionally trying to infuriate me?"

"No, Hades. I'm trying to wake you the fuck up. Because if you don't figure this out soon, I'm going to be left with no choice but to claim her without you."

The world shakes around me as he gives me some sort of mental shove, one that knocks me completely off-kilter.

I start to fall, the realm around me going black as my concept of reality tilts.

And I suddenly find myself facedown in my bed.

I blink into the familiar mattress, my head aching like I've been buried beneath a pile of a thousand columns.

Maybe I have.

With Morpheus, it's impossible to know what's real and what's not.

Except his words... those were very real. All truths. Threats masked as calmly worded statements.

Grumbling, I push up off my bed and look around.

I have no idea how long I've been here or how I even returned. Knowing Morpheus, he knocked me out with some sort of sleep spell.

Groaning, I roll off the mattress. "If you made me miss my date with my wife, I will hunt you down and kill you again, Cousin," I say.

I swear I hear him chuckle in response.

But it's probably just in my head.

"Arse," I mutter.

Then I head to the bathroom. Because late or not, I need to shower the remnants of a ruined realm off my head and shoulders.

Afterward, I'll go track down my wife.

And consider what Morpheus suggested about kissing her.

SERA

"Pɪᴘ!" I ᴡʜɪsᴘᴇʀ-sʜᴏᴜᴛ, ғʀᴜsᴛʀᴀᴛᴇᴅ ᴛʜᴀᴛ ʜᴇ's ɴᴏᴡʜᴇʀᴇ to be found or seen.

Maliki stands nearby, his expression skeptical. "You're sure this soul of yours is real, yeah?"

"You're sure I'm an Omega, yeah?" I toss back at him.

His lips twitch. "Touché, sweet mystery. Proceed in beckoning your pet spirit."

I grit my teeth and try again.

Nothing.

"Come on, Pip," I say, exasperated. "They're making me move, and I don't want to leave without at least saying goodbye."

"*Making* is a strong word choice, as well as inaccurate," Maliki inserts.

I glare at him. "Nothing about my life is a choice, Maliki. Everything has been predecided because of an evil soul. So if I want to say I'm being forced to do something, you can bet that it's true."

Some of his amusement slips. "Sera…"

My eyebrow lifts as I wait for him to finish whatever he's about to say. But he falls silent. Just my name, his voice laced with so much apology that I know he's feeling sorry for me. "Please don't pity me."

"I don't."

"You do," I correct him. "Life is never fair. I accepted that a very long time ago."

More sorrow enters his golden eyes, forcing me to look away.

And as I do, I spy a little flurry of color in my bedroom.

"Pip!" Darting to the door, I look inside and see him floating near my bed with his hands behind his back, his head turned down.

There's a solitary dead flower on my pillow.

"Where have you been?" I ask him.

He floats around nervously, his fiery orb-like eyes darting up as Maliki joins me in the doorway. Pip instantly scurries back toward the wall, his cloak rattling in a way that makes it look like he's shaking.

"What is that on your bed?" Maliki asks slowly. "And where is your little soul?"

I frown. "He's right there." I point at Pip, who is now gaping at me with wide eyes, like he can't believe I just gestured toward him. "What's wrong, Pip?" He begins to shake, true sorrow painting his features. "Hey," I say, softer now as I start to approach him. "What's going on? Why are you so spooked?"

Maliki snorts. "Now there's a good ghost joke."

"Shh," I hush the unhelpful assassin and focus on Pip. "Can you write to me?"

Pip shakes his head, his gaze flickering between me and Maliki.

My brow furrows. "I don't understand. You always write to me."

"He doesn't want me to see him," Maliki says. "Assuming he's a real soul and just playing hide-and-seek in the in-between."

I glance back at him. "What?"

"I can't see him," he reiterates. "But you're saying he's here, right?"

"Yes." I look at Pip, who is again staring at me with a look of betrayal. "You don't want Maliki to know you're here?"

Pip nods, his expression somewhat angry now, like he's mad that I've already spoiled that plan.

"Why not?"

"Because he thinks I'll escort him back to the Soul Yards," Maliki says. "Right?"

Pip cocks his head a little, then nods again.

"Maliki isn't going to do that," I promise Pip. "I won't let him."

The assassin unhelpfully chuckles at that.

"Right?" I say, shooting him a glare.

Maliki lifts his hands in mock surrender. "If you say this soul is your pet, I won't take him away from you."

Pip folds his arms in a way that tells me he doesn't believe Maliki.

"He's not my pet," I mutter. "Pip is my friend."

My little soul perks up at that, the skirt of his cloak starting to sway as he dances.

"And as my friend, I would like you to come with me to the palace," I continue to Pip. "To stay with me."

"As a pet," Maliki adds under his breath.

I cast him another withering look. "You are not helping."

He lifts his hands again. "Sorry, sorry. I'll let you tame your friend."

My gaze narrows even more. "I'll tame you."

He laughs. "I think you've already started, little mystery."

I'm not sure what he means by that, so I go back to ignoring him and give Pip all of my attention again. "Can you please come out of the in-between?"

Pip drops his arms, but his movements still appear to be uncertain.

"If you prefer to hide, that's fine," I tell him, aware of how that feels. "But will you come with me to the palace?"

My little friend sways, the answer unclear.

"If he's not agreeing, it's not because of you," Maliki says. "He's probably afraid Hades will send him to the pits."

"The pits?" I repeat as Pip begins to shake again.

"A place where judgment occurs," Maliki explains darkly.

Pip starts to float into the wall.

"I won't let that happen to you," I promise Pip. "I... I'll talk to Hades." The uncertainty in my voice is clear to my ears and obviously to Pip, too. My shoulders sag. "It's okay, Pip. I understand if you want to hide here. I would stay with you if I could."

He floats out of the wall again and comes a little closer, seeming to be undecided again. His eyes are so sad. Yet the way he vibrates tells me how terrified he is of everything we're discussing.

"What if I promise to help you?" Maliki says, his eyes on the door to my bathroom.

I frown. *Does he think Pip is over there?*

"If you know who I am—which I assume you do and

that's why you're hiding—then you know my offer is valid. Hades won't touch you if I say you're mine."

Pip seems to be considering him.

Meanwhile, Maliki is still talking to the bathroom door.

I bite my lip to keep from grinning. Because it is kind of amusing.

Especially since Pip is floating even closer to him now, near enough to touch his side.

"You have ten seconds to decide, lost soul," Maliki says. "Don't make me start counting."

Pip lifts his arm, only for Maliki to spin away from him.

"I may not see you, but I can feel you."

Pip's eyes smile as he tries again, causing Maliki to whirl away.

"Stop fucking with me, soul. I was being nice."

I cover my mouth to stop from laughing as Pip does it a third time, which results in Maliki growling.

Then his eyes find mine, and everything stills. The fight in him disappears, and he shakes his head. "Your pet is trying to make you laugh."

"Pip," I say, reminding him of his name. "And yes, I think so."

The cloaked soul floats to my side, and Maliki glances down at him, his gaze narrowing a bit. "What the fuck are you wearing?" he asks, telling me he can see Pip now.

Pip does a little twirl to show off his cloak.

Maliki snorts. "That's ridiculous."

My little spirit pauses, then places his hands on his hips. Or I assume he does, anyway. Then he begins a game of charades whereby he reveals one bony finger, gestures toward me, mimes touching me, and then falls on the floor with a soundless thud.

After a moment, he lifts his head up and looks

pointedly at Maliki as he tugs his cloak down over his exposed finger.

Maliki stares at him in bewilderment. "Well, I'll be shadowed. You're a smart little soul."

Pip bows, then rights himself again and twirls.

"Yeah, you'll do," Maliki decides out loud, heading for the door. "He wears that cloak to protect you, by the way. In case you didn't know that." He pauses to glance at me over his shoulder. "One touch of his bones, even a brush, would kill you instantly. So he covers himself in case you get too close. I think he likes you."

With that pronouncement, he walks into my living area, where he collects my plant.

"Shall we go?" he calls back to me.

I gaze down at Pip, who is dancing around happily again.

"For the record, I like you, too," I tell him.

He blows me a kiss, then floats off after Maliki.

Watching him overcome his nervousness so quickly makes me kind of wish I were a little ghostlike soul, too.

Maybe then I wouldn't be so terrified of returning to the palace.

Or of the dinner I'm going to attend tonight.

Alone.

With Hades.

If only I were a little soul, I muse. *Instead, I'm paired with an evil one determined to ruin my existence.*

Yay me.

MALIKI

Home sweet home.

Except there's nothing sweet about it.

Not with Sera feeling forced to be here and her little spirit pet glancing around nervously.

Styx, how did everything escalate so quickly?

I don't even mean coming here—that part at least makes sense. Sera should never have left in the first place.

No, I'm thinking about my whatever-this-is with Sera.

I almost kissed her earlier.

Fuck, I almost did a lot more than kiss her. I wanted to devour her. When she made those comments about being my *task*, I wanted to show her just how I handle my business.

It was a stark need, one that physically hurt me to tame.

Death it. I need to finish this job and shadow off somewhere to try to find my head.

Except I won't be able to.

Because the notion of leaving Sera here to face Hades alone makes me want to break something.

He's been such a colossal dick to her. I've never really seen him interact with women. I always assumed it was out of loyalty to Persephone. Now I'm thinking it's because he has no idea how to talk to a female.

Clearly, all those times he watched me fuck taught him absolutely nothing.

I mean, yes, I'm not exactly a gentle lover. But I always ensure my bedmates are satisfied, and that includes emotionally if that's what the woman requires.

Styx. Who am I kidding? I've never stuck around long enough to cuddle. But the women I fuck typically don't want that anyway.

Sera is different, though.

Last night was different.

I fell asleep with her. I... I held her for nearly twelve hours. And it felt so fucking right.

Just like having her up against the wall.

I meant every word I said to her about this assignment and how I want to taste her.

Shadows, do I want to taste her.

I close my eyes and nearly miss a step up the grand stairs of Death's Palace.

I really need to focus and stop thinking about Sera's mouth.

Instead, I take in her other features and study her expression. Most visitors gawk at the obsidian decor and fiery chandeliers. But not her.

Because she's seen it already.

Pip hovers by her side, looking anxious but alert, his protective glances reminding me a bit of a guard dog.

How did this thing escape my notice? I wonder.

He must have hidden in the in-between whenever I was near.

But he's corporeal now and obviously watching out for Sera.

An ally, I decide.

Then I remember how he almost burned down her kitchen, all the comments about Pip suddenly making sense.

Okay, so he's an ally with a penchant for chaos.

Yeah, I can work with that.

I just have to convince Hades to let Sera keep him.

That'll be a fun task. He'll probably make me promise him something in return.

Fine.

Pip clearly makes Sera happy. That's worth more than whatever favor Hades will extract from me.

Once we reach the top landing, she tries to turn left, no doubt heading toward her old room. "Other way," I say, causing her to pause.

She gives me a puzzled look.

"Your new accommodations are in Hades's quarters," I explain.

She swallows. "Oh."

"If it's any consolation, my rooms are also in his part of the palace," I tell her.

Sera's expression brightens a little, the reaction one that has my chest warming. She likes that I'll be close by. I can't admit it aloud, but I like it, too.

Except that also means I'll be near her when she's with Hades.

And that… that sends a cold bolt of reality through my veins.

Fuck.

She's not mine. I know that. I've *known* that. I don't even want a mate, either. It's not all that conducive to my lifestyle or my choice of occupation.

Yet there's something about Sera that makes me desire something new.

That desire is one I can't explore. I don't even want to define it. So I kill the instinct to investigate the *something* that my desire leads to and instead focus on giving Sera a proper tour.

"There's an enchantment down this hall that reroutes uninvited guests to a different part of the palace." I look at her. "Hades is very particular about who he allows into his private rooms."

She nods. "I'm familiar with some of the magic in the palace, but only what Alina and her mates have shared with me."

"The enchantments they probably told you about are likely exclusive to Orcus's wing. Hades's quarters are a completely different beast when it comes to protection charms. There are magical adornments everywhere and deadly consequences when it comes to any potential tampering."

I don't add that all of this is a result of trust issues. I think she already understands that part, along with the cause for said trust issues.

"Which means Pip may or may not be allowed through," I add, glancing at the little ghost. "If we get separated, I'll talk to Hades and fix it, okay?"

The soul looks at me with widened flames in his hollowed eyes.

"Trust me," I add, causing Sera to look between us.

Her lips curl a little when Pip nods.

I almost stop to stare. Because fuck, she's beautiful.

I've known this since I first laid eyes on her. Yet the attraction feels more potent now. More *real*.

I should not have pinned her against that wall.

It's fucking with my head.

Giving myself a mental shake, I continue until we reach a specific set of columns. There's nothing noteworthy about them; the entire corridor is decorated with these skull-adorned pillars. But this is where the enchantment lives. I recognize it, as I've lived here for a very long time.

However, I impart some wisdom to Sera so she can find it more easily until she memorizes the path, too. "This is exactly nine pillars in from the stairwell," I tell her. "That number doesn't really mean anything except that I used to count every time I went back to my room. Because this is where the divide occurs."

Her nose scrunches. "Do I need to do something special to go the right way?"

I shake my head. "No, you're already precoded with access based on your aura." That's not exactly how it works, but it's the best way for me to explain it. "So the second you pass these pillars, you'll automatically be in Hades's wing."

She frowns. "Then the pillars being set number nine doesn't really matter, right?"

I cock my head, considering. "No, it… still matters."

"Why?"

"Because the first thing that's going to greet you when you pass through these pillars is probably going to be growling and have three heads."

Her eyes widen. "*What?*"

"It's fine. They won't hurt you. Just try not to run,

though, okay? Howl, in particular, is really fond of chasing."

"Howl?" she repeats, sounding incredulous.

I just nod, then step through the enchantment and sigh when Ossa growls at me. "Hello to you, too, princess," I drawl.

She bares her teeth.

Meanwhile, Howl and Mort yip excitedly and force their big body to move right for me.

Only, they freeze when Sera tentatively moves through the threshold.

Her eyes round upon seeing the three-headed beast, and she promptly backs up and out of view.

I follow her and see Pip waiting nervously on the other side.

It's a strange sensation, slipping between the barrier, which I guess is more of a *veil*, but I do it anyway so I can see and hear Sera. "They won't hurt you," I repeat gently. "They're basically Hades's familiar. And he can't harm you, so they won't either."

The look she gives me is filled with disbelief. "What in the thorns is that thing?"

My lips twitch at her use of *thorns* in that sentence. She's fucking adorable.

"It's a dog," I tell her.

"That thing is *not* a dog. It's a wolf beast!"

I shrug. "Okay, I can agree with that description. But at least you know where the Cerberus legends come from now."

She blinks at me. "Cerberus?"

"Right. Greek mythology probably wasn't taught in your backward schools." I sigh. "Look, just… just come in with me. They're going to jump, and Ossa is probably going to try to take my head off, but it'll be fine. Watch me and you'll see."

Her brow furrows. "You want me to watch the beast take your head off?"

"I said *try*. Very important word in that sentence. Now stop being a coward and walk with me." I step back through the threshold and wait.

Sera's indignant little huff precedes her entry, followed by a muttered "Coward. Yeah, okay, I'll watch them kill you."

I chuckle at her cute little comeback, then spread my arms in anticipation of getting mauled by Howl and Mort.

Except they don't jump on me at all.

Instead, I find them sitting patiently, their three heads trained on Sera. She stares back at them, her body locked in a position that suggests her mind is trying to decide if she should fight or flee. "Don't run," I warn her again.

"Easy for you to say," she mutters.

Ossa cocks her head.

"Don't," I say, my voice sharp as I focus on the troublesome one of the trio.

Naturally, she ignores me.

But she doesn't snarl at Sera. She... I frown. *Is that a wolfy grin?* I marvel, my jaw basically falling to the floor as Ossa's tongue lolls off to the side of her now-open mouth.

Howl gives a little yip, causing Ossa to snap at him like she's saying "Shut up." He lowers his head, and she resumes her smile.

Sera stares at the three-headed creature, her brow furrowing. "They're not trying to take your head off."

"No, they're... being strangely calm." I don't think I've ever seen them sit like this for anyone other than Hades. And he usually has to issue a stern word to accomplish it.

Movement out of the corner of my eye has me turning to watch Pip float cautiously through the threshold.

Ossa instantly bends her head and growls, causing Sera to glance at the source of her agitation. Seeing Pip, she instantly steps in front of the soul, her shoulder nearly touching his cloak.

He backpedals into the wall so fast that it has Howl and Mort instantly taking notice, their stares guarded. But it wasn't the three-headed wolf-dog Pip was trying to escape; it was Sera's nearness.

Definitely an ally, I think, smiling as he cautiously returns and keeps a safe distance from his human. He obviously has some practice with ensuring he doesn't accidentally touch her.

"Please don't attack him," Sera says softly when Ossa growls again. "And, um, please don't attack me."

Ossa stares at her with a confused expression. Then her tongue lolls again, and she begins to pant.

I blink. "I have never seen her act like this before."

Upon hearing my voice, Ossa returns to her usual mode and snarls at me.

And promptly looks back at Sera... to begin panting again.

Howl and Mort both exchange a glance, look at Ossa, and instantly follow suit, giving all three heads an adorable puppy façade that I know is absolutely false.

Pip peeks out from behind Sera, then cautiously drifts closer.

Which is when it dawns on me that the little soul had no problem crossing the threshold.

Well, I'll be damned, I think.

The magic is specifically programmed to only allow certain individuals and their familiars, something I know because Fleur is allowed to fly through these halls—because of her connection to me.

Pip automatically being granted entry means he's somehow tied to Sera.

I note that as something to mention to Hades. It gives even more reason for him to allow the little soul to stay.

Unless, of course, being a soul makes him capable of flying through wards. But I doubt it. Otherwise, we would have stray souls all over this part of this palace. Hades is a damn magnet for them, thanks to his ties to the death world.

Clearing my throat, I say, "Shall we continue, then?"

Ossa growls in response, making me shake my head.

"We've been over this, little beast. You don't scare me."

She snarls again.

I roll my eyes. "Nice to see you again, too."

Ossa humphs in response.

"Can she understand you?" Sera asks slowly.

"Yep," I drawl. "All three of them can, but Ossa is the leader of the pack. And she happens to hate me."

The alpha-like female snaps at me, confirming my commentary.

"Meanwhile, Mort and Howl love me."

Both heads look my way and give me toothy grins but almost immediately go back to studying Sera.

Pip circles the beast while they're occupied, his head cocked. When Ossa notices him, she gives a little sniff but otherwise ignores his presence.

Because Sera asked them not to attack him, I realize, fascinated. *She's tamed Hades's pet just by walking through the enchantment.*

I nearly laugh.

But I'm too engrossed in the situation to let my amusement show.

Instead, I start to walk by the seated beast and smirk when Ossa doesn't even acknowledge my presence. Normally, I would be covered in dog drool by now from Mort and Howl and have at least one puncture wound from Ossa.

However, my sweater—which I grabbed before we left —and jeans are perfectly intact.

Excellent.

I continue down the hall as Sera skirts around the three-headed beast to follow me.

When I glance back, it's to find her nervously checking over her shoulder as the dogs trail behind her, their stances suddenly guarded.

They're protecting her, I marvel, still utterly captivated by this development. Their behavior, coupled with Pip's ability to pass through the ward, has me floored. *Hades is going to hate all of this.*

Which just adds even more enjoyment to the situation.

Unlike Sera, Hades doesn't deserve to feel happiness. He needs to fucking grovel.

And I plan to tell him that as soon as I see him again.

SERA

This side of the palace feels different. Colder. More remote. *Deadly*.

And not just because of the giant wolf creature following me down the dimly lit corridor.

I glance back at the beast again and note the way their heads are all pointed at different angles as they take in every inch of the hallway.

Ossa, Mort, and Howl.

Each one of them has a collar around their respective necks, just like a dog would, but they're all joined in the same body.

It's unnerving.

But also kind of amazing.

Who controls the legs? I wonder as Ossa stares down a column lined with more skulls. They're like ancient pillars but made of bones. I want to believe it's just decoration. However, I fear they're actual remains.

These decorations didn't exist near my previous

accommodations in the palace. Although, the dark colors and general gothic atmosphere did.

Reaper is the one who taught me that term, saying how Gothic architecture is a favorite of his.

I didn't really understand it until he started showing me pictures on a screen of other building types. He seemed to take great pleasure in teaching me and Alina things about the "real human world."

The more I learned, the more I wondered what it would be like to visit.

I still wonder that today but don't dare to hope that I'll ever be permitted to see it.

No, my fate as the Bride of Death is pretty much sealed now.

A fact that seems quite clear to me as I once again look back at—

"Oof," I mutter as I walk into a wall.

Er, not a wall.

Maliki.

Shaking my head, I slowly face forward once more and find him staring down at me in amusement.

Which is when I realize he caught my hip with one hand to keep me from falling when I ran into him.

And he hasn't let go.

If anything, he pulls me closer. "You all right?" he asks, his voice soft, his lips slightly curled. "Or are you still freaking out?"

"I'm not freaking out," I counter, scowling. "I'm fine."

"Hmm," he hums. "Yes, you are. More than fine, actually." He winks and releases me, leaving me to gape at his back.

What does *that* mean?

It sounded like something one of the fae at the bar would say to me.

But Maliki makes it so much sexier. His compliment rolls over me like a hot wave, exciting my nerve endings.

And I'm right back to thinking about the way he pinned me against the wall.

The almost kiss.

His admission.

I shiver despite the heat rushing to my cheeks and nearly melt on the floor.

But he distracts me by saying, "This is your room."

I swallow and look at the nondescript black door framed by skulls. "Looks inviting." It's a joke, one he clearly gets because he snorts.

"This is the Netherworld Kingdom, trouble. And you're the Bride of Death."

With that pronouncement, he grabs the skeleton hand, twists it like one would a knob, and pushes the heavy door open.

I pinch my lips together. "I think I prefer the standard doorknobs from my last two accommodations."

"Hades decorated his own wing" is Maliki's explanation.

I don't need him to say more than that. The grotesque decor makes a lot of sense. "I can't wait to see the inside," I mutter.

Maliki chuckles again and leads the way inside, then he steps out of the way so I can see the interior.

Biting the side of my cheek, I gingerly enter and half expect to find a bed lined in bones.

But I'm pleasantly surprised to discover a room full of color.

The door magically closes behind me, keeping the three-headed wolf from following. Though, I'm rather certain the beast can't fit through the threshold.

However, Pip enters just fine—through the wall—and

begins investigating the space while I gape at the flowered walls.

Petals and vines and leaves are embedded in the rocky texture, making my lips part. The plants are not real. I can see that from here. However, the details are incredible.

"Wow," I breathe, taking in the interesting scenery. "I don't even recognize what these are supposed to be, but they're pretty."

I walk over to touch a vibrant orange flower that reminds me of an Oriental lily.

"It's beautiful," I whisper, stroking the silky texture.

Maliki doesn't comment, but I turn to find him rotating a familiar pot on the table.

It's the one from my hut.

He grabbed it before we left, then it disappeared when he shadowed us up here.

Part of me wants to ask how it ended up in my rooms, but as I glance around, I realize it's not the only thing that magically ended up here.

With a hint of suspicion, I go to the bathroom and freeze when I see that the space is larger than my entire home in the village. There are two double sinks—one on each side—a huge walk-in shower, and a tub that looks like it's meant for bathing the wolf beast.

Holy fae, I breathe, touching the obsidian marble as I walk by the sink closest to me. The fixtures are all gold and silver, the opulence rather startling.

But what's really impressive is the windowed wall of the shower, like through the glass. "It looks like a rainforest outside," I marvel out loud, noting the way the mirage moves. "Like it really looks as though you're staring right into the forest."

Maliki joins me and pops his hip against the door

frame, his arms folding. "Mine is just a black slate wall," he tells me. "But I prefer it that way."

I smile. "That doesn't surprise me."

I leave him to go investigate the closet like I intended when I first arrived and find all my belongings from the hut taking up a fraction of the space. The rest is full of gowns and other items, with one hanging alone, a note attached to it.

Narrowing my gaze, I walk toward it—which takes a lot longer than it should, considering this is just a closet, but the room is *huge*—and pluck the paper off the deep red dress.

If you'll honor me with your presence at dinner, I would love for you to wear this…
Yours,
Hades

I frown. He made dinner sound like a mandatory affair, but this note almost implies I have a choice.

I don't.

I know that.

Which is why I huff a laugh at the stupid letter, ball it up, and toss it on the floor—where it lands beside a pair of silver heels.

I glare at them. "He would make me wear heels."

They're a special form of torture, especially ones like those with the pointed ends and four inches of height.

I roll my eyes. *Fine. Whatever*. I'll wear the damn outfit if it appeases him. It's the least I can do, I guess.

"Sera?" Maliki asks, his voice right behind me. He looks around me to see the dress, his brow pinching. "You don't have to do anything he asks, you know. You can tell him to fuck off."

"Says the man he hired to convince me to marry him," I return, arching my brow.

Maliki sighs. "He didn't *hire* me. He just gave me the task. But like you, I can also tell him no."

"Have you ever told him no?" I ask, curious. "Have you ever declined an assignment?"

He shakes his head. "No, I haven't. But he's never given me one I disagree with… until now."

My eyebrow lifts a little higher. "You disagree with your current assignment?" The question comes out slowly, the air between us seeming to thicken with some sort of foreign tension.

"I disagree with convincing you to do something you don't want to do," he replies, taking a step toward me. "And I disagree with this situation. I know you feel obligated now that you've learned what Persephone did to him." He shifts even closer to me, his palm cradling my cheek. "But you're not Persephone."

Oh, how I wish that were true.

But it's not.

And there's one simple way to explain why. So I ask him, "Can an entity survive without a soul?"

He stares down at me, his chest brushing mine as he closes the remaining gap between us.

"Should an innocent entity be held liable for the sins of a past life?" he counters, his gaze falling to my mouth. "Should an eternal bond between souls impact potential claims on any and all future reincarnations? Even when it's clear said reincarnation is not only unmarked but also untouched?"

My lashes flutter, his soft words seeming to swirl around me in a kiss of forbidden energy. "Once a soul is assigned to an entity, is there even such a concept of freedom or choice? Or is it all dictated by fate?"

His forehead touches mine. "I refuse to believe that fate would be this cruel," he whispers. "You don't deserve to pay for Persephone's sins, Serapina. And I'm going to ensure you don't have to."

I pull back to look up at him. "What do you mean?"

But he just shakes his head, his jaw clenched tight. "All of your things from the hut should be here. If anything was missed, let me know and I'll retrieve it personally."

I frown, confused by our abrupt conversation switch. As well as his sudden aloofness. "Maliki…"

"I'll be back to check on you in a bit," he says, not looking at me. "And I'll ask for some food to be sent up as well."

With that chilling line, he vanishes, leaving me staring at my closet with a mixture of bewilderment and annoyance.

And a tiny bit of frustration.

Because for a second, I thought he might kiss me.

My thumb brushes my lower lip, my mind conjuring sensations and fantasies of what it may have been like. And I suddenly find myself craving something I shouldn't.

A real first kiss.

Not in a dream.

But in reality.

With Maliki.

MALIKI

I SHADOW INTO MY ROOM, AWARE THAT HADES IS ALREADY there waiting for me.

Because he sent me a fucking summons.

It was like a bloody doorbell going off in my head, right as I was considering giving up my life in exchange for a kiss.

"Have you taken to spying on me now?" I ask Hades as I appear. Because there is no way this summons wasn't timed on purpose. "You're the one who told me to seduce her. Remember?"

He stares at me from my favorite recliner chair, his hand on Fleur as she purrs in his lap. She looks up at me with big blue eyes, not caring at all that we haven't seen each other in almost a month.

No.

She's too busy enjoying Hades's hand on her nape.

Traitor, I think at my familiar.

Granted, she's probably pissed that I've been gone. But the reason I've been gone is currently petting her.

Ironically, he's also the one who has been feeding her in my absence. So she probably doesn't view the situation the same way I do, despite our mental connection.

We have a strange bond, one formed throughout the last two hundred years since I saved her from a psychotic Midnight Fae.

So she's not *technically* my familiar. She's a conjured animal with immortal life. And I imprisoned her former master.

It's complicated.

And irrelevant to the current situation. "What do you want, Hades?"

He hasn't said a word, his contemplative gaze giving nothing away. "Well, now I want to know what you meant by reminding me that I told you to *seduce her*. What did my summons interrupt?"

I stare at him. "Really? You're going to sit there and pretend like you have no idea how close I just came to kissing Sera?"

His eyebrow arches. "I trust you implicitly, Maliki. So no, I was not spying on you. And no, I was not aware of how close you just came to kissing *my mate*. But please, elaborate."

Those last few words are underlined with power and possession.

My jaw ticks.

He merely stares at me, his patience steadfast.

Shaking my head, I leave him with my cat and head into my bedroom. I'm not in the mood to verbally spar right now.

I need a shower.

Preferably a cold one.

Stripping out of my sweater, I kick off my boots and socks, then rip off my jeans and leave them on the floor.

Hades can see everything, including the fact that I'm aroused. And I just do not fucking care. He's seen me naked more times than I can count. Styx, he's witnessed me do a lot without clothes.

Fucking voyeur.

Normally, I don't mind. I enjoy exhibitionism.

But what Sera and I have shared lately is… it's ours.

It's confusing.

It's wrong.

Growling, I walk into my bathroom and directly to the shower, which starts automatically when it senses my presence. The temperature also magically adjusts to match my mood.

Which means the water is scorching hot.

I slam my palm against the rocky wall, my opposite one going to my throbbing shaft. "*Fuck.*" I'm furious and I'm burning. It's a dangerous combination.

My shadows ripple across my skin, seeming to hum in response to my lethal desires.

Movement behind me has the hair along my nape standing on end.

Hades's steps are silent, but his power is loud. It's suffocating. It's a presence in and of itself.

"Does she want you to kiss her?" he asks softly, his question carrying over the sound of the rainfall because his words are laced with dark energy.

I ignore him and bend my arm, leaning into the wall as I slowly stroke myself to thoughts of Sera. Her mouth is so fucking perfect. So plump and pink. The kind of lips that men dream about having wrapped around their cocks.

Styx, just thinking about that has me picturing her on her knees.

My grip tightens, my chest burning with the need for release.

But I don't want to give Hades the satisfaction of watching me explode. Even though he should see it. Witness what *his mate* does to me. How he's torturing me by dangling a piece of forbidden fruit just within my reach, all while holding me above the fiery pits of the afterlife.

One wrong touch and he'll drop me.

And I'm almost beyond the point of concern.

I don't know how it's come to this.

Except that's not true.

I've been watching this woman for months, memorizing her facial cues and speech patterns, observing her strength, noting the way she masks hurt feelings and worries.

She's strong. Fierce. Yet soft and innocent. *So fucking innocent.*

"She's not playing a game," I grind out.

"I'm starting to wonder if that's true," Hades responds, reminding me that he's intruding on my personal space.

Though, I suppose it isn't *my space*, is it?

He owns this palace.

And I'm fairly certain he thinks he owns me, too.

I finally look toward him and find him leaning against my counter, his long legs stretched out and crossed at the ankles, his hands in his pockets.

He arches a brow. "Surprised?"

I'm not sure what he's referring to. Surprised that he's here? No. Surprised that he's wondering if what I said is true? "Yes."

He smirks. "Me, too."

My palm drops from the wall as I turn to face him fully, my opposite hand still on my dick.

He notices but doesn't comment. "What do you want, Hades?" I ask him.

"Right now or in general?" he inquires.

"Both," I say, knowing my answer doesn't actually matter. He'll tell me whatever he feels like sharing.

His gaze captures and holds mine. "I want you to respond to my previous questions about my mate because I'm thinking about asking you to kiss her."

My back stiffens. "Are you going to tell me to fuck her?" I demand, far too aware of his kinky preferences.

He frowns. "I said *kiss,* not *fuck.*"

I glare at him. "So you'll let me kiss her but not fuck her?"

His jaw clenches. "Are you deliberately trying to provoke me, Maliki?"

I huff and return to my shower, done with this conversation. He says something I purposely tune out while I dampen my hair, then I pointedly give him my back as I work on lathering my hair up with shampoo.

His gaze practically burns against my skin when I pick up a soap bar and use it to cleanse myself—all while not looking at him.

Yet I can feel him very much admiring me.

It's always been this way, his eyes on me with a mild curiosity that is borderline erotic. But really, it's an evaluation. Like he wants to make sure I'm sexually competent for his uses.

I've waited eons for him to do something other than *watch.*

Not because I want him to touch me or fuck me. That's not my interest.

No, my desire has always been to *share.*

I want to feel him inside a woman while I fuck her, to experience his power as we take a female to new heights.

That is my kink.

I like pleasure.

Giving it. Receiving it. *Sharing it.*

And I know he would be masterful in bed.

So I've spent millennia proving to him that I can keep up. That I, too, know how to command a bedroom.

Yet all he's done is *watch.* And now he wants to watch some more?

"No," I tell him after I'm done rinsing off. "No, I will not fuck her for you." I grab a towel and use it to dry myself off. "If you want me to touch her, then you'll have to touch her, too."

"I said *kiss,*" he reiterates through his teeth. "I also don't think she wants me to touch her."

"And whose fault is that?" I ask him, tired of this circular discussion.

Leaving him, I head for my closet, not caring at all that my hair is still dripping with water.

Naturally, Hades follows. "How are you going to feel when you find out this is all a lie? That Persephone is playing a game and manipulating you?"

I grab a pair of sweats and turn around to face him. "She's not Persephone. And you can't punish Sera for the sins of your soulmate."

His jaw ticks. "Then answer me hypothetically, Maliki. How would you feel if you found out she's just a deceptive Omega with a penchant for betraying her lover?"

"I imagine I would be pretty furious," I admit. "Which is why I've supported you in this quest for well over a thousand years. I may not fully understand your fury, but I respect it, Hades. And that's why I'm asking you to hear me when I say that Sera is an innocent being who has been paired with a not-so-innocent soul. That's not her fault. So please stop trying to punish her for it."

He frowns. "I'm not punishing her."

I give him a look. "I was just in her room. You covered it in fake greenery. She loves it right now. But I know your intention—you want her to miss life and realize that everything is dead here. Just like your heart."

Okay, that last sentence was a low blow.

But I'm in a bad fucking mood. My dick is still hard. I have no sexual outlet. And something tells me if I shadow somewhere right now, Hades will just fucking follow me.

"The accommodations are a moot point in this discussion," he says.

I fold my arms, my skin still somewhat damp. The sweats I'm holding are probably going to get wet.

That's fine. I'll just put on another pair.

"Be straight with me, Hades. What are we actually discussing? Because for a God who claims to hate games, it certainly feels like we're playing one right now." He's practically daring me to touch his mate. That's not only dangerous—it's asinine.

He's an Alpha.

I'm a fae. Albeit a unique one. But I don't stand a chance against his wrath. He knows this. So why tempt me to fight him?

"Morpheus thinks I should kiss… Serapina."

My eyebrows lift, not just at what he's saying, but at his use of the name *Serapina*. I don't think I've heard him refer to her as anyone other than Persephone.

He runs his fingers through his hair and starts to pace. "His reasoning is unfortunately sound," he goes on.

"Yes, it's always unfortunate to have a reason to kiss one's mate," I deadpan.

Dark eyes glance at me, irritation evident in their depths.

But he ignores my commentary and continues by saying, "He says if I want proof that the human isn't in possession of my mate's memories, then a simple kiss should do. If she reacts like Persephone, then I'll have proof she's lying. And if she doesn't…"

"You'll finally realize she's *not* Persephone," I finish for him, impressed by Morpheus's suggestion.

I've been trying to get through to Hades for months.

Maybe I should have requested some feedback from Morpheus, since he clearly believes Sera is telling the truth about not remembering anything.

To me, it's just logical. Sera hasn't even embraced her inner Omega yet. So how could she remember said Omega's memories?

Hades's opinion is that she's done something to mask her instincts. Or, more likely, her mother did something to hide her inner Omega.

I still think the latter could be true.

But I think it was without Sera's knowledge.

"Omegas can't resist an Alpha's call or his charms," Hades says, still pacing. "If I kiss her, I'll be able to coax out her reactions quite quickly. And, more importantly, she'll have a difficult time taming her response. Which means, in theory, she'll be too mindless with lust to put on a performance."

I nod. "From what you've told me about Omegas, that makes sense." They have a hard time controlling their needs when turned on. Especially when in heat.

Hence the reason Hades was waiting for her to go into estrus—he wanted her mindless so she would be forced to answer questions truthfully.

235

Of course, he could also try holding her over a death pit—a concept I would have approved a year ago.

But not today.

I would push him in if he tried to do that to Sera.

Him kissing her, though? Yeah, that's fine with me. Styx, I would even enjoy watching him knot her.

Being cruel to her is where we have a problem.

"The problem is, I don't think she wants me to kiss her," Hades says, his steps pausing right in front of me. "So I'm going to ask you again—does my mate want to kiss you?"

MORPHEUS

I whistle, calling for Pip to meet me outside on Serapina's balcony.

It's a massive space, one that boasts a fountain of bloody water and two small gardens crafted from stone. I suppose it's beautiful on a surface level. But I understand the hidden context beneath. And due to that, I'm not all that keen on Hades's exterior decorating choices.

Alas, the barrier spell Hades has implemented prevents me from entering Serapina's suite. However, it doesn't protect her rooftop terrace from my presence.

Could I break through it in an urgent situation? Yes. However, I would prefer not to alert my cousin of my intentions at the moment.

He can no doubt sense my nearness. However, numerous visits over the last year will have him wondering if it's a new arrival or just a lingering presence in the air.

By the time he figures it out, I'll be gone.

Pip floats out through the glass and does an excited little twirl upon seeing me.

I hold out the bag I've brought for him and set it on the balcony. "Can you make sure Serapina—"

The door opens before I can finish speaking, a pair of pretty blue eyes instantly finding mine. She blinks, her lips curling down as she steps out onto the dark marble patio. The dueling moons above shine down upon her, illuminating her hair in a shimmer of golden waves.

"Uh, hi," she says slowly, her gaze going to the item in my hand.

"Hi." I set the bag on the floor. "There's a lamp inside —the one you need for your plant," I explain. "I was going to give it to Pip."

"I see that," she murmurs, glancing between me and the cloaked soul. "Um, thank you."

"You're welcome," I reply.

She smiles shyly.

And when she doesn't say anything, I ask, "Are you… all moved in, then?"

She snorts and shakes her head. "Yeah, by some bizarre magic, apparently I am." Her nose wrinkles. "I told Maliki all I wanted was my plant and Pip, but he somehow moved it all up here."

"I actually think Hades may have assisted with that," I inform her softly. "I saw him leave your place a bit ago with his arms full of clothes."

Sera stares at me. "What?"

I shrug. "Omegas are usually quite attached to their garments, you know, for nesting."

Her eyes round. "He thinks I'm going to nest?"

"Well, once your Omega instincts come in, yes." I frown at her. "You don't think you'll crave a nest?"

"I..." She blinks. "I haven't considered it."

"But you know what a nest is?" I press.

Her lips twist, and her gaze goes out to the Netherworld Kingdom below. "Alina has told me a little about it—how she makes a bed for her and her mates. And she told me it's instinctual, but that's really all she's said."

I nod, understanding. "Nesting is a very private affair for an Omega with her circle. She probably didn't know how to share more details. It'll also be unique for you. Because every Omega nests differently."

Or, apparently, sometimes Omegas don't nest at all, I think, a little perplexed by this development.

"Don't you ever feel proprietary about your personal space?" I ask her, curious. "Specifically, your bed?"

She shrugs. "I've never really owned my own space until the hut, and I didn't get to stay there long."

"Do you miss it? Do you want to return there? Perhaps to grab your blankets?" Because I noticed Hades left her sheets behind. Maybe it was because they smelled like Serapina and Maliki—a scent that left me more than a little intrigued as to what they did in that bed.

Serapina frowns. "I miss what my home represents— freedom. But I understand now that I'll never be free. How can I be when my soul is so evil?"

I take a step back, her question seeming to hit me right in the heart. "Your soul is not evil, Serapina Everheart. Do not ever say something like that again."

Her gaze narrows. "My soul destroyed an entire realm. Wasn't that the point of yesterday's lesson?"

"The point was to share our history and teach more about Mythos Fae," I reply, moving toward her again. "Not to promote incorrect assessments regarding your soul's virtue."

"Okay, then how would you describe her actions?" she counters when I'm only a foot away from her.

I stare down into her pretty eyes, my palm itching to grab her nape.

Evil is such a horrible word. So unfair. So *cruel*.

But I suppose what little she knows would lead her to that assumption.

"I would describe Persephone's actions as unknown," I tell her honestly. "Hades believes she betrayed him. I think she was manipulated by her mother because he didn't properly guard his mate."

I don't tell her this to paint him in a negative light. It's merely the truth.

"Hades never desired a mate-circle because he refused to share his Persephone. But there's a reason Mythos Fae Alphas form clusters around their Omegas—to protect them." I give in to my need to touch her and reach up to tuck a strand of hair behind her ear.

She shivers, the action one that delights me to no end.

So I let my touch linger, the backs of my fingers tracing her soft jawline as I add, "Omegas are our Goddesses. They create life. They bring light to our world. And they are literally the stars of our universe. But not all Alphas believed in worshipping our Goddesses. Some wished to enslave them instead."

It's a sad history.

But she needs to know the truth to understand Demeter. And perhaps it will help her understand Persephone, too.

"Come, let's relax, and I'll continue our lesson. If you'll oblige me?"

Serapina's blue eyes hold me captive as I await her decision. For I will never force this female to do anything she doesn't desire. But I will absolutely do whatever it takes to win her affection.

"Okay," she says. "But only because I want to learn more."

I smile. "Of course."

My hand drops from her face but reaches for her palm as I gently tug her over to a bench seated in a fake garden. It's a cruel re-creation of one of Persephone's favorite places in our home realm. Because instead of life, the plants are all made of rock.

They're dead.

Cold.

Frozen in place with a moon that bathes them in dull yellow colors instead of vibrant pastels.

Yet Serapina looks upon the creation with wonder, her gaze flitting over the statues of fire lilies with open curiosity.

This is how I know she isn't connected to Persephone's memories.

Because if she were, there would be tears in her eyes right now, not stars.

I've seen Persephone in this very garden, not up close, but from afar, and I know how much she adored those flowers. She nursed them every day, showering them with life while I hovered in the mist, just out of reach.

She wasn't mine to touch, thanks to Hades's reluctance.

Oh, I could have interfered. I could have forced him to share.

But it would have broken Persephone's heart to have her Alphas fight over her soul.

And so, I let them be, even though my heart shattered in the process.

Swallowing, I glance up at the sky and fight the urge to

growl at the memories flooding my thoughts. My anger. My fear. My *agony*.

I knew what was brewing in the Mythos Fae Realm, as did Hades. Yet he never thought anyone would breach his infamous walls.

He was right, of course. No one overtook his perimeters. *Because the enemy was already inside the gates.*

I stretch my arm out on the bench behind Serapina as Pip dances around the flowers, his antics reminding me a bit of a puppy enjoying his time outside. It's so innocent that I nearly smile.

But there's nothing humorous about what I need to tell her.

"To understand the past, we need to revisit dynamics. Alphas are the protectors, therefore stronger than the rest. We're powerful, right?"

She nods. "I've gathered that."

I smile. "You've barely seen what we can do, but that's because you're an Omega, and Alphas know to temper their energy around your kind. I don't want to call you fragile, as that's not the correct term, but you are smaller and softer than my brethren."

This should be rather evident to her already since she's a foot shorter than me and weighs a fraction of what I do.

"It doesn't matter if the Omega is male or female; they all possess a petite stature in comparison to that of an Alpha," I explain. "And, unfortunately, some Alphas feel that strength equals superiority. Therefore, they believe in taking what they want and forcing everyone else to pay homage in exchange for survival."

That's why the Mythos Fae Realm has self-destructed.

Without Omegas to soften the Alphas of our world, many have become feral versions of their former selves, thus joining the ranks of those who feel the need to dominate.

They've created camps where Betas serve to survive.

Others have created wastelands.

And some—like Hades and me—have found other kingdoms to live within.

But before I can explain that to her, I have to address the point of this discussion.

"Some of the Alphas who believed in their inherent superiority decided that Omegas were theirs to take and own, and essentially turned their mates into slaves."

Serapina's eyes widen, her discomfort causing my chest to ignite in a purr.

It's an automatic reaction. I just want to soothe her.

Clearing my throat, I say, "Sorry, that's a natural reaction to your distress."

"It's okay," she says, leaning toward me. "I… I don't mind. Though, I find it interesting you can speak while making that sound."

My lips twitch. "Haven't you heard a cat meow while purring?"

"Only once or twice," she admits, her gaze going to Pip as he jumps off the terrace. "What are you—"

The soul comes right back up and does a flip in the sky.

"I think he noticed your discomfort, too," I say, amused. "He's trying to make you smile."

She blinks at Pip, then looks back at me. "I don't mean to react. It's just the notion of being a slave…"

I nod. "I understand, little dreamer. Many Alphas did not agree with this mentality. But, unfortunately, there were enough who did. It caused a lot of strife between our kind, as well as a few battles. Omegas were taken from their mates, forced to breed, and…" I trail off, not wanting to go into too much more detail.

All she needs to understand is that it was a tumultuous time.

"Something to remember—and I apologize if this is repetitive information, but it's important—Alphas can only procreate with Omegas and vice versa. Also, Alphas and Omegas only ever produce Alpha and Omega children."

I study her features to make sure she's following me before going on.

"So Betas are essentially a different species of Mythos Fae that are compatible sexually with other Omegas and Alphas, but they can't accept a knot. So they can't produce offspring," I tell her.

This is important.

Because it leads into what I want to tell her about Demeter.

But I can tell by Sera's expression that I've lost her somewhere, and I suspect I know exactly what's confused her. "What's a, um, knot?"

It takes everything inside me not to grin at that beautiful question. "It's how an Alpha ties to an Omega... during sex."

Her eyes widen.

"Don't let it alarm you," I murmur. "Omegas love being knotted. I've been told it's immensely pleasurable, particularly as it extends climaxes for minutes. Or, if you have a really good Alpha, it can go on for hours."

Pip floats by and does another cartwheel-like motion, but Serapina is too busy gaping at me to see him.

I have to cover my chuckle with a cough, as I don't want to make her more uncomfortable. But her reaction is truly adorable.

Her cheeks are a bright red, her lips slightly parted.

My purr strengthens, mostly because I'm enjoying her

reaction and I want to reward her. But it functions as a way to keep her calm, too.

"Right, well, as I was saying, it's important to understand how Alphas and Omegas mate because then you'll also infer that all Omegas have one Alpha parent and one Omega parent. Same with Alphas, actually. But the Omegas are the important part here."

"Okay," she whispers, her cheeks still red as she not so subtly glances down at my lap and then right back up at my face.

Wondering what a knot looks like, little dreamer? I long to ask her.

But I don't want to tease her.

Not yet, anyway.

So instead, I go on to explain why I'm ensuring she knows this important distinction.

Because some Alphas were not happy about the fates of their Omega children.

And Demeter was one of the loudest voices of that dissent.

When I explain this to Sera, she loses some of the color in her face. "Did she think Persephone was taken against her will?" she asks me.

"Yes," I reply. "She wasn't, though. Persephone loved Hades. That much I witnessed myself. But Demeter didn't trust the affection between them. She didn't trust *any* Alpha around an Omega. I think it's safe to say she went a little mad."

It's an understatement.

Demeter was absolutely insane.

Which was what made her so dangerous.

"I'm telling you all of this so you can understand that there are multiple facets to every story, and while Hades may believe that Persephone betrayed him, I don't. I think

245

Demeter forced her hand. I can't prove it. But I would like to try."

Serapina studies me. "By accessing her memories."

I shrug. "Perhaps. Another option is to make Demeter talk. But regardless of the method, I need you to believe that your soul isn't evil. Because even if Persephone helped her mother, I don't think her intention was ever to harm the Omegas. I think she wanted to save them."

"From the Alphas who were enslaving them," she says.

I dip my chin. "Yes. And maybe something went wrong. Or perhaps Demeter tricked her into that fate. Irrespective of that, I know without a doubt that Persephone's soul isn't evil. And on top of that, I know that *you* are not evil. Nor do you deserve to pay for the sins of another person's choices."

She swallows, her gaze glittering with unshed tears. "Then why has fate forced us together?"

"Because fate knew you could handle whatever is coming," I reply without missing a beat. "You're strong, Serapina. You're brave, too. And you have compassion." These are all traits I've identified throughout the months of observing her but have positively confirmed just in the few times we've met.

Serapina is an amazing female.

And she's going to be an incredible Omega.

Leaning in, I brush a kiss against her forehead. "I think that's enough for today," I whisper. "Besides, I hear you have a date with Hades later."

She shudders as I pull back. "Yeah. He left me a dress."

"Is it sexy?" I ask.

Her brow furrows. "Excuse me?"

"Is it a sexy dress?" I repeat.

"I... I guess."

I smile. "Good." I lean toward her again and tap her

on the nose. "Make him beg, Omega. Because the God of Death deserves to fucking crawl."

With that, I stand and leave her gawking up at me as I walk back to the bag I left on the patio floor.

"Pip?" I call again.

The little soul zips right over and stands at attention.

"Can you please put this next to her plant?"

He gives me a mock salute and takes the handles gingerly in his hand—which he covers with the cloth like I showed him—and disappears into Serapina's new quarters.

Casting my intended one final look, I say, "If you ever want to talk to me, just dream of me. I'll be there for you in a breath, sweetheart. Always."

SERA

I STARE AT MYSELF IN THE FULL-LENGTH MIRROR OF MY closet.

About an hour ago, I received a note telling me that Hades would be here in sixty minutes to escort me to dinner. I don't know who wrote it, just that it appeared shortly after Morpheus left. I saw it on the table next to my pot and the gift bag Pip brought in for me.

After setting up the plant light, I went to shower and prepare myself for dinner.

And now I'm wondering if Morpheus's idea to make Hades beg is a good or a bad idea.

Because this dress is… revealing. I don't think I've ever worn something so risqué. The gown is backless, and the V-neck exposes a lot more of my breasts than I'm used to.

And the slit up my left leg… yeah, that's going to be dangerous for sitting.

Plus, the shoes, which I'm holding in my hand, are probably going to make me fall.

Chewing on my lip, I consider changing. There are a lot of other options in the closet. There's no reason I need to wear this specific gown, right?

The fact that Hades picked it out for me should actually make me *not* want to wear it. However, Morpheus's words fueled something inside me that forced me to at least try the dress on.

And now I'm regretting it.

"Yeah, I'm totally going to change," I tell my reflection.

"Why? Does the gown not fit?" a deep voice asks, making me jump backward and right into a hard, masculine wall.

Spinning around, I gape at Hades's large presence in my closet. "Where?" I sputter out. "How?" I clear my throat. "Do you not know how to knock?" I demand.

He frowns down at me. "I did."

"What?"

"I knocked on your door, and when you didn't answer, I came looking for you." He glances over his shoulder. "Well, first I met Pip. *Then* I came looking for you."

My eyes widen, the shoes dropping to the ground with a loud thud—one that rivals my racing pulse. "*Pip.*" I rush around Hades, my heart in my throat. "Pip!"

He floats into view, his blue eyes large as he looks around for whatever has me so concerned.

"You're okay," I whisper, falling to my knees in relief. "Oh, fae, you're… you're still here."

My little friend creeps closer and lowers himself into my view.

If I could hug him, I would.

"I thought you might be gone," I tell him, recalling what Maliki said about the pits. "I would never forgive myself if something happened to you… because of me."

"Why would something happen to him?" Hades asks, a

note of irritation in his tone. "Has someone threatened your familiar?"

I blink at Pip, then slowly look back at Hades. "My familiar?"

"Yes. Or he's something to you, anyway. That's why my wards let him through. You're bonded." He shrugs. "*Familiar* is the best term for now. But tell me why you thought he was gone."

I stare at him and swallow. "I... You said you met him. I thought you may have hurt him." Fae, I sound ridiculous. Like a weakling.

I hate this.

I don't want to be meek.

But I feel so lost.

Morpheus helped put some things into perspective. Perhaps Persephone's intentions came from a good place, so she's not as evil as I once believed. However, she still caused so much pain.

And the only way to right those wrongs is to remember what really happened.

Which means embracing my Omega soul.

I only wish I knew how to do that. And I really wish I knew how to make Hades stop hating me.

Because the Hades in my dreams...

My shoulders fall. I don't even want to compare them now.

The reality is nothing like my fantasies.

Pip glides away as Hades approaches. I can't hear him, but I can feel him, his aura so dark and angry that everyone can probably sense his presence.

"Serapina," he murmurs as he crouches in front of me.

I startle, his use of my real name causing me to glance up at him.

"I would never harm a creature that's bonded to my

soulmate," he tells me. "The moment I felt him cross the wards, I accepted him. But even if the wards had rejected him, I still would have re-spelled the barrier to grant him entry because Maliki said you personally requested his presence here."

Each word is delivered with quiet precision, his patient tone unlike anything I've heard from him until now.

It renders me speechless.

Because I don't know how to interpret this side of Hades. *Why is he being so nice to me?*

"And as much as I love when an Omega kneels for me, this is neither the time nor the place." He holds out his hand. "Please stand."

Every part of me shivers at his request, his silky tone caressing me in a way I don't quite understand. I lift my palm to his before I even realize what I'm doing, like my body is designed to obey his.

He pulls me up, his strength seeming to bleed into my skin through that simple touch alone. I shudder, my eyes nearly falling closed as a hum of electricity thrums through my veins.

Fae, I've never felt anything like this.

I almost weep when the sensation disappears, his hand dropping to his side.

"How would you feel about having dinner here instead?" He gestures toward the dining table, which is a lot bigger than the one from my place in the village. "We can also invite Maliki."

"I…" I nearly close my eyes in frustration at my hoarse voice.

Morpheus says Omegas are Goddesses. I've heard Orcus say that about Alina, too.

So how do I become one?

By not being meek in front of the God of Death might be a good start, I tell myself.

But I'm definitely not off to a great start tonight.

I give myself a mental shake and force myself to meet Hades's dark gaze. "Eating here is fine. And if Maliki is hungry, then invite him."

Hades nods.

And disappears.

I blow out a breath and grab the sides of my head. "You're doing really great, Sera," I chastise myself. "Super great."

Spinning back around, I return to my closet to find something more comfortable to wear.

But then I recall Hades's outfit. *A suit.*

All black.

Sexy.

Gritting my teeth, I search for my discarded shoes instead and pluck them up off the floor.

Pip watches as I return to the living area, his movements curious as I sit down and start trying to figure out the straps.

Naturally, Hades returns while I'm in the process of trying to put on the ridiculous heels. His gaze runs over me with interest. "The food will be here soon. As will Maliki."

I nod, pretending to care, and try to tighten the strap on my right foot.

When it looks secure enough, I switch to the left, only to have the shoe taken from my hands as Hades goes down on one knee before me. He sets the heel on the floor and picks up the one I already fastened, then places it on his thigh to inspect it.

My heart skips a beat as he undoes my work and gently secures it at a different angle, one that's a lot more comfortable.

I swallow when he lowers my foot back to the floor, only to grab my opposite ankle and bring it up to his muscular leg.

This feels… intimate.

"I don't understand why you're doing this," I whisper.

His gaze lifts to mine, and I realize that we're the same height like this—with him down on one knee and me seated on the couch. "We're soulmates, Serapina. That means you're mine to care for. And I haven't been doing a very good job of that lately."

That's twice now that he's used my real name and not called me Persephone.

Does that mean he's starting to believe me? To understand that I don't know anything about their history?

He studies my expression for a moment before returning to his task. He's just finished securing the heel when Maliki shadows in wearing a suit that matches Hades's.

Fae. I'm pretty sure I just swallowed my tongue.

I… I don't know what I'm supposed to say or do right now.

Fortunately, Hades saves me from having to speak as he sets my foot back on the floor and stands. "Thank you for joining us, Maliki."

"You promised popcorn," Maliki replies. "I love popcorn."

Hades snorts. "We both know *popcorn* isn't why you agreed to be here."

Maliki merely smiles, then looks around Hades to meet my gaze.

And promptly stops smiling as his eyes run over my dress. "Bloody shadows, Sera…"

My lips twist as I glance down. I'm not at all surprised to see the slit has run up to my hip—thanks to my squirming on the couch while trying to sort out my shoes —and my boob is half out of my gown, too.

"In my defense, I didn't pick this dress," I mutter as I force myself up off the couch. "Hades—"

I cut off on a yelp when I twist forward, the heels even higher than I realized. My arms fly up to brace for landing, only to be caught in a masculine grip instead and spun before I could accidentally punch him in the face with my flailing hands.

Yeah, this is going really well, I decide. *I've never felt more graceful in my life.*

The sarcastic thoughts make me wince as I go limp in Hades's grip. He holds me from behind, his lips at my ear. "How about you sit down again and I take those shoes off, hmm?"

"Feel free to take the dress off, too," I grumble.

Then I stiffen as I realize what I just said.

"That is not what I meant," I say quickly as I try to push myself away from him. But his grip is too tight.

"Calm down," he tells me, his torso suddenly rumbling with a sound I know very well now.

A purr.

It's different from Morpheus's reverberations, though. His are almost like a low hum, the kind that lulls someone into sleep.

Hades's purr is a deeper growl, one that instantly steals my fight.

Instead, all I want to do is roll into him and rub myself all over his chest.

Because wow.

Wow.

That's an alluring echo, one that lulls me into a state of immediate comfort as Hades guides me back down to the couch.

But as he goes to one knee again, I snap out of my daze and say, "No. I want to leave the shoes on."

Because now they feel like a challenge.

I couldn't stand in them before… so I'll try again.

And while I might hate every moment of wearing them, I'm determined to see it through. To gain some of my dignity back. *To be Sera*.

Hades looks at me. "All right." He resumes his standing position and holds out a hand. "Want to try again?"

I consider batting his palm away, but that feels childish. So I accept his help up and focus on balancing. Then I fix my dress since I still look ridiculous.

So much for being sexy, I think, huffing at the stupidity of it all.

Once I'm done, I glance up at Hades. "How do I look?"

His gaze is as black as night as he replies, "Like a Goddess."

SERA

I pinch my side, convinced I'm dreaming. This feels too much like one of my nightly fantasies to be real.

"Like a Goddess."

Fae, I wish that were true.

But I accept the response with a smile. When I asked how I looked, I expected him to confirm that I adequately fixed the dress.

Instead, he caught me off guard with his reply. So now I have no idea what to say.

"Maliki?" Hades prompts. "Compliment my wife."

My blood heats from the command underlining his tone. Plus the possessive way he worded the demand.

My wife.

Part of me wants to point out that we're not married yet.

But a stronger part of me wants to hear Maliki's response.

He moves forward to stand beside Hades, his golden

irises swirling with interest as he takes his time looking me up and down. "*Goddess* is a good description," he murmurs. "You're our very own Aphrodite, sweet mystery."

My brow furrows. I have no idea who or what an Aphrodite is.

"She's the Greek Goddess of Love," he tells me, likely seeing the confusion in my expression. "I have no doubt her myth was inspired by an Omega like you."

"Wasn't Aphrodite also the Goddess of Lust?" Hades asks conversationally.

"Beauty, lust, *sex*," Maliki murmurs. "Though, that last one may be attributed to Venus. But the compliment remains."

Hades nods. "It's appropriate."

I shiver, their words warming my veins even more. They're talking to each other like I'm not standing right here.

"Now escort my wife to the table and help her find her seat," Hades demands. "I'll go help Lyon bring in dinner."

He vanishes before either of us can comment, his crisp scent the only remaining indicator that he was just here.

Maliki takes his spot, his lips curling. "Feeling overwhelmed, trouble?"

I swallow and nod. "A little."

He reaches for my hair and tucks it behind my ear, then traces my jaw with his fingertips. "Don't worry. I'm still your protector. No one can touch you, not even Hades."

"Isn't he the one who hired you?" I ask, incredulous. "Can't he just relieve you of the task if you try to stop him from hurting me?"

"Hades didn't hire me," he reminds me. "And he would never hurt you, Sera," he says seriously. "I know you may

257

feel otherwise, given the situation, but in time, you'll understand my certainty."

His expression is so earnest I can tell he really believes that.

I wish I could, too. I wish I could be like Pip and trust easily. Have faith. Enjoy hope.

Alas, pessimism is my friend.

So I simply reply, "We'll see."

Maliki palms my cheek, then glides his fingers back into my hair and pulls me into an unexpected hug.

"I told you I don't want your pity," I mutter into his suit jacket as his free arm wraps around my waist to hold me against him.

"I don't pity you, Sera," he murmurs against my ear. "I just don't have the ability to comfort you with a purr, so I'm using my warmth instead."

My lips curl at both his words and the way he holds me. "I like your hugs," I admit.

"Good. Because I like hugging you," he whispers.

My eyes close as I revel in his strength. It's different from Morpheus's purr and Hades's touch. They all provide contentment in unique ways. But Maliki's warmth is the one I trust most.

Rather than overthink the reasons for that trust or how his actions may have been inspired by me being an assignment, I simply let him soothe me.

Just like when I fell asleep in his arms.

Fae, was that only last night?

My sense of time is severely skewed. I feel like I've lived through a dozen lifetimes over the last few years.

Maliki buries his face in my hair. "This dress is fucking killing me, Sera."

I frown. "It is? How?"

His palm goes to my nape, giving it a squeeze, as his

opposite hand explores my bare back. "It makes me want to touch something that isn't mine to touch, trouble."

My lips part as understanding crosses my mind. "Oh." I have no idea how to respond to that because I... I don't want him to stop. Which is probably wrong. I'm engaged to his... his boss? His friend? I don't really understand his relationship with Hades.

Fae, I don't really understand *my* relationship with Hades.

"All I want to do is explore every inch of your exposed skin." He traces my spine down to where the fabric hugs my waist. "Which I know will lead to me wanting to reveal more of you."

I shiver at his admission, at the fantasy it creates in my mind.

Hades told Maliki to guide me to the table. To help me find a chair. And suddenly, all I want is to go to the bedroom instead.

I don't need food. I ate a few hours ago when Maliki sent a snack to my room.

In fact, I don't think I'm hungry at all.

"I meant what I said when I called you Aphrodite," Maliki adds, his mouth at my ear again. "She was a temptress. The most beautiful Goddess alive. A myth, of course. But you are so very fucking real, Sera."

A tremble works through me as he kisses my temple.

"I've struggled to keep my hands off of you, choosing survival over giving in to this forbidden need," he whispers. "I'm starting to think dying is a small price to pay if it means tasting you before I depart."

My stomach twists, his words doing strange things to me. He keeps talking about death being worth the risk. "I don't want you to die," I tell him.

"Then perhaps you should consider asking your husband for mercy," a deep voice rumbles behind me.

I stop breathing, his tone rippling through me like a wave of dominant energy.

Yet Maliki doesn't stop stroking my back. "I'm not apologizing," he says. "You left me here with her in a dress you knew would bring me to my knees. So consider me begging, *my lord*."

Hades hums, the sound one that seems to vibrate throughout the room as he grabs my hip from behind.

My eyes widen, his heat bleeding into my back as he sandwiches me between his large, masculine form and Maliki's lethal one.

"Do you hear that, little mate?" Hades asks silkily, his opposite hand going to my chin to tilt me back to look at him. "Maliki is begging me to kill him."

I gape at Hades. "Please don't," I whisper. "He hasn't done anything wrong."

"Oh?" Hades arched a brow. "But he's touched someone who doesn't belong to him."

Because I belong to Hades.

Rather, *my soul* belongs to him.

But does my body?

"I should have a say in who can touch me," I tell him, my voice lacking the necessary conviction to properly deliver the comment. But I'm thinking out loud. "You can't kill Maliki for hugging me."

"Can't I?" Hades asks, his tone suggesting I may need to reconsider my stance.

However, I don't want to reconsider anything.

"It's my body. I choose who touches it." There, that came out stronger.

"I see." Hades searches my gaze, his expression giving

nothing away. "And do you want Maliki to continue touching you, *wife*?"

We're not married yet, I nearly reply, the boldness coming from somewhere within. Maybe from the part of me that feels frustrated with my fate.

Every decision in my life has been made by someone else.

The Day of the Choosing.

Demeter's Gardens.

Coming to the Netherworld.

My engagement to Hades.

Maliki being assigned to guard me.

But the way I feel about Maliki is *my* choice. He gives me warmth. Happiness. *Humor*.

And now he's giving me comfort with his touch.

So I answer Hades with a stern "Yes."

His eyes glitter as he stares down at me. "Good. Then consider him a wedding gift."

My lips part. *A wedding gift?* I repeat in my head. *What does he mean by that?*

"Please my wife, Maliki," Hades demands. "Your life depends on how much she enjoys your *touch*."

Black flames dance in his irises as he utters those words, his focus entirely on me despite his words being for his enforcer.

I swallow, and Hades tracks the movement with his gaze, his fingers still clasping my chin. "This stops the moment you request it," he tells me, his voice softer than a second ago. "Just say my name and this all ends. Understand?"

Not really, I think. Primarily as I don't understand what *this* means. Yet I nod anyway. Because it feels like the right response.

"He won't hurt you," Hades adds. "And neither will I."

His statement feels like a vow. However, I don't know if I can trust it.

Hades may not hurt me physically, but I have no doubt he'll annihilate me mentally. The hatred and anger still simmer in his gaze, along with another emotion I can't define.

Possession, maybe?

Whatever it is, it's hot and stoking the inferno flickering in his stare as he looks at my mouth. His thumb traces my lower lip, and he might as well have lit me on fire.

Because my skin *burns* from that short caress. Like he's marked me as his without ever having kissed me.

"Maliki," he murmurs. "Begin."

"I'm not your puppet," Maliki returns, his palm flattening against my lower back. I'm certain Hades feels it since he's still holding me tightly from behind. And I see the knowledge of it flash in his features.

"Definitely not a puppet," Hades says softly. "But if you want to play with my wife, you'll adhere to my commands."

Maliki hums, his hold loosening as he pulls back from my hair. "Release her to me," he tells Hades, issuing his own form of a demand. "If I'm going to pleasure your wife, I need to be able to see her eyes."

Flames erupt across my skin.

Pleasure your wife.

He means *kiss your wife*, right?

That's a form of pleasure.

That's what he intends to do.

Right?

"As you wish," Hades says, guiding my chin forward until I meet Maliki's gaze. Then Hades's fingers slowly trace my jaw, all the way back to my ear, where he tucks away my hair and exposes my neck.

Hot lips meet my tender skin, right above my throbbing pulse point.

"Enjoy your wedding gift, pet," he says, then lets go of my hip and takes a step back.

But he doesn't leave.

I detect his presence behind me like a wall of intensity, his gaze a palpable sensation I feel roaming over my exposed back.

"Ignore him and focus on me, Sera." Maliki's tone is laced with a gentle command, one that has me nearly swaying in his arms.

Because this is too much.

Yet not nearly enough.

I have no idea what he intends to do to me. Or if Hades is planning to just stand there and... and *watch*.

However, the idea of it has me burning all over.

Not with mortification, but with *excitement*.

Fae, what is wrong with me?

"Sera," Maliki says again, his palm cupping my cheek. "Remember what Hades said. Say his name and this all stops, yeah?"

What all stops? I want to ask. *You touching me?* Because I don't want that to stop.

So I guess I'm never saying *Hades* out loud ever again.

That's fine.

I'll just call him *my lord* like Maliki does.

Yep.

Okay.

Maliki smiles. "I think your wife is lust-drunk."

"It does appear to be that way," Hades replies, his tone lacking ire. If anything, he sounds intrigued. "Are you going to keep teasing her or kiss her?"

"Hmm," Maliki hums. "I'm not sure yet. You know how much I enjoy foreplay."

"I do," he says as something pops in the background.

I glance back, startled by the sound, and see Hades holding a bottle of something. It looks like bloodpagne, a type of bubbly drink that some of the fae like back at the Den. He pours it into a glass, then takes a sip while holding my gaze.

That's when I realize the table is full of food.

I have no idea when he carried it all in. I'm not sure I care.

Because I'm still not hungry.

"Sera," Maliki says, his hand on my chin—just like Hades's was before—as he guides my focus back to him. "I'm the one touching you right now. Not your mate. So I want your undivided attention. Understand?"

Swallowing, I nod. "Yes."

"Good girl." He brushes my mouth with his thumb, stoking the fire Hades left behind, and lifts me in the air with his arm around my lower back.

I gasp, my hands instantly going to his shoulders for balance as he begins to walk. "Maliki…"

"I warned you that this dress makes me want to reveal more of you, Sera," he says, his steps sure despite his gaze locking with mine. "I'm going to remove it."

My eyes widen. "*What?*"

He simply smiles. "That's not your husband's name."

MALIKI

Styx, Sera's innocence is going to undo me.

I usually prefer experienced females, but there is something undeniably erotic about having the opportunity to teach this woman about bedroom play.

Hades follows as I carry her into the bedroom, his presence louder than his steps. Though, I can tell he's trying to tone it down—for his mate.

His fiancée.

His wife.

They're all the same words to him and to me. She's *his*. I respect that. But I'm about to make her mine, too.

He's going to regret offering to share her with me.

Because I'm pretty sure I'm about to become addicted to Serapina Everheart. Styx, I probably already am, and I haven't even kissed her yet.

Big blue eyes stare up at me in wonder as I set Sera on the floor beside her bed—one she hasn't even slept in yet. It's much larger than her old one, something that will benefit us in time.

But for now, I simply cup her jaw and stare down into her eyes. "Like I said to Hades, I adore foreplay. Which is why I'm going to kiss you everywhere else before I properly taste you."

Her pupils dilate, her fingers seeming to dig into my shoulders. "Oh" is all she says, the word coming out in a breath.

I take that to mean she's okay with my intentions.

However, for her, and *only her*, I'll be a gentleman and go slow.

I press my lips to her cheek first, then her jaw, and gradually begin to trace the column of her slender neck. When I reach her thundering pulse, I hum in approval.

She's aroused.

Which is precisely what I want from her. *Pleasure*.

And not because Hades told me to *please his wife*. But because I *want* to please her.

Shadows, I want to do a lot more than that.

However, I'm making this experience about her. Hades may think this is about confirming her truths, but that's not my goal. I'm simply using this opportunity to my advantage.

I want her.

And if this is the only way Hades is going to let me have her, then so be it. I'll make sure she enjoys every second and thinks about me for the rest of her existence. Every time he knots her, thoughts of me will drift through her mind, too.

Thoughts of what I did to her with my mouth.

My hands.

My tongue.

That'll be my satisfaction. My lasting gratification.

I'll probably spend the rest of my long life craving her after this, but I'm willing to pay that price for just one moment of bliss.

Tonight she's *mine.*

And I'm going to show her exactly what that means.

Nibbling on her neck, I run my mouth back up to her jaw and higher to her ear while my palms skim up her sides. "You're so fucking beautiful, Sera," I tell her. "I've been fantasizing about you for weeks, wondering what this body would look like beneath my hands. How you flush when you're turned on. The sounds you might make while I stroke your bare skin and tease you with my mouth."

She shudders against me. "W-weeks?"

"Maybe even longer," I admit, my fingers reaching the straps of her stunning gown. I pull one over her shoulder, just to test her reaction, and grin when she trembles again. "You turned away all those fae. But you're not telling me to leave now, are you?"

She shakes her head. "No. I…" Her throat bobs, suggesting she's trying to swallow. "Please don't leave."

My smile deepens. "I'm not going anywhere, trouble." I nip her earlobe, then draw my lips back down to her bare shoulder and place a kiss where her strap used to be. "What color do you think her nipples are?" I ask Hades, curious as to whether or not he has any guesses.

While I wait for his response, I trace her quivering collarbone with my tongue, aware that he instructed me to only kiss her. And that I'm doing a lot more than that.

Though, he's not trying to stop me.

He also said to *please his wife.*

So this is me doing just that.

Besides, I am technically kissing her, too.

"Pale murberries," he says. "The kind that have been in the sun for just the right amount of time, making them juicy and sweet and fucking *delicious*."

I've never had a *murberry* before, so I assume that's a fruit from the Mythos Fae Realm.

"Let's see if you're right," I reply, testing both his possessive instincts and Sera's willingness for more.

He doesn't reply.

And my sweet, innocent mystery simply trembles.

So I tug on the strap a tad more to begin exposing her tit, all while monitoring her for any signs of discomfort.

Her breathing quickens—a sight that enhances her already exquisite chest—and a delectable little flush creeps along her neck.

I glance up to see her staring down at my hand, her lips parted like she can't believe I'm doing this. But she's not trying to stop me. And nothing in her features says she wants this to end.

So I finish freeing her breast, then look down to take in the color. "Rosy pink," I murmur, very much approving. "I bet they turn a beautiful red when sucked."

Like cherries, I think, inhaling. *How appropriate.*

Her natural scent has always been sweet to me, but now I realize what fruit she reminds me of—*cherries.*

The aroma is a beacon for my tongue, making me want to taste her even more than I already do.

Releasing her strap, I move my hand to her breast and gently thumb her erect nipple. "Gorgeous, Sera," I praise her.

The hitch in her breath confirms it was the right thing to say.

No one has seen her like this. She doesn't need to tell me that for me to know. She may have handled those flirtatious fae in the bar with the skill of a professional, but she's very much untouched.

Her background wouldn't have allowed for it.

Yet she masks her innocence well.

Because she's a Goddess.

And her *God* is currently at my back.

I half expect him to yank me away from his mate, but instead he just moves to my side with a drink in one hand and his other in the pocket of his slacks. "Murberries," he murmurs. "And I agree. They'll redden nicely if given the appropriate attention."

I glance at him and meet his gaze.

He's daring me to push him. I can see it in his expression, the way violence brews in his gaze like a dark thunderstorm.

He should know better than to tempt me into his version of madness.

Because I'll follow him every time. *For fun.*

Holding his gaze, I lower my mouth to Sera's breast, then close my lips around her rose-colored tip and *suck.*

His nostrils flare in response, his arousal as potent as his fury.

I'm touching his mate, and he's torn between demanding more and killing me. It's an erotic disposition, one that has me returning my focus to Sera as I swirl my tongue around her taut peak.

She releases a delicious moan, prompting my arm to slide around her back to pull her tightly against me as I introduce my teeth to her sensitive skin.

I don't bite hard, just enough for her to feel the sting before laving it away with my tongue. Her hand on my shoulder moves to my hair, holding me to her breast as I hollow my cheeks and show her just what I can do with my mouth.

"Maliki," she breathes.

And fuck if that doesn't make me hard in an instant, the way she says *my* name in response to *my* touch.

Not *Hades*.

Not *stop*.

But *Maliki*.

Fuck. Yes.

Hades hums, reminding me that he's still here. Usually, he's silent while I play. Seated in a corner. Brooding.

Yet this time, he stands right beside me, not missing a single second of what I'm doing to his mate. I would almost bet that he wants to touch her, too.

But he refrains, instead sipping his bloodpagne while I expose her other breast and feast on her rosy nipple.

She doesn't taste like cherries; she tastes like *sin*.

And it's a sin I'll happily indulge in for as long as I'm allowed. Because Styx, this female is the sweetest temptation I've ever had the pleasure of enjoying.

By the time I finish worshipping her tits, she's panting and clinging to me with her head tossed back in a beautiful display of carnal need.

But my gaze goes to those stunning peaks again, and my lips curl. "Cherry red."

"Indeed," Hades murmurs, his voice seeming to make Sera quiver.

He may intimidate her, but she likes that he's here. And she absolutely enjoyed what I just did to her.

It makes me want to do *more*. To take *more*. To see how far I can push Hades. To see how much Sera will let me do to her.

So I finish dragging both of her straps down her arms to reveal her flat stomach, all while the God of Death watches.

She isn't wearing a bra because of her backless dress.

Which has me wondering… "Do you think she's wearing panties?" I ask aloud, my question for Hades.

His answer will tell me if I should proceed… or stop.

While I wait for his decision, I admire Sera's topless state. Her flush has spread, giving her pale skin an alluring, pink glow.

"I'm guessing no, as I didn't leave any out for her to wear," Hades tells me. "Show me if I'm right."

I wait a beat, studying Sera's reaction to his demand. She rights her head to look at him and then at me, her eyes rounding. "I warned you, mystery," I tell her. "I said this dress made me want to touch you, which would result in me wanting to expose more of you."

Her nails dig into my scalp like she's trying to hold on to me because she might fall. I straighten and stare down at her.

"Do you want to tell us if you're wearing panties?" I ask her. "Or do you want me to find out on my own?" I tug a little on her dress, allowing her to feel it pooling at her hips.

"I…" Her lashes flutter. "I don't want this to stop."

My lips curl. "That wasn't my question, Sera. There's a lot more I can do from the waist up." I lift one hand back to her tit and give it a little squeeze and pull her even closer until my mouth is hovering over hers. "So if you want this to be the line, I can work with that."

I allow her to feel my breath, my heat, *my desire*.

She quivers in response, her mouth parting beneath mine, like she's trying to invite my tongue inside for a thorough introduction.

"All it takes is an answer, trouble. Do you want to tell me what's under the dress? Or should I find out on my own?" I ask softly, my thumbs teasing the exposed skin of her hips.

LEXI C. FOSS

Her voice is a sultry whisper as she replies, "Find out."

My abdomen tenses, her words nearly dropping me to my knees.

Because *Styx*, this female is all innocent seduction. Like she was born to be *fucked*.

And maybe she was—she's an Omega. From what Hades has told me, they're notoriously insatiable. Shadows, I hope that's true. I want to spend hours, days, *years*, worshipping this female.

With my mouth still hovering against hers, I push the fabric down her legs and allow my thumbs to discover the truth. "No panties. Just smooth, soft skin."

Hades emits a low growl, one that has Sera clutching me on a moan, her body seeming to react to his possessiveness. Or maybe it's just an Alpha talking to his Omega. I don't know, but the way she rubs against me in response has me feeling like I'm the one benefiting, not him.

"I can smell my wife's slick," Hades says, his voice low, purposeful, *furious*. "I think she wants you to taste her, Maliki."

"Mmm, the feeling is mutual," I reply, aware that I'm playing with fire.

He's probably going to kill me for this, even though he promised he wouldn't.

So I might as well do exactly what I want and pay the consequences later.

"I'm going to kiss you now, Sera," I tell her, my words a warning for her—and underlined with meaning for Hades.

Because he asked me to *kiss* her earlier, saying he wanted to observe her reactions.

Well, I'm going to do just that.

It's not my fault he didn't specify *where* he wanted me to kiss her.

He also told me to make sure she enjoyed this.

So technically, I'm doing exactly what he requested. Just in my own way.

Grabbing Sera's hips, I lift her from the ground, causing the dress to fall the rest of the way off, then I place her on the bed. "Head on the pillows, mystery," I tell her. "Legs spread. I want to see your pussy."

Her widening eyes tell me she's never heard that word out loud before. But she's familiar with it.

I'm not sure I want to know how or why she knows that term.

Not that it's going to matter in a few minutes. Because I'll be the only male she can think about as soon as I get my mouth on her.

With a slight quiver in her movements, she does as I request and slowly spreads her legs.

"Wider, wife," Hades says as he walks around the foot of the bed. "If Maliki is going to feast on your cunt, then he needs more room to work."

Fuck.

He never participates like this.

Never tells my women what to do.

But this isn't *my* woman.

This is *his* woman.

And he wants to give me to her as a wedding gift.

I'm aware of how fucked up this is, but as Sera shifts to obey Hades's command, I realize that I just do not care. All I want to do is *lick*.

Pulling off my jacket, I drape it over the edge of the mattress. I need more flexibility, which is why I remove the tie, too. And unfasten the top button of my shirt, as well as the ones on my wrists.

Formalities are one of Hades's quirks, not mine. But the way Sera watches me roll my sleeves makes me

273

LEXI C. FOSS

wonder if I should start wearing outfits like this more often.

By the time I finish, her skin is flushed an even darker crimson, and her sweet pussy is practically dripping with need.

I place a knee on the mattress and start toward her as Hades sits on the bed beside Sera. He's close enough to touch, yet he simply stretches out his legs to cross them at the ankles and continues to enjoy his beverage.

While watching.

I've always enjoyed having his eyes on me while I work. That's one of my kinks.

But this is different.

He's never sat on the bed while I've played.

And I find that I rather *like* this change.

Which doesn't surprise me. I've longed to share a woman—*properly*—with him for eons.

Perhaps that'll happen with Sera.

Assuming he doesn't kill me for making his mate come all over my face, I think.

Ah, but what a beautiful way to die is my next thought as I kneel between Sera's splayed thighs.

"Fuck, Sera. I've never seen such a needy pussy." I draw my finger through her slick folds, which has her eyes widening in response like she can't believe I just touched her *there*. But she moans in the next breath, her concerns already forgotten. "You're so wet, sweet girl."

"Welcome to being with an Omega," Hades murmurs. "Now stop stalling and give my wife what she needs."

HADES

I can't decide if I want to kill Maliki or encourage him to do more.

He has my mate naked and wet and panting. *For him.*

It's an infuriatingly arousing situation.

I know what he's capable of, so I'm aware that he's being gentle with Serapina. Because he believes her to be inexperienced. Naïve. *Innocent.*

And thus far, every reaction she's provided suggests he's right.

She's physically different. I expected that. Her skin is paler than Persephone's was, her features pinker as a result.

But it's more than that.

Her moans are different. Her pants are a foreign cadence. The way she went from shy to bold was unique.

Persephone always supplicated, her role as an Omega intrinsically ingrained in her from birth. Oh, she could take on the role of seductress, too. But there was always a shy quality to it. And she often relied on her slick to entice me to knot her.

Scents are a powerful tool for Alphas and Omegas. Growls and mewls, too.

Serapina hasn't mewled once, even after I growled.

And she doesn't seem to understand the power of her natural aroma.

That haven between her thighs is a fucking beacon, yet she didn't present herself the way an Omega typically would. Instead, she had to be told to spread her legs.

I watch her face as Maliki presses a kiss to her inner thigh, his intention clear as he begins a path upward.

Part of me expects Serapina to open her eyes right when he meets her core and stare directly at me.

But she doesn't. Instead, her head falls back on a gasp of shocked delight as he begins to work her with his tongue.

The stark wonder in her features has me reaching for my zipper and adjusting my pants because *fuck*. That expression makes me want to slide my cock through those pouty lips and fuck her mouth while Maliki devours her cunt.

It's such an intense need that my balls actually tighten.

I haven't been with anyone since Persephone.

A lot of outsiders assume I use Maliki as a lover, but that's not our relationship. I... I just like to watch him perform.

Yet this is different.

The pleasure I feel watching him feast on my wife's pussy is unlike anything I've experienced with him. Perhaps unlike anything I've *ever* experienced.

Memories, though, are finicky. So it's hard to compare the present to the past, especially in terms of sensations.

Though, I do know this is the most intense interaction I've faced in a very long while.

I'm so damn hard that my knot *hurts*.

However, I need to see this through, to watch my mate —my *intended*—fall apart.

I thought a kiss would do, but the moment Maliki began exploring the boundaries of my tolerance, I decided to see where this would lead.

Because an orgasm is impossible for an Omega to fake.

"Maliki," Serapina breathes, her fingers threading through his thick hair again as she holds him to her slickened center. "I… I feel…" Her face is red, the color matching her hard nipples.

I almost want to lean over and take one between my teeth. *And bite*. Mark her as mine. Ensure Maliki sees it and knows it, too.

But I don't want to interrupt her pleasure, either.

"Shh," Maliki hushes her. "Just enjoy the sensations, little mystery. I'll guide you to where you need to go."

His palm runs up her inner thigh toward her sex, his finger slipping inside her as he meets my gaze.

My jaw ticks. Only *my cock* belongs inside *my mate*.

But the sweet little moan she releases in response has me instantly calming.

Fuck, this is insane.

I should not be letting Maliki do this. *She's mine. My mate. My wife.*

However, she's *enjoying* his ministrations.

And if there's anyone I can trust with my soulmate, it's my best friend.

I force myself to take another sip of bloodpagne, my mind barely registering that I've almost finished the glass.

All I can see is Maliki's tongue as he swirls it around my mate's clit.

All I can hear is her responding whimpers.

All I can *taste* is slick-scented air.

I adjust myself again and set my glass to the side.

Then I try to focus on Serapina's beautiful heart-shaped face again. So unlike Persephone's oval-shaped one. Even their lips are different.

Yet I sense my mate's soul inside this stunning human.

It's a conundrum I don't understand, and it has me wondering if this… is wrong.

Can I lust for a woman who is so very different from my mate? Or is it allowed since she's a reincarnated version of my true mate?

Are they one and the same?

I fist my hands at my sides.

There's still a small sliver of hope inside me that this female is lying, that Persephone has been there all along.

But as she clutches at Maliki and bows up off the bed, that sliver melts away.

My lips part in awe at the display before me, the way Serapina's back arches, presenting her tits. The way she moans another man's name. The way she shakes, like she's lost all control.

And the way her eyes… *remain closed*.

That's the action that tells me everything I need to know.

Persephone always loved to see the stars when she climaxed. As a result, her eyes… were always open.

I swallow, my chest suddenly tight.

Her soul is here. I sense it. Feel it. *Know it.*

But this woman, this human… *isn't my Persephone.*

She possesses my mate's soul.

However, Serapina isn't my mate.

She's not my wife.

She's not mine.

Which is a serious fucking problem.

Because that orgasm she just experienced rippled through my Alpha senses like a fucking beacon. And it had nothing to do with me being in the room beside her.

I would have felt that pull from twenty realms away.

An Omega has just come into her prime.

It's a notorious call, one I haven't felt in over two thousand years.

And every Mythos Fae Alpha in existence just sensed it, too.

"We're about to have company," I say to Maliki, rolling out of bed.

He must sense the urgency in my tone because he pulls his mouth away from Serapina's pussy and looks at me. "What kind of company?" he asks, his tone as serious as ever despite my soulmate's slick dripping from his chin.

I hold his gaze, my jaw tightening. "*Alpha* company."

And my wards are not built to handle their style of aggression.

Which means we only have one choice.

We need to run.

The Netherworld Fae Series continues with *A Nest of Lies*...

Continue the series with *A Nest of Lies*…

I'm being hunted by all of Mythos Fae kind.
Why?
Because I'm about to go into my first heat.

For years, I've just been Serapina the human.
Now, I'm Sera the Mythos Fae Omega.
And apparently I harbor millennia's worth of secrets inside
my soul.

So not only am I trying to discover the memories hidden
somewhere within my mind, but I'm also on the run…
With three irresistible fae.

Hades, the God of Death.
Morpheus, the God of Dreams.

Maliki, the Enforcer of Death.

I'm pretty sure their presence is going to inspire my heat to overtake me sooner rather than later.
Which will leave me a mindless, vulnerable mess.

Can I trust my new guardians to protect me?
Or am I going to find myself twisted up in a nest of lies?

I'd better unravel the threads soon.
Because the feral Alphas are not the only ones hunting me…
The truth is coming.
And it might just destroy us all.

Author's Note: *A Nest of Lies* is book two of the Netherworld Fae trilogy and ends on a cliffhanger.

USA Today Bestselling Author Lexi C. Foss loves to play in dark worlds, especially the ones that bite. She lives in North Carolina with her family. When not writing, she's busy crossing items off her travel bucket list, or chasing eclipses around the globe. She's quirky, consumes way too much coffee, and loves to swim.

Want access to the most up-to-date information for all of Lexi's books? Sign-up for her newsletter here.

Lexi also likes to hang out with readers on Facebook in her exclusive readers group - Join Here.

Where To Find Lexi:
www.LexiCFoss.com